HARLEQUIN
ROMANTIC
SUSPENSE

COLTONS of
COLORADO

TO TRUST A
COLTON COWBOY

DANA NUSSIO

ISBN-13: 978-1-335-73814-1

50625

EAN

"How long have you been receiving the texts?"

"About three weeks," Kayla answered.

"And you waited this long—" Jasper stopped himself. "I'm glad you trusted me enough to tell me."

"At first, it didn't seem like a big deal."

"Can I see them?"

Her stomach churned with misgivings as he read.

"They're all from different numbers. And the threats are escalating. Whoever they are, they're getting more desperate for you to tell them what they think you know. Do you have any idea what the messages mean?"

"No clue. I mean, they seem to think I know where something is hidden. But what and where, I don't know."

"Do you know of anyone who has something against you?"

This time she just shook her head.

"Could it have anything to do with your—" He stopped. "Sorry. I had to ask."

"I don't think it's about my dad. Why would it be?"

"We should take this to the police."

"What would we tell them? That someone's prank-texting me? It hasn't even reached the level of—"

"Scaring the daylights out of you? I think you're already there."

Dear Reader,

I am so pleased to share my story in The Coltons of Colorado series. I get a kick out of writing stories in the Colton world and getting to know these families, as warm and loyal as our own but with more tantalizing secrets and a little gunfire. In *To Trust a Colton Cowboy*, I enjoyed having the chance to invite so many of the characters from earlier series titles into my story. The Thanksgiving celebration was definitely an adventure!

I loved exploring trust in Kayla and Jasper's love story. Their struggles, resulting from their respective fathers' actions, spoke to me as well. Many of us can relate to the pain these two experience after being let down by those they love. Though both characters have opportunities for growth and healing in this story, I didn't attempt to show those journeys as complete. As is the case for all of us, healing takes time.

I hope you enjoy this story and the other eleven books in The Coltons of Colorado series. I can't wait to cheer on the other Colton family members as they search for answers and find the reward of love along the way. Learn more about me and sign up for my newsletter through www.dananussio.com; connect with me through Facebook and Twitter; or drop me a line on real paper at P.O. Box 5, Novi, MI 48376-0005.

Happy reading!

Dana

TO TRUST A COLTON COWBOY

Dana Nussio

HARLEQUIN

ROMANTIC
SUSPENSE

Special thanks and acknowledgment are given to Dana Nussio
for her contribution to The Coltons of Colorado miniseries.

Recycling programs
for this product may
not exist in your area.

ISBN-13: 978-1-335-73814-1

To Trust a Colton Cowboy

Copyright © 2022 by Harlequin Enterprises ULC

For questions and comments about the quality of this book,
please contact us at CustomerService@Harlequin.com.

Harlequin Enterprises ULC
22 Adelaide St. West, 41st Floor
Toronto, Ontario M5H 4E3, Canada
www.Harlequin.com

Printed in U.S.A.

Dana Nussio began telling "people stories" around the same time she started talking. She's continued both activities, nonstop, ever since. She left a career as an award-winning newspaper reporter to raise three daughters, but the stories followed her home as she discovered the joy of writing fiction. Now an award-winning author and member of Romance Writers of America's Honor Roll of bestselling authors, she loves telling emotional stories filled with honorable but flawed characters.

Books by Dana Nussio

Harlequin Romantic Suspense

The Coltons of Colorado
To Trust a Colton Cowboy

The Coltons of Grave Gulch
Colton Nursery Hideout

The Coltons of Mustang Valley
In Colton's Custody

True Blue
Shielded by the Lawman
Her Dark Web Defender

Visit the Author Profile page at
Harlequin.com for more titles.

To my own hero, Randy, who keeps me fed while on deadline (and, let's admit it, the rest of the year, too), helps me block fight scenes, and listens to me whine when my characters are misbehaving. None of this would be possible without you.

A special thanks to Jeannie Watt, the gracious real-life rancher who helped me build Jasper and Kayla's world; to Bait, the very real pup that served as inspiration for ranch dog, Bandit; to my editors, Patience Bloom and Carly Silver, for believing in me and putting up with my constant suggestions; and to my agent, Chip MacGregor, for helping me chase my dreams.

Chapter 1

Kayla St. James sat crisscross on her bed, cocooned by darkness and a snarl of blankets, her lit cell phone shifting in her trembling hands. She could no more stop staring at the screen than she could still her body from rocking.

We know you know where it is!

Again, she shuddered from more than the cold, though overnight lows in Blue Larkspur had already set November records, and pregnant clouds hugging the Colorado mountaintops predicted a white Thanksgiving. The unsettling sensation of being watched, more than the imperfect heating inside her tiny private room in the Gemini Ranch's bunkhouse, peppered her arms with gooseflesh.

She gulped air, but even the familiar smell of horses and the vanilla diffuser she used to mask it refused to calm her. She hadn't felt this vulnerable, this targeted, since that day two years before when the cops had arrived to take away the only thing she'd still had to lose.

As the screen blackened, she tapped the glass to awaken it. White letters reappeared inside a gray bubble and cast light. Shadows from the old armoire and the three-drawer bureau, her stack of library books protruding at the top, were better than the near-complete darkness in what had once been a storage area. She'd added flourishes of dried flowers and her precious snow globe to brighten the space since even a cowgirl working on a dude ranch deserved pretty things, but they all but vanished now into the darkness.

Before the phone could steal the last of the light, she tapped the screen and read the message again.

We know you know where it is!

The words themselves might not have alarmed her—other than the "we" that she couldn't identify and the "it" that made no sense—had this been the first text she'd received. Or the second. Or the twentieth. That the vibration of its arrival had yanked her from a frightening dream in a collision of colors and sounds and that the message came on the heels of a more threatening text the night before had sharpened its teeth.

Though aware that she should tuck the phone under her pillow and try to claim a few more minutes of sleep, as elusive lately as privacy in the main area of the bunkhouse, Kayla couldn't resist scrolling to the message from the previous night. It showed one of the other phone numbers—she'd counted at least six now—but they had to be from the same sender. Or *senders*.

Tell us or else!

Though her hands shot open, and the phone dropped onto the covers, she still couldn't look away from the menacing words. Her heart raced like a horse given rein to gallop, and her lungs squeezed as if she'd sprinted across an open pasture herself. Who was sending the texts? What were they looking for? Why did they think *she* would know where to find it? And the biggest question of all: What would they do to her if she couldn't give them what they wanted?

The not knowing was killing her. She'd faced foes before. Classmates who'd bullied the girl with a convict father. Banking officials unwilling to grant another extension on her mortgage. The Liar who'd once said he loved her. At least those situations made sense. These invisible threats were different. How could she protect herself when she couldn't see them coming?

Kayla crossed her arms and squeezed to stop the trembling and then untangled herself from the covers. She was overreacting. No one had tried to hurt one of her horses or held her at gunpoint. Even if they tried, she was no delicate bluebell. She could pull a calf or rope a steer as well as any of the ranch hands, and none of them could match her riding skills. She also knew how to use her .22 pistol and old Remington bolt-action rifle. If her pursuers were snakes and pesky coyotes, anyway.

Choosing to close the messages, she shook her head as the time flashed on the phone. Just after two o'clock.

But since more sleep was out of the question for her, she slid her feet into her slippers and tied her hair in a low ponytail with a band she kept on her wrist. With her phone as a flashlight, she pulled an extra fleece over her sweats and tiptoed through the tight space.

She opened the door just wide enough to squeeze through while avoiding the squeak. In the main area, slivers of brightness from the outdoor safety lights, seeping past the blinds on the structure's few windows, made it possible for her to put her phone in her pocket. But since she both dreaded the next message and worried that she would miss one, she couldn't bring herself to shut the dang thing off.

Kayla shuffled along the narrow walkway toward the kitchen on the opposite end of the building. As she passed the line of bunk beds, only the lower mattresses occupied during the slow season, when they operated on a skeleton crew, she paused to see if she'd awakened anyone. The blanketed lumps of her fellow ranch hands only continued their chorus of snores. She shivered anyway, and then shook her head hard.

It was ridiculous for her to suspect that one or more of these men could have tried to terrorize her with those texts. Even as a practical joke. They worked together and ate meals side by side. Most even slept in the same building, if not technically in one room. They treated her like one of the guys, too. Well, not Hank, but even that old-school cowboy had done nothing more offensive than to continually offer to "help out the little lady."

She hurried to the kitchen, where she heated water in the microwave for tea, hoping it would clear her head. Back at the long wood table, her hands wrapped around the mug, she stared out over the softly lit bureaus on one side of the building and then back to the beds on the opposite wall.

She'd been living and working on the Gemini for close to two years now and had been content until just three weeks ago. That truth was surprising, even to her, given her family's tragic history with the father of the ranch's twin co-owners. She'd justified the job in her mind, too. Just a step in her plan to someday buy back The Rock Solid. Somehow, she'd convinced herself she could count on those sleeping coworkers to have her back without putting a target on it.

Now she didn't know what, or *whom*, to believe.

The same men she'd thought she knew also had her cell number. Using a few burner phones and some prepaid minutes, they could easily have been the texters. Not just them. She'd suspected every man who visited the ranch, from the farrier to the equine veterinarian to the regular food delivery driver for the main lodge kitchen. All of them except for...

"Why not Jasper Colton?"

Her hand jerked, causing steaming liquid to pour over the mug's rim and onto her fingers. She winced and stuck a burned knuckle in her mouth as she shot a look back to her sleeping roommates. Had she just spoken *that name* out loud? Just her luck, one of them would awaken and ask why she'd called for their boss in the middle of the night. If she could answer that, maybe she could also explain why, on a ranch filled with potential suspects, she'd never once doubted the innocence of *Judge Ben Colton's son*. Even if she'd been right not to blame the sins of the father on the child, she'd taken charity to an extreme.

That Jasper had the bluest and most intense eyes she'd ever seen didn't qualify as an excuse, either.

Kayla closed her eyes, rested her elbows on the table and lowered her head into the cradle of her hands, guilt forming a knot in her throat.

"Sorry, Dad," she whispered.

Mike St. James already had to be frowning down on her from heaven as she gave riding lessons to pampered princesses on the Gemini while the land he'd entrusted to her care rotted not far away. She could only imagine the disappointment and betrayal he would feel knowing how much attention she paid to her boss's habit of shoving his longish strawberry-blond hair out of those eyes. And how he wore the hell out of a pair of snug-fitting Wranglers and a tight black T-shirt.

Images of the man she had no business noticing *ever* pushed her up from the table. Her body seemed confused about what to do, her chest tightening while warmth spread over her neck. She tried to ignore both as she washed her mug at the sink. To rein in the dis-obedient turn of her hormones lately, she'd steered clear of her boss, a tougher assignment given that she'd also been dying to get her hands on his adorable new puppy. But when she'd passed him in the barn yesterday, she'd had an unexplainable urge to tell him about the texts.

What had she been thinking? It didn't matter that she'd caught him watching her again with that un-masked sadness, as if he wished that he could make up for what his father had done to hers. How could she have been tempted to *trust* any man, particularly a Colton? Just because she'd been around Jasper long enough to know that the scruff he wore on the fawn skin of his upper lip and chin covered a baby face didn't mean that she really knew him. Beyond her late parents, she'd learned the hard way never to put her belief in any creature that didn't have hooves, paws or claws, and she couldn't start now.

Kayla jutted out her chin and then crept back to her room to clean up in the small bathroom and change into her work clothes. She might as well get an early start on chores, maybe do some extra cleaning in the tack room. Keeping busy would help her avoid Jasper and any additional temptation to confide in him. If only her gut would stop telling her that deep down Jasper Colton was a good man. One who would help her find the answers if he could.

She reminded herself of a more important truth: she'd been wrong about people before.

Jasper Colton would have sworn that of the many names others could call him, *slouch* wasn't one of them. Until this morning. Grumbling, he jammed one foot into the leg of his jeans and stumbled past his rumpled bed, knocking over a stack of books, while pulling on the second pant leg. He paused only long enough to zip and button before snatching a suspect Henley and a flannel from the armchair that doubled as a hamper. With his bare feet protesting each step on the frigid hardwood floor, he rushed to the window to open the blinds.

Daybreak already outlined the lesser mountain peaks with pink and orange promise and sneaked past the cypress pines and snowcapped cedars that embraced the Gemini's one hundred acres of open pasture. How could he have overslept? Just two weeks into the slow season, and he'd lost his edge. No Colton could afford to do that, not this year with Ronald Spence, a living ghost from their late patriarch's corrupt legal past, running free now and leaving the whole family waiting for the other boot to drop.

But he had no time to worry about guilt or innocence or escaping his late dad's shameful legacy through honest work. Right now, his only focus needed to be on the cattle that, like always, would expect a meal at sunrise. Based on the look of the sky, that breakfast bell would ring in about half an hour. Worse, they wouldn't even be able to put the horses to work since *someone* had failed to feed them out in the pasture two hours earlier to give them time to digest.

Jasper yanked his shirt over his head, slid his arms into the flannel and grabbed his cell phone and a pair of clean wool socks. He didn't bother answering Aubrey's text, since his twin already knew *where the hell* he'd been, anyway. Sneaking a few extra hours of shuteye and setting a lousy example for their employees.

Would anyone believe him if he blamed the dog?

As if Jasper needed more reasons to feel guilty, plaintive whines filtered from the laundry room before he'd even made it downstairs. He'd neglected another creature this morning, even if technically a three o'clock potty break still counted as morning. The whines turned to scratches as Jasper's footfalls neared the door. He yanked it open.

"Sorry, Bandit."

The forty-pound blur of black and white didn't wait for the rest of his apology, tripping his owner, claws skittering on the wood, as the pooch raced for the front of the house. Paws were scratching at the door by the time that Jasper caught up. Nothing like a brand-new puppy to flip a home sideways. Well, new to him, anyway. He'd thanked his lucky stars when the nine-month-old pup had become available for adoption at the beginning of the month, just when he'd decided that the Gemini needed a dog. The purebred Australian Shepherd had seemed like a perfect fit for the ranch, since this American herding breed traced its heritage to the sheep herding dogs in Australia. Now, with this particular pup, he wasn't so sure.

He pointed to the brown grass, dotted with curled leaves and spots of both frost and snow. "Pick a spot, buddy. Pronto. We're late."

While the pet did its business, Jasper ducked back in to check the laundry room. Thankfully, there'd been no accidents, and the auto-feeder had kept the poor boy from starving. That made one of them. Jasper grabbed a protein bar on his way through the kitchen and then put on his insulated rubber work boots, heavy jacket and felt Resistol cowboy hat.

Outside, he squinted as he opened the door of his old pickup, the wind stinging his cheeks and burning his eyes. But as he climbed into the cab, four wet paws scrambled behind him.

Bandit settled into the passenger seat, happily panting and ready for a ride.

"Glad you've made yourself at home."

After wiping the dog's paws and his own jacket with the towel that he kept on the floorboard these days, he patted the puppy's head, despite its poor manners. Who could resist those adoring pale blue eyes and that pink-and-black-spotted nose? He couldn't.

The truck's starter hiccuped more than usual, but finally it relented. With the defroster blasting, he raced down the hill and over the bridge toward the barn. Already, the structure pumped with morning activity while the massive green tractor idled on the road, the first fourteen-hundred-pound hay bale primed in its front-end loader.

Aubrey met her brother just as he stepped into the lit barn, the dog at his heels.

"Nice of you two to join us," she said, her dark blue eyes peering at him over the top of her eyeglasses.

His sister's words lost some of their venom when she crouched to scratch Bandit's ears. Jasper rolled his eyes. He wasn't the only one on the Gemini who'd fallen in puppy love.

"Enjoy your beauty sleep?"

"Didn't get much of that," he scoffed. "I was up a few times to make sure Bandit hadn't forgotten his house training."

"If you'd let him out of his puppy prison in the laundry room, he could serve as a live alarm clock for you." She stood again and tucked escaped strands of long blond hair back under her hat. "Apparently, you need one."

"Maybe."

"Still think it was a great idea snatching up an animal that washed out in service-dog training? Could have been a sign."

"Shhh!" He covered Bandit's ears with his insulated work gloves. "He was in the wrong job. Aussies are herding dogs. He'll be great on the ranch. Just you watch."

"If it doesn't work out, he can be an oversize lap dog, too." She pointed to the pup that wiggled its behind as if music played in the background. "Also, if you plan to bring him to Thanksgiving dinner, you'd better get on his training. Luckily for you, the holiday falls late this year, but he still might not be ready for a prime-time Colton family gathering."

His sister had a point. They wouldn't need more to worry about while hosting Thanksgiving for the whole family, with plus-ones and more, at the newly renovated lodge.

"Don't worry. He'll be ready," he assured her. "And it will be a wonderful, relaxing holiday for all of us. We all need it, after last month."

"If Spence could threaten Mom and Alexa right on the street, what else is he capable of?"

"I don't think we want to know."

As they stepped back outside, they exchanged a look that sent a shiver down his shoulders. Their mom's trip to the emergency room following that confrontation had terrified them all, even if it had turned out to be only a panic attack. It could have been so much worse.

"We missed you at dinner last night. Luke made pot roast. Wish you would occasionally accept our invitations."

"You know how much I love being the third wheel, but I'll try."

His breath sending a filmy white cloud into the air, Jasper trailed after her to the west corner of the barn, where they could see the road.

"Well, some of us have to go feed." She pointed to the tractor and then started in that direction.

"Sorry about the horses," he called after her. Though ranch tasks were shared, he usually made it his job to feed the horses each morning and then help drive them into the corrals for guest rides or regular health checks.

She stopped and looked back. "What'd you say about the horses?"

As if in answer to her question, a rumble of hooves filtered from the side of the barn. Bandit barked and leaped, but Jasper grasped the dog's collar. He held on while he stepped over to get a better look.

Though the early light and the distance made it difficult to determine which horse trotted their way, he could easily identify the rider. This went beyond the reality that, besides his sister, there was only one other woman living on the Gemini. Kayla St. James sat a horse, taught horseback riding and spoke to equines like no one else he knew. Of course, while he'd been asleep on the job, Kayla would have ensured that the horses were fed on time.

Even with all that cold-weather gear hiding the sweet curves that he always tried—and failed—not to notice, Kayla rode with a statuesque grace as she approached them, the horse slowing to an amble. The animal and rider appeared to have been formed together in an artist's mold, two parts of a single whole.

Lucky horse.

He knew he should look away, but he couldn't do it. Not for the first time, he wondered what it would be like to unravel the dark brown braid she often wore beneath her hat and let the silky-looking strands slide through his fingers. How it would feel to have those startling green eyes stare at him with the kind of admiration she reserved for a fine piece of horseflesh. Or for her to smooth her hand over parts of him the way she tenderly brushed withers and flanks. His skin beneath all those layers of clothing betrayed him by tingling and warming. He'd never appreciated his long canvas duck coat more.

When Bandit yipped and yanked against his hold on the dog's collar, Jasper startled. What was he doing thinking about his *withers* and *flanks* when it came to Kayla St. James? Or letting his mind wander her way at all, even if she was a natural beauty, requiring no more cosmetics than sunscreen and lip balm. In his case, she should have worn a neon off-limits sign on the front of her insulated overalls.

Straightening, he sneaked a peek over his shoulder and winced. Aubrey, who should have reached the tractor by then, stood watching him, her grin as wide as those times when she'd busted him sneaking chips from their mother's pantry. For the millionth time in their thirty years, he was grateful that they didn't share twin telepathy or any of that nonsense.

He cleared his throat and gestured to the rider. "Looks like Kayla already tended to the horses."

"Good thing *someone* picked up the slack," Aubrey said. "I bet she misses caring for the livestock on her own ranch."

His sister's words hit him like a poke to the solar plexus. Was she reminding him that he should steer clear of the pretty cowgirl? As if he didn't already know the reasons why he should. He signed her paycheck. That should have been enough to throw ice water on his romantic notions. But that didn't begin to cover this roadblock created when their disgraced-judge father sentenced a little girl's possibly innocent dad to prison.

Where he'd *died*.

Jasper lowered his head, the silk wild rag scarf tied at his throat brushing his chin. It didn't matter that he couldn't get this strong, amazing woman out of his mind. No movie date—even with extra-butter popcorn and a box of Junior Mints—could ever make up for Kayla losing her childhood, for her dad never getting the chance to prove his innocence or for the downward spiral that resulted in the loss of both Kayla's mother and the family's ranch. For someone only twenty-six years old, she'd already experienced a lifetime of loss, and he couldn't change that for her, no matter how much he wished he could.

"We're lucky to have her," Aubrey said when he didn't respond. "She wouldn't be here at all if she had any other choice."

"Probably not," he managed, though he should have said *absolutely.*

To end the uncomfortable conversation and to resist the temptation to continue watching Kayla's approach, he pulled an extendable leash from his coat pocket and snapped it to Bandit's collar. That prompted his sister's grunt of objection, but at least it was only about his pet training and not his personal life.

"Luke's waiting for me." Aubrey pointed to the tractor, where her fiancé, Luke Bishop, now sat inside the cab. With a wave, she hurried to climb in and sit on the buddy seat.

Though Jasper didn't miss the couple's long kiss before driving off, he refused to be jealous of his sister, or any of his eleven siblings, some of whom had found love this year, often while facing down danger at the same time.

Dating hadn't been at the top of his priority list for the past few years anyway, since the Gemini had become his whole life. Not that he'd ever been a hero in the dating game. Funny how few women found his need to question their motives—a gift from dear old dad—endearing. Lately though, his social pool consisted of one off-limits ranch hand and a revolving selection of adventure-seeking guests. Since he never mixed business with pleasure, that was that.

But something had changed when Aubrey and Luke announced their engagement. Nothing like watching his twin and *business partner* planning her spring wedding to make a guy rethink his life. If even Aubrey had found a way to fit romance into her busy schedule, then did that mean that it was time for him to consider settling down, and maybe try to trust someone, too? Well, either take that step or embrace his life as a bachelor.

When his gaze shifted back to the rider who'd just slid from the saddle ten yards away, Jasper blew out a frustrated breath in another puff of white mist. He didn't have to make any decisions about his future today, but if he wasted more time pining after *this* woman—one who had every reason to despise the whole Colton family—he wouldn't need to choose between companionship and isolation. That choice would be made for him.

Chapter 2

In the expanding morning light, Jasper recognized the horse that Kayla guided with a lead rope as Reina, a sweet part-Arabian mare. As she neared him and the dog that was still pulling on the leash but had stopped barking, Kayla paused to give the horse's shoulder a good rub. Just out of reach for both man and animal.

"Good morning, boss."

"Morning, Kayla."

"Oh. Sorry… Jasper," she corrected. Her pink complexion, already flushed from the ride, edged toward magenta.

He turned so she wouldn't see his wry expression. In his thoughts, the two of them had been *awfully* familiar. Yet even after all this time, Kayla still wasn't comfortable calling him by his first name. Since he expected her to continue to the arena once she determined that the dog wouldn't startle the mare, she surprised him by hesitating there. She shot a few glances over her shoulder, as if she expected one of the other ranch hands to catch up with her, though she'd ridden in from the upper pasture alone.

Was she waiting for him to acknowledge that she'd covered for him that morning? Given that most of their conversations involved nothing more riveting than the bountiful or meager alfalfa crop or the arrival of new salt-and-mineral licks for the cattle, it made sense that waiting for deserved recognition would make her nervous. But this was extreme. She seemed more skittish than her horse.

"Hey, thanks for doing the feeding this morning."

Her dark brow lifted as though his words confused her, and she shifted her boots in the dirt. Finally, she nodded. "Just doing my job. I was up early, anyway."

She blinked, and her gaze shifted to the side in a way that tempted him to ask her why, even if she had been awake, she'd decided to start work earlier than everyone else.

"Well, I appreciate it," he said, instead. "Still can't believe I overslept."

He pointed to the dog that continued to pant, the bit of give that Jasper had provided on the leash pulled taut between them. "Not getting much sleep with the new puppy."

"You mean that little guy?"

Kayla let the horse's lead rope drop to the ground and cautiously approached the dog as it choked itself trying to reach her. A few feet away from it, she stopped. Whatever had been on her mind before seemed to disappear as she beamed at Bandit, the tension around her full lips smoothing.

"So, you're the one keeping the boss awake?"

She took another step forward and paused again, lifting her gaze to meet Jasper's. "Is it okay?"

"He'll have a coronary if you *don't* pet him."

He chuckled as she extended her gloved hand, fingers folded beneath, for the dog to sniff. Bandit barely managed a whiff before diving in, hindquarters and trademark Aussie docked tail wiggling. The tinkling sound of Kayla's laughter filled the air as she kneeled close to the puppy, earning multiple kisses. She chuckled again as she brushed off her damp cheek with her coat sleeve.

Great. Now he was jealous of a horse *and* a dog.

"I can't believe you haven't met Bandit up close yet. He's already insisted on greeting almost everyone."

But then Kayla always seemed to be elsewhere when he was working in the barn or the other outbuildings. She even took most of her assignments from Aubrey, as if purposely avoiding him. He must not have been as discreet with his staring as he'd thought.

"How could I have missed meeting this sweet guy?" She spoke in a singsongy voice to the dog. "Who's a good boy? Bandit's a good boy."

And a chick magnet. Jasper couldn't look away as she buried her face in the puppy's furry, damp neck. Whether or not it was in his best interest to draw Kayla St. James closer to him, he wished he'd thought of adopting a pet sooner.

As she stood with Bandit still bouncing around her legs, she twirled the part of the leash that hung slack now. "What's this all about? A ranch dog can't be tied down like this."

"I know. He has to be free so he can protect—"

She flinched as if he'd hit her with something more powerful than a response. Stepping back so the dog could no longer stretch to reach her, she tilted her hat lower over her brow and sneaked another peek behind her.

He followed the direction of her gaze. Only layers of brown, gold and deepening green of pastures and trees extended behind her and upward until they broke at the lightening gray sky. His stomach tightened, anyway. What had she been looking for?

When she met his gaze again, he cleared his throat and said the first thing that popped into his head. "I'll saddle up Shadow and catch up with the rest of you in the upper pasture."

She stared at her boots, shifting her weight from one to the other. "After the cattle are fed, I'll continue riding the fences for the rest of the morning."

"Yeah. Well—" He stopped himself from saying something ridiculous like she shouldn't ride alone. The ranch hands regularly completed the solitary task of checking the fences along the property's perimeter and outside the pastures for breaks. That job was critical to prevent cattle from escaping or predators from invading. How could he tell her he suddenly wasn't comfortable with her riding by herself? "Uh. That'll work."

Having missed the whole drama that had played out in Jasper's head, Kayla strode back to Reina. The horse must have sensed a new tension as it shuffled its forehooves. Kayla brushed a hand through the animal's mane, but her actions were too quick to soothe.

She earned only a snort of disapproval. Maybe a cute puppy had helped her to forget about it for a moment, but something wasn't right.

"You doing okay?" The words were out of his mouth before he could stop them.

Kayla glanced over, chewing the corner of her lip, a nervous habit he'd always found endearing. Now something about it prickled his scalp.

"Sure. I'm fine."

How had he never noticed what a terrible liar she was? Unlike some of the people in his past who lied without apparent guilt. He suspected that Kayla usually stuck close to the truth. She avoided his gaze as she brushed her fingers through Reina's mane again. Gentler this time. The horse settled, but Jasper wasn't so easily fooled.

"If you're not here about the horses this morning, then was there something else you wanted to tell me?"

"Nothing I can't handle."

His breath caught as a thought struck him, his gut clenching with foreboding. "Did one of the guys say something—"

He cut off his words, trying to reconcile the vile idea with any of the men he'd thought he knew well.

Kayla had started to guide Reina to the west side of the barn, where she would help load the next hay bale when Luke and Aubrey returned with the tractor, but she stopped and faced him again.

"Of course not," she said with a huff. "You know better than that."

At least he hoped he did, which let him catch his breath. How could he explain his clenched fists or that his first instinct had been to think only about protecting her while not even considering the impact a sexual harassment lawsuit could have on the ranch? He pressed his hands to his sides, trying to unfold his fingers without her noticing.

"Anyway, if someone had said something, don't you think I'd be able to handle it?" Still holding the rope, she crossed her arms over her duck coat.

"Are you kidding? I would worry more about the other guy."

The straight line of her lips refused to curve. Like the ground, her green eyes had taken on a coating of frost.

"Good."

Without looking his way again, she continued around the barn. As her employer, he should have reminded her never to take a matter like that into her own hands, but he doubted she would be receptive at the moment.

He couldn't blame her for being annoyed with him. Kayla was no damsel in distress, and she was a darn good ranch hand. At about five foot nine, she stood taller than some of the men and not much shorter than his six feet. No way would she be impressed with his instinct to protect her.

Only after horse and rider disappeared around the corner did Jasper realize that Kayla had never told him why she'd come to him. Whether she'd planned to say something, or he'd just been an unwelcome witness to her unease over something she planned to keep private, he shared her jitters now.

Next to him, Bandit whined and pulled on the leash, trying to catch up with her.

"I get it, buddy."

Just like the times when Jasper sensed that coyotes had moved too close to the herd, the hair on the back of his neck lifted. Kayla had kept checking behind her as if she'd thought someone was following her. No… *chasing her*. He had to know who or what it was and try to help her, even if nothing would ever make up for the tragedy his dad had created for her family. And even if she'd never want anything to do with him again.

Still, he'd learned to trust his instincts, and this one told him that she needed *someone*. He might not be her choice of helpers, but he would just have to do. He petted his puppy's head and grinned, an idea forming in his mind. If Kayla thought that he was above using the horses she loved or the dog that already adored her to get her to open up to him and maybe even trust him a little, she'd be dead wrong.

Kayla stomped to the front of the barn, where several hay bales were already stacked for the tractor's return. The horse that she led tossed its head and snorted when they finally stopped. She regretted causing Reina's rare frustration, but she could relate to it. First, she'd almost spilled her guts to Jasper *again*, and then he'd automatically assumed she'd come to tell him about a problem she couldn't handle herself. She hated it even more that he had a point. If she were forced to trust someone eventually, he wouldn't be the worst choice she could make.

She stepped to the corner of the barn. An uncomfortable feeling tinged her relief when she found no one there. She refused to call it disappointment. Had she *wanted* him to follow her and ask more questions? Would she have told him if he asked the right ones?

Nearer to the closed door, she craned her neck to catch a glimpse of the tractor that should have returned down the hill by now. What was taking Aubrey and Luke so long? She needed to know which feeding stop they were on, so she could ride out and meet them there. Didn't they understand that she couldn't afford any lulls in activity this morning? She wouldn't tell Jasper, but she'd appreciated the distraction that feeding the horses had provided. The last thing she needed now was extra time to think or worry.

Tell us or else!

She shivered as the words invaded her thoughts again, her gloved hand automatically shifting to her jacket pocket, where she'd stowed her phone. Though she'd received no additional texts since this morning, dread still swelled in her throat, making the frigid air even more difficult to breathe.

Us. The messages always came with plural pronouns, suggesting multiple senders. Just how many of them were there? Were they nearby? Could they see her now? She shivered as her gaze swept over the open pastures, the few ranch buildings and guest cabins appearing like toys in the distance as they dotted the tree-lined backdrop.

Swallowing, she pulled out her phone, yanked off a glove and tapped the screen to check it one more time.

"Getting paid to play on your phone?" Jasper followed his words around the corner as he sat tall in Shadow's saddle.

Kayla fumbled the phone, managing not to drop it, though her glove slid to the ground. Her chest tightened. All morning, she'd been bracing herself for an attack from the rear, and somehow she'd missed Jasper's approach. On horseback, no less.

She returned the phone to her pocket and bent to retrieve the glove. "Sorry. I was just—"

"Killing time?"

"Something like that."

He clicked his tongue so that the horse moved a few steps closer. When they were near enough that Kayla could have reached out to pet Shadow, Jasper watched her from his advantaged position. She turned away and climbed onto her horse's saddle.

Jasper glanced up and down the paved roadway. "Guess everyone's moving in slow motion this morning. Except for you, anyway. You never said why you were up so early."

"Couldn't sleep."

Now that was an understatement, even if he seemed to accept it. Before he had the chance to ask more questions, she posed one of her own.

"How'd *you* get here so fast?"

He patted the arch of Shadow's neck and delivered one of his closed-lip smiles that probably made weaker women swoon. She reminded herself that she wasn't one of them, even if she'd occasionally bristled at female ranch guests who flirted with him. Strange how he'd always seemed oblivious to their attention.

"Funny discovery. Did you know that if you *ride* a horse rather than to just walk one with a lead rope, you can get where you're going quicker?"

"I've heard that somewhere."

She allowed him his joke, but she couldn't help giving the saddle a once-over to see if Jasper had taken any shortcuts in preparing the horse, just to catch up with her. Boss or not, she'd speak up if he failed to provide proper care for one of the horses. But the pad and blanket beneath the heavy Western saddle, the front and back cinches, and even the headstall appeared to have been properly positioned and secured.

"Did I miss anything?"

He smiled again, and this time, her tummy did a little flip. Either he'd moved efficiently through the steps of tacking a horse, or she'd been waiting longer for the tractor than she'd realized.

"Not that I can tell without checking the cinches myself."

"Be my guest."

"That won't be necessary." As a thought crossed her mind, she shot a look to the corner of the barn. "Wait. Where's the dog? You can't lock him in the truck all day, you know."

Jasper folded his fingers in a hand flute and whistled. Bandit rounded the building and bounded up to the horses so quickly that it slid on an icy spot, paws finding no purchase, and landed on its rump. Both horses whinnied and stomped.

"Good boy," Jasper said anyway.

"Sure you shouldn't have him on a leash?" she asked with a smirk.

"Had to trust him sooner or later."

She shifted in the saddle, Jasper's words coming too close to her thoughts about *him* earlier. "Glad you figured that out."

"He needs to run off some energy. Like you said, I shouldn't tie him down."

"You're taking your dog-training advice from me? What do I know?"

He pointed to Bandit, now sitting near Reina's hooves and looking up at Kayla, whining.

"You're a horse whisperer. Bet you know something about dogs, too." He gestured to Bandit again. "He can't seem to get enough of you."

Jasper straightened in the saddle as he must have recognized the double meaning in his words. The color in his cheeks deepened. For someone who'd been concerned about one of the guys saying something inappropriate, he'd come close himself. "Uh. Sorry."

"We always had dogs on The Rock Solid," she volunteered, to steer past the uncomfortable moment.

He settled back in the saddle. "You see. You *do* know something about them. We never had any pets when I was growing up. With twelve kids, including three sets of twins and a set of triplets, Mom already had her hands full."

"I bet she did." Though she'd met many of Jasper's siblings over the past two years, as an only child, she still couldn't wrap her head around the idea of having so many brothers and sisters.

"Somehow, she handled the chaos," he said. "She's pretty amazing."

Kayla didn't miss that Jasper said nothing about his father. Come to think of it, neither he nor Aubrey had ever mentioned the man in her presence, though they had reasons to tiptoe around *that* subject with her. Before, she'd thought her family and the families of others to whom Ben Colton had denied justice were his only victims. Now, as the faces of the man's dozen children and their mother paraded through her thoughts, she wondered.

Jasper stared down at his saddle horn, his shoulders curled forward, as if heavy thoughts weighed on him.

"Butch and Wyatt," she blurted, surprised by her sudden need to lift some of that weight for him.

He drew his brows together.

"Our dogs," she clarified. "My parents named them for Butch Cassidy and Wyatt Earp."

"An outlaw and a lawman. Interesting mix."

Kayla nodded, glad he didn't mention that their fathers had also been on two ends of the criminal-justice spectrum, at least for a while. The irony had been that the judge was the guilty one, while her dad was innocent.

"Anyway, I wondered if you would help me out as I retrain Bandit. We have different expectations for him since he won't be a service dog. I need to prepare him to help with the cattle. Plus, I don't want to leave him at my house when Aubrey and I host Thanksgiving dinner, so…"

"You're kidding, right? You can't retrain him in that short amount of time."

"I could…with *your* help."

"That isn't a good idea." In fact, she couldn't think of a worse one. A plan like that would require her to spend time with Jasper and would give her the chance to be tempted again to confide in him.

"Clearly, Bandit would disagree."

Kayla lowered her gaze to the ground, where the pup sat on its haunches, too close to Reina's hooves for her liking, and stared up at her with yearning. She averted her gaze to stop her heart from melting.

"Isn't there anyone else on the ranch who could—"

"I would pay you overtime, of course. I wouldn't expect you to help for free."

She shook her head. "I'm not the right one—"

"Can you name anyone better?"

Quickly, she cataloged the faces of her coworkers and even her other boss. Sure, several had expertise with Red Angus, Hereford and even Charolais cattle, but they came to her with questions about the horses. Though the others might know something about dogs, this puppy seemed to have chosen her.

"Well, can you?"

"Fine. I'll help." Because she felt as if she'd been ensnared in a trap and that she'd practically stuck out her foot and waited to be caught, she couldn't resist adding, "But there's no way he'll be ready for a holiday appearance."

"As long as we try—"

The tractor interrupted whatever he'd been about to say by finally rumbling down the hill. Without waiting for him to finish, she clicked her tongue to signal for Reina to get going. As she rode toward the tractor, she forced herself not to look back. She could only hope that Bandit and, more importantly, its owner hadn't followed.

When the massive machine met her on the road and stopped, Aubrey popped out of the cab onto the step.

"Is everything all right, Kayla?"

She wished her bosses would quit asking her that.

Aubrey studied her face and then glanced beyond her to Jasper. She squinted as if attempting to decipher what had just taken place between her and her brother.

"I'm fine," Kayla answered too late. "Just wanted to see which stop you're on for the feed."

"Oh. Headed to the west side of the lower pasture."

"Good. I'll meet you there."

The mare didn't need coaxing as they headed off

the road and back to the horse trail. Before, the wind that came at her face like pinpricks had bothered her, but now she appreciated the cold on her heated cheeks.

Once she could no longer see those near the barn, she directed the horse to trot and then to canter. She was running, too, she recognized with a frown. But what could she do? She had to put distance between herself and Jasper. Even if that meant traveling, alone, in the same direction she'd ridden from earlier when she'd been convinced someone lurked behind each bank of trees. Now she longed for the comfort of those sheltering firs.

Why did Jasper have to be so easy to talk to, just when she'd felt vulnerable enough to let someone in? And why had she let him use that cute puppy to get closer to her?

Was she afraid of him? A resounding *no* flashed in her thoughts, which should have worried her more than any text, no matter how threatening. Jasper Colton was dangerous to her, all right. Just danger of another sort.

Chapter 3

Jasper guided one of his favorite older mares, Dory, into the barn two days later, just as Vince Little led Marco toward the exit. Marco, a quarter horse gelding that they'd added to the Gemini's stock the year before, swung its head and snorted, but the American paint mare, with its huge swashes of brown and white, ignored the other horse and continued stepping carefully, favoring its left forefoot.

As the two unsaddled horses passed, Vince paused and pointed.

"Kayla will want to look at that one."

"I'm sure she will." Jasper grimaced as he examined the animal's gait again. "We'll also call in the vet as a precaution. Poor girl. Hope it's nothing serious."

"Kayla would be the one to know."

Jasper was counting on that. Since riding off two

days before, leaving him behind with curious looks from his sister and future brother-in-law, she'd avoided him. He couldn't use Bandit as an excuse to spend more time with her if she constantly dodged them both. So, though he didn't relish seeing any of their horses in pain, he appreciated that Dory's sore foot would at least give him another reason to talk to Kayla. Why he kept trying when she'd made it clear that she didn't want to confide in him, he couldn't answer.

As he stuffed his gloves in his coat pockets, Jasper scanned the yawning barn from the wide aisleway, floodlights shining down on recently swept floors, to the numbered stalls lining each side of the building. Aside from the ranch hand, him and the two horses, the place looked empty, the iron-and-wood sliding doors of the stalls gaping open. He understood how Kayla might need a break after examining about thirty quarter horses, Appaloosas and paints for foot and health issues that the farrier or the vet would need to address before the holiday. But her absence right then, when she had to know he would bring in the final animal, seemed to be more than that. It was personal.

Another equine snort brought his attention back to Vince, who tightened his grip on Marco's lead rope, the high-strung horse continuing to sidestep in protest.

"Guess somebody didn't like anyone messing with his shoes," Vince said. "Even Kayla."

"Or maybe it rankled him that you pulled him away from the pretty little lady."

At the sound of that voice, both men glanced back at the barn's main doors. Hank Moore stood in the opening, a saddle hoisted over his shoulder. Immediately,

Jasper's fists clenched so tightly that the rope dug into his palm. His jaws ached from grinding his molars.

"You think that's funny, Hank?"

The ranch hand blinked, and his mouth fell slack. "Sorry, boss. Just joking—"

"Just nothing. I've told you before that we won't tolerate sexist comments around here. You're all doing the same job. You're equals."

Hank raised his free hand in surrender, though his wide eyes suggested he still didn't understand Jasper's outburst.

"I didn't mean anything by—"

"I don't *care* what you meant. Don't let it happen again. It doesn't matter how hard it is to find good help around here…"

Jasper willed his fists to loosen but let the threat hang heavy in the dusty air. When Hank nodded and stared at his boots, Jasper shot a glance back to Vince. The other man gawked as if he'd just reported a cattle stampede. For a few seconds, no one spoke, the only sounds coming from the horses shifting their hooves on the floor.

What was wrong with him? He never raised his voice to employees. Not even last July, after Charlie Clark's practical joke had resulted in a setback in renovations.

Hank cleared his throat. "It won't happen again."

Jasper wished he could say the same about his own behavior. Though he'd always had a reputation for being easygoing, around Kayla St. James, he couldn't keep his cool even if he were standing inside a refrigerator truck. Unfortunately, no one appreciated the odd protective instinct she inspired in him less than she did.

"See that it doesn't. Now, don't you two have work to do?"

"Yessir," Vince answered for them both.

Jasper could imagine the looks the men had given each other as Hank hefted the saddle onto one of the racks in the tack room, and the two of them hurried out of the barn, taking the gelding with them. He couldn't let what they thought matter to him. Though he might have been oblivious to workplace antics that made one of his employees uncomfortable before, that stopped now. And if he *had* been oblivious previously, he shouldn't have been—no matter how he felt about any of those involved.

If only the employee in question hadn't stepped out of the third stall just then. Jasper's breath caught, and his eyes were probably wider than Hank's had been. Without her hat, her braid mussed from hours under it, and her coat unbuttoned over her overalls, Kayla leaned on the wall separating two stalls. She crossed her arms. Jasper didn't have to ask if she'd overheard the conversation where he'd swooped in like an action hero to defend her honor. Or how she felt about it. Her body language and flat expression said it all.

"What was that about?"

"Nothing." Guilt had him cramming his free hand in his coat pocket.

"Didn't sound like *nothing*."

Jasper expected a stream of words to follow that would have made ranch guests blush, and some that should never be spoken to an employer. But she just stood there, waiting for him to explain himself.

"I'm sorry," he said when he couldn't take it anymore. "You said you could handle it, but—"

"You're the boss."

Her words stated the dull finality—truth with neither adornment nor defense. Jasper rolled his lips inward. Usually, he loved the title of boss, but now it sounded like a slur. He would have preferred to hear her tirade.

The side of Kayla's mouth crept up in a smirk. She either wasn't as furious with him as he'd thought, or she was covering it well.

"I've got to know, what was the look on Hank's face when you called him out?"

For a few seconds, Jasper could only stare at her.

"Don't leave me hanging."

"But I thought—"

"That it was ridiculous to go off on him over something so minor? Fair point. But if Hank called me 'little lady' or 'darlin'' one more time—" She shook her head, closing her eyes. When she opened them again, she stepped away from the wall. "Anyway, not my dude ranch, not my corral of horses."

She appeared pleased with her new take on the old Polish proverb about circuses and monkeys, a hint that she had no say in the way he ran his business. Something about it bothered him. No matter how many ways she reminded him that they were employer and employee and needed to remain in their respective corners, he wished he could forget it.

"Speaking of horses…"

At least one of them was clear about the role she played on the Gemini. Kayla stepped forward, her movements jolty as she reached out to take Dory's lead rope from him. Unprepared for her sudden approach, he couldn't let go quickly enough to avoid brushing her hand. She jerked back as if he'd burned her, an irony since the heat from her fingers spread through *his* frozen skin.

As he sneaked little breaths and willed his pulse to slow, Jasper couldn't stop staring at her hands. She clasped them in front of her now. Calloused like his, they were badges of honor, earned through hard work and dedication to the animals and the land. Some men might not have found her hands attractive—nails unpainted and trimmed short for the job, skin pink and wind-chapped. But just the idea of Kayla's touch set enough fires on his skin to burn down the barn.

She had no idea how she affected him, anyway. Her focus, now and always, remained on the horses. Trying to follow her example, Jasper draped the end loop in front of him so she could grab it without touching him again. Whether that was for her protection or his, he chose not to analyze.

Gripping the rope, she clucked to encourage the mare to follow her into the stall. At the horse's first step, Kayla stopped and looked back.

"You didn't tell me she was hurt."

"I didn't get the chance."

She lifted a brow. If he hadn't been fighting her battles, whether he had the right to or not, they already could have addressed the horse's injury.

"I don't know if she had a misstep, kicked something or what, but she's been babying that foot ever since we started over."

"Is that why you don't have Bandit with you?"

"Sent him off with Luke for a tractor ride so he wouldn't be under her hooves."

Though he expected a crack about him spoiling the

puppy or confusing Bandit about the identity of the pack leader, she nodded.

"Makes sense. She might not have been as patient with him when she's hurting. Let's get a look at it."

She leaned close to the horse's ear and whispered encouraging words. When she tugged the rope again, the mare trailed unsteadily.

Jasper followed her into the stall, slid the door closed and bolted it, while Kayla tied the rope to a hook on the wall. She continued speaking in soft tones.

Though the door was only solid wood at the bottom, with black wrought-iron bars at the top, the spacious stall seemed smaller than usual. The air heavier. The only thing keeping the space from feeling downright intimate was the one-thousand-pound beast that Kayla had positioned between them.

Rather than to begin an examination right away, she used a soft-bristle brush from the tack basket on the wall to clear dust from Dory's coat in long, smooth strokes. Once the mare relaxed, Kayla traded the brush for a hoof pick, carefully rounded the front and stopped at the horse's right foreleg.

"It's going to be okay, sweetie. I know it hurts."

Jasper was anxious to know the extent of the injury, but he kept quiet to avoid startling the animal. They needed Dory to trust the ranch hand enough to let her see the tender foot. Kayla rested her hand on the horse's shoulder and slowly slid it down the leg, past the knee to just above the fetlock joint. Then she waited. After a few snorts, the mare lifted its leg.

"Good girl," Kayla crooned as she held the injured hoof between her hands and used the pick to clear dirt so that she could get a better look. "We're going to make it feel better."

Just watching those tender ministrations made Jasper's throat thicken with emotion. A Florence Nightingale in bulky layers and muck boots. None of the horses on the Gemini were hers—she'd been sure to point that out—but she cared for them as though they were. She treated them like dear friends. Though he refused to be jealous of a horse twice in the same week, he resented any lucky human who would one day be on the receiving end of Kayla's care.

After a few seconds, she gently lowered Dory's foot to the ground and stepped back.

"Do you think it's serious?" he asked in a low tone.

She held her chin between her thumb and forefinger, studying the horse, before shaking her head. "I don't see any cracks, abscesses or evidence of seedy toe. It could be just bruising, but I'll have the farrier give her some extra attention and give the vet a heads-up. Until they visit, she'll need some TLC and a stall in the barn for a few days."

"You're the boss on this one."

Kayla had returned to the horse's near side, but now she studied him over Dory's back. Though she probably thought he was joking at first, something must have convinced her otherwise because she nodded. "I'll make sure she's getting the best care possible."

She let the horse nuzzle her hand and reached into her pocket to pull out a sugar cube. Sore foot or not, Dory quickly nibbled the treat.

"You're the horse expert, but I hope you know that I would do anything to make sure that all the animals are safe as well." Jasper blinked, realizing he hadn't mentioned his business partner, who was an equal part in that commitment. "Aubrey, too."

"I know you would."

Her declaration surprised him. Jasper watched her over the horse, looking for answers as she had before. This time, their gazes caught. Lingered. Warmth spread in his chest. For a flash of a moment, the enormous animal and all those other barriers between them didn't seem impossible to navigate after all. When her amazing eyes shifted to the side, and she turned to face the wall, he wondered if he'd imagined the whole thing.

"I'd better get back to the bunkhouse for dinner." She busied her hands collecting tools. "It's Charlie's turn to cook, and it's usually almost edible, so…"

With her arms full, she gestured with a movement of her head, silently asking Jasper to open the stall door. He swallowed. If he were smart, he'd just let her go. Already, he was imagining possibilities between them that didn't exist. Couldn't. But today was the most they'd spoken since she'd arrived on the Gemini, and he wasn't ready for this moment to end.

"He thought I'd been replaced by an alien," he blurted.

She looked up again. "Who thought *what*?"

"You know… Hank. You asked me about the look on his face."

Her lips lifted in a real smile that crinkled the corners of her eyes, and he knew instantly he would do or say anything to make her smile like that more often.

"Good," she said. "He deserved a little shaking up."

"I would tell you he's a product of his generation,

but that's no excuse." He shook his head vehemently. "I meant what I said earlier. I won't allow it."

Her smile slid away, and she seemed to lose herself in her thoughts. Like the other morning, her discomfort made him uneasy as well.

"Please don't fire him on my account. He hasn't done anything really. And as I said before, I can handle—"

"I'm not going to," he said to interrupt her. "At least not yet."

He waited for her nod before he continued. "Anyway, if I did fire any of the ranch hands, it would only be punishment for the rest of us. Same amount of work, fewer people to share it."

"Hank will be on his best behavior from now on. I know it."

"I hope you're right." That she wouldn't meet his gaze made him wonder if she was as certain as she wanted him to believe. "If not, he'll have more to worry about than just losing a job. He'll have *you* to contend with."

She chuckled, but that ended abruptly when the loud vibration of a cell phone startled them both. Kayla fumbled in her pocket for hers, forgetting about the items she'd balanced in her arms. Two brushes and the hoof pick toppled to the hay-covered stall floor.

"Such a klutz." She scrambled to pick up everything.

Jasper unbolted the stall door, and she hurried out, continuing down the aisleway to the tack room. He couldn't help but to follow, convinced that at least one of the answers he'd been looking for had to do with that phone.

When he caught up with her, she'd already hung up

the equipment and had her back to him. He approached until he could see the light of her screen.

"What's the message?" he asked over her shoulder.

Kayla slipped the phone in her coat pocket and scanned the room as though checking to see if they were alone. She turned to face him.

"That? It was nothing important."

"Didn't sound like *nothing*." He crossed his arms and repeated her words from earlier.

Just like before, she tilted her chin up with defiance, but now her skin looked pale, her eyes too bright.

"I keep telling you that I can handle—"

"Sure about that? Are you certain you can take on whatever that is—" he paused to point to her pocket "—without backup from anyone at all?"

He trapped her gaze until she finally lowered it to her boots. Still, he waited. Finally, she shook her head.

"Then tell me, who is after you?"

She lifted her gaze to meet his again in that same resistant pose, but her chin quivered, and she couldn't stop blinking. His gut felt so heavy that he could have sworn he'd swallowed a block of cement. He was certain nothing she could say would worry him more than just seeing her fear on full display. Until she spoke.

"That's the problem. I don't know."

She pulled out the phone again, opened her messages and turned the screen to show him.

Your time is running out!

He froze. He'd faced down black bears and a few rattlesnakes before, even people targeting his family, but without knowing all the details of the threats, he'd still never felt a sense of doom like this before. Or the determination to throw himself in front of a bullet.

Whoever was coming after Kayla would have to get through him first.

Chapter 4

Kayla stared out the pickup's windshield into the fully dark six o'clock sky, bewildered over how she'd ended up there, on the bench seat next to the man from whom she'd sworn to keep her distance. More than that, forty pounds of wet and contented canine lay draped across her lap. When she scooted farther from Jasper, the puppy only resettled over her legs, resting its snout on the door handle.

"Sorry about Bandit." He handed her a towel.

"You could just drop me off at the bunkhouse. I'll be fine."

Jasper continued to look straight ahead, headlights illuminating the fast dance of snowflakes pouring from the sky, the windshield wipers thudding, trying to keep pace.

"You said you'd come to my place so we could talk about this."

"I know what I said, but maybe it wasn't a good idea. I was a little overwhelmed."

It wasn't fair. He'd caught her at a weak moment. First, their unsettling exchange in the stall, and then another text. She hadn't been thinking clearly enough to avoid sharing her secret with him, let alone to dodge his request that might have been a demand.

"And you're not overwhelmed now?"

He had a point. It was too late to turn back, anyway, in the situation or on the road. They'd already caught up with Luke to pick up Bandit and had long since driven past her living quarters. Now Jasper pulled up to his own house, illuminated by ordinary porch lights. Several of the motion-activated type flipped on along the cabin's exterior as they parked. Though Kayla had gotten a few looks at the cabin from the trail, and even from the road, she'd never been inside.

Jasper opened his cab door. "Well, we're here. Let's go inside and scare up something to eat. Then we can talk about what's been happening to you and come up with a plan."

As much as Kayla regretted telling him about the texts and hated the idea of relinquishing control, Jasper's idea sounded solid. Comforting, even. That should have worried her.

"I can't move until the dog gets off of me."

"He's just making sure you're okay. Remember, he was training as a service animal. Now he's being a canine weighted blanket."

"You mean when he wasn't a stellar student?" Kayla sensed Jasper's frown in the darkness, so she added, "He's doing a fine job."

"She's all right, buddy. Come."

Bandit followed his instructions, and Kayla trailed after them. After using the cast-iron bootjack on the porch, she stepped into the doorway in her wool socks. She couldn't help hesitating though, not ready to barge into her boss's house.

Beyond its amazing, paneled ceiling design and A-shaped window grouping in the front and back, the house was more simply appointed than any of the guest cabins she'd toured. The main living area featured only a woodstove, sturdy furniture, a television and a braided rug on the hardwood floor, plus a stack of books on the table. Still, it looked like a palace when compared to the slowly decaying structure she and her mother had shared after her father's imprisonment. The home she still would have returned to, if given a chance.

"Aren't you coming in?"

Jasper hurried around, fluffing a flattened pillow and draping a wadded sherpa throw over the back of the couch. Bandit darted after him, intent on starting a game of keep-away. Finally, he led the pup into the laundry room for dinner. On his way back, he nabbed a few sweatshirts from the chair arm and collected dog toys scattered on the floor. He left the books where they were.

"Sorry. Bandit and I weren't expecting guests."

"I'm definitely not dressed to be one," she said as she glanced down at her overalls and sock-clad feet. What was the matter with her? Dinner with the ranch hands was always a come-as-you-are thing. Did she believe she needed to step it up in Jasper's house?

"Good thing it's casual around here."

"Your place is nice," she said, to change the subject. "A little different from the bunkhouse."

"Yeah. Sorry about that, too. Pretty basic living there."

"It's a roof over my head."

Their gazes met as both recognized that if not for the Gemini, Kayla wouldn't have had a place to live.

"And the guys would *kill* to have my private room."

Jasper shot another glance her way over that unfortunate choice of words. He gestured for her to follow him into the galley kitchen.

"Let's eat."

As if in response, Bandit ran out of the laundry room and into the kitchen, clean but for a few dishes in the sink. As Jasper washed up, reheated lasagna on individual plates and prepared salads, Bandit whined and begged, following him like a shadow as he moved back and forth in the narrow space. The pup even popped up on its hind legs and tried to paw food off the counter, earning a firm reprimand. Jasper led the dog back to the laundry room and closed the door.

By the time that he returned, Kayla had already washed her hands and located the silverware drawer to set the table. Just as she finished, he sat across from her.

"Maybe he really won't be ready for Thanksgiving."

"He needs some training. But locking him up won't teach him anything, either."

"I know," he said miserably.

"He's a good boy. He'll get it."

Jasper didn't look so sure.

As the scents of oregano and basil filtered from her plate, Kayla focused on her food, surprised to discover she was famished. Welcoming the change since she hadn't had an appetite for a week, she dug into the lasagna, barely taking time to breathe between bites.

"This is amazing. Did *you* make this?"

"I like to eat," he said with a grin. "And though Mom enjoys having her kids around, she doesn't always appreciate us just showing up at mealtimes."

She took another bite and closed her eyes, savoring it. "Don't let any of the other ranch hands know you can cook like this, or you'll have a line out your door at dinnertime."

"Luke already knows, but he's a good cook himself. Aubrey appreciates that."

They returned to their food. Though her confession about the texts remained as an elephant in the kitchen, overfilling one of the four chairs at the dinette, she was relieved to have a break before they discussed it. A few minutes to breathe more easily than she had in days.

Only after they'd finished eating did Jasper set his napkin aside, signaling that the time had come for them to talk.

"How long have you been receiving the texts?"

"About three weeks."

"And you waited this long—" He stopped himself and tried again. "I'm glad you trusted me enough to tell me."

Her fork clanged to her plate. She picked it up and set it on her napkin. She was certain that if he'd asked her to *trust* him earlier, she never would have been able to tell him.

"At first, it didn't seem like a big deal," she said.

"Can I see them?"

Swallowing, she collected her phone from the kitchen counter where she'd left it. After opening her messages, she scrolled back to the date of the first text and handed him the device. Her stomach clenched with misgivings as he read. Had it been a mistake to tell him after all? Was it too much to risk, letting anyone in?

He clicked out of the app and set the phone on the table.

"They're all from different numbers. And the threats are escalating." At Kayla's nod, Jasper continued. "Whoever they are, they're getting more desperate for you to tell them what they think you know."

She couldn't help shivering at that. Desperate people did unimaginable things, like when she'd made a cop, enforcing the court-ordered foreclosure on her family's ranch, drag her out of the house.

Jasper watched her for so long that she couldn't help but squirm, the cushion on the wooden chair scooting beneath her.

"Do you have any idea what the messages mean?"

"No clue. I mean, they seem to think I know where something is hidden. But what and where, I don't know."

"What about *who*? Do you know of anyone who has something against you? Or who would want to frighten you?"

This time she just shook her head.

"No parent of a child you've given riding lessons to, displeased with your efforts?" He dismissed his own suggestion with a brush of his hand. "Why am I asking that? You get glowing reviews every time."

Even if discussing the texts out loud made them more real, she couldn't help smiling at the comment, like many he'd made since she'd started work on the Gemini. Her Colton bosses always ensured that their employees felt valued.

"No violent ex-boyfriend with an axe to grind?"

This time she rolled her eyes, even as the idea made

her want to shift in her chair again. Of anyone, she should have been the one to carry a sharp weapon around The Liar, just to make him leave before he could stomp on her heart. Bill Blevins wouldn't be the texter, anyway. Her ex was strange, but not violent. And by now, his fascination with relatives of convicts would have escalated to those of death-row inmates, so he would find her even less appealing.

Kayla blinked, as she realized that Jasper was still watching her, still waiting for an answer.

"I don't date anymore, and the guy I turned down for prom has probably gotten over it." The Liar came after that, but she didn't share that part.

The corner of Jasper's lip tipped upward before flattening again.

"Could it have anything to do with your—" He stopped and focused on his folded hands. "Sorry. I had to ask."

"I don't think it's about my dad. Why would it be?" She crossed and uncrossed her legs, and then shook her head to dispel the supposition that loitered. "He was innocent, you know, and your father put him away."

Jasper nodded, that familiar sadness appearing in his gaze again.

"I hate this," she admitted. "I don't usually spook easily. But with these messages, the not knowing is getting to me."

"We should take this to the police." He planted his hands on the edge of the table.

"I don't think that's necessary."

"We even have a contact in the Blue Larkspur Police Department. Chief of Police Theodore Lawson is a friend of my mom's. More than a friend." He seemed to consider his words and then added, "Also, my sister Alexa's boyfriend is Dane Beaulieu, a new detective with that department."

Kayla knew Alexa well; the US marshal often came to the ranch to ride Reina.

Still, Kayla shook her head. "What would we tell them? That someone's prank-texting me? It hasn't even reached the level of—"

"Scaring the daylights out of you? I think you're already there."

"I know I've overreacted. But the threats, so far, have been vague."

"I don't think 'Your time is running out!' is vague."

Her knees wobbled like gelatin under the table. "I've seen better intimidation than that in the comments on a social media post."

Jasper blew out a breath. "Fine. We'll wait. But we should ask a few of my brothers and sisters to look into it. Unofficially, of course."

"They don't need to do that." She'd already let one Colton know about her problem. The last thing she needed was to involve more of them.

Jasper gave a determined nod, letting her know that he wouldn't surrender that point.

"Morgan and Caleb. They're the ones most involved with The Truth Foundation. They might be willing to check it out. Or maybe Dominic. He's the FBI special agent. Or Ezra. He's the retired army officer who started his own security business."

Kayla already knew these details. She couldn't explain why, but she'd made a point of remembering facts about Judge Colton's children when she met them. Like

Jasper, several of them seemed to be trying to make up for their father's wrongdoings.

"Forget the local police," she said. "We'll take it straight to the FBI. Next, you'll be bringing in a SWAT team."

He sat back and crossed his arms. "Take this seriously, will you?"

"I am, but I'm also trying not to make too much out of it."

"Don't make too little, either."

She couldn't tell him that joking about it kept her from coming out of her skin. "How do you know your siblings wouldn't take it to the local authorities, anyway?"

"They won't if I ask them not to."

Her chest tightened at just the thought of having people in her life whom she could rely on so completely. She resisted the voice inside suggesting that Jasper might be one of them.

Still, she raised her hands in surrender. "Okay. Check in with the Colton justice crew, and I'll lay low until we find out something more."

She expected him to celebrate his win like most of the men she knew would, with loud-mouth comments or at least a victorious grin. Instead, he stacked their plates and carried them to the dishwasher, skipping his victory lap entirely.

When he finished loading, he returned to the table and gripped the back of his chair. "I'm also not comfortable with the idea of you sleeping out in the bunkhouse."

"Where exactly do you expect me to sleep?"

He gestured through the kitchen to the living room beyond it.

Kayla's mouth fell open, her hands immediately damp. "You mean here?"

"It's not a *horrible* idea." He lowered himself into his seat.

"That's exactly what it is."

"Just for a few days while my siblings check things out." He gestured to the living room and back to the kitchen. "This place has three bedrooms. You can choose between the one with the queen and the one with bunk beds. You'd even have your own bathroom."

She shook her head while he delivered his real-estate agent pitch. "Not a good idea."

"Are you saying you wouldn't enjoy a break from the bunkhouse?"

"What I'm saying is you haven't thought this through." She pushed back from the table and paced through the kitchen all the way to the woodstove before marching back. "What would we tell the rest of the staff? What about your sister and Luke?"

"Nothing. It's none of their business."

"Everything on the Gemini winds up being *everyone*'s business. This might be a huge ranch, but it's also like its own small town."

With an open hand, he indicated the chair where she'd been sitting. She sat again, planted her elbows on the table and waited.

"The rest of the staff is too busy to worry about—"

"Are you kidding? If I stayed here, you and I would be the story du jour. Hank, Charlie and Vince, the kitchen staff, the custodial staff—heck, even Luke and Aubrey—they would all think we were *doing* some business."

Her cheeks burned. How could she have just mentioned having an affair with her boss *to* her boss? Worse, her mutinous skin betrayed her by tingling all over. If she needed another reason to know that playing house with Jasper Colton would be a horrible idea, she'd found one.

Though Jasper appeared to take a keen interest in his kitchen cabinets, the flush on his neck gave away his embarrassment.

"They won't think that." He brushed his hand through his hair the way he often did when he removed his hat, but this time did it roughly enough to yank strands out by the roots. "Even if they do, who cares?"

"Speak for yourself. Nobody will accuse *you* of trying to move up from the bunkhouse to the big house. They'll say it's like Aubrey and Luke all over again."

He scoffed at that. "The situations aren't close to the same. Luke was in hiding after the exposé he wrote on that organized crime syndicate. You're the only staff member Aubrey shared that secret with, by the way. And, though Luke helped out, he never lived in the bunkhouse."

"So, what you're saying is this would be worse."

Shrugging, he appeared to concede the point. Then his smile vanished as quickly as it had appeared. "We have to figure out something to keep you safe, especially with a few guests still coming in next week."

"What makes you think that I'm safer here than I would be in the bunkhouse? Even if I didn't know how to handle a weapon, I would still be surrounded by three men rather than one."

"How do you know that one of them isn't sending the texts?"

Kayla stiffened. He'd keyed into the fear that kept

her up at night, so she struck back. "How do I know *you* aren't sending them?"

"Guess you don't."

She shouldn't have felt guilty for taking the shot since he'd provoked her. But the flash of hurt in his eyes tugged at a tender place inside her that she was always careful to hide.

"I'm not," he added in a low voice.

"I know."

The admission was out of her mouth before she could stop it, and based on his wide-eyed look, it had surprised them both. She braced herself for him to ask *how* she knew. How could she explain a conviction that came from deep in her bones? She'd been wrong before, she reminded herself. Around Jasper, she needed to record that truth and play it on repeat.

Though he didn't ask the question, the hurt in his eyes vanished.

"I have another idea."

Kayla blew out a breath. "Can't wait to hear it. The last one was a doozy."

He gave her a mean look and continued. "We'll tell everyone that you're staying here to help me train Bandit."

"No one's going to buy that story."

"They should. It's the truth. You said you'd help me get him ready for Thanksgiving dinner, and you've already seen how much work he needs with his table manners." He crossed his arms and nodded at his own idea.

"We'll tell our story. They can believe whatever they want. We'll neither confirm nor deny. It's the perfect cover. Then while everyone's busy sleuthing out details on some imaginary romance, we can be ruling out staff members, so we can look at other potential suspects like maybe the bad guys who got your father in trouble."

"Neither confirm nor deny?" Kayla squinted at him, focusing on his ill-advised plan since the creeps who took advantage of her dad were long gone now. She and Jasper had both endured their share of scuttlebutt over sins that weren't theirs—or even true, in her dad's case—and yet while she avoided public scrutiny at all costs, Jasper didn't appear to care. He would even let the others believe they were lovers just to protect her. She didn't know what to make of that.

"You might have to deal with the humiliation of people thinking you took up with this ugly mug, but at least you'll be safe."

At his grin, the tingles were back. She was so busy trying to tamp them again that she nearly missed his next words.

"They're probably already thinking it, anyway."

Her ears became impossibly warm. "They were? Why?"

"The thing with Hank in the barn. I should have handled that differently."

She sighed. He was right. No matter how Jasper had presented modern workplace standards, Neanderthals like Hank would still think he'd been defending his girlfriend.

"You also missed dinner tonight," he added.

The guys sometimes had dates and skipped meals. On a rare occasion, one even got lucky on a Saturday night and didn't come home at all. But she had been as steady as rain, never missing a meal until that night.

Not having her own vehicle and being forced to borrow someone's truck whenever she needed something at the store contributed to that. Having left them in the barn, her fellow ranch hands wouldn't have to stretch too far to guess that she and Jasper had been together.

"So, the plan is already in the works." He brushed his hands as if the matter was a fait accompli.

"I haven't agreed."

"But you'll be safe here," he insisted. "It's not as good as my mom's house, where my brother Gideon added a security system and a driveway gate with a keypad, but you saw the motion-detection lights all around the house. It seemed like a good idea after everything that happened with Luke and the sabotage on my little sister Naomi's reality show."

She could feel his gaze on her, willing her to look up from the table. Finally, she did.

"If the texts escalate into something more, at least, you'll be able to see who's coming," he said.

Kayla squashed the shiver inside her before he could see it, not ready to give in, despite the solid points he'd made. "I still think I could stay at the bunkhouse. You could even drive by a few times a night just to make sure everything is all right."

"We've already discussed that the danger might be inside."

When she opened her mouth, searching for another argument, he held up both hands, asking her to stop.

"And then there's Bandit. You don't have a guard dog at the bunkhouse." He pointed to the laundry room door, which had been closed before. Now it stood wide open.

"Guard dog? You mean that little guy?"

She pointed at the puppy scampering through the kitchen toward them, having escaped its prison.

Jasper frowned down at his pet. "How'd you get out here?"

But the pup was too busy giving Kayla kisses, tail nub wagging, to listen.

"Maybe the door didn't latch? Or he learned how to open it."

"That wouldn't be good news. What am I going to do with you?"

Jasper scowled but eventually kneeled down in front of Bandit to receive his own dose of puppy affection. He looked up at Kayla from his spot on the floor.

"Look, you need to stay safe, and I'm desperate to get this little guy situated before the turkey goes into the roasting pan. So, let's make a bargain." He extended his hand and waited to shake hers. "I would consider it a personal favor if you would stay."

She stared at his hand. "Well, if it means that much to you, then fine. You have yourself a houseguest and dog trainer."

Kayla realized her mistake the moment she let him grip her hand and felt the strength and surety in his. She pulled back quickly, hoping he wasn't watching her. She sensed that he was. The tingles returning at full force, she crossed her arms and tucked the offending hand between her arm and rib cage.

She'd learned two things today, one she'd suspected before and the other she would never have guessed. First, Jasper Colton was the kind of person who would do something big for another person, even if it came at a cost to him, while trying to convince the recipient that the roles were reversed. And second, the man who'd volunteered as her backup or protector or whatever he was might be more dangerous to her than whoever was threatening her.

Chapter 5

"Are you sure you have everything you need?"

Jasper trailed down the hall after Kayla, from the linen closet to the only main-floor bedroom, where they'd left her duffel. He'd piled the flannel sheets and towels in her arms so high that she had to tuck the top one under her chin. Good thing his mom had convinced him to purchase some guest linens "just in case," or he wouldn't have had anything to pair with those decorative comforters besides a sleeping bag or a horse blanket. Even better thing that he hadn't offered to carry the sheets for Kayla. She probably would have marched right back out in the snow in just her jeans and crewneck sweatshirt with the Gemini logo on the front.

"I think so," she said, glancing over her shoulder back at him, "unless you want to pile a foot spa and the minibar on this stack."

"I'll look into getting a minibar, but I can offer you a fine canine assistant in the meantime."

"Only the best, I see, at this five-star hotel."

He'd expected her to clean up when he dropped her off at the bunkhouse. The type of work they did required showers *at the end* of the day instead of in the morning, after all. But the lavender that wafted from Kayla's messy knot of damp hair as she hurried to the room took him by surprise. Not that he minded the aroma of cattle, horses and honest sweat that clung to their clothes, but her alluring scent threatened to caress him from the inside out, making his own shower earlier pointless. He'd already started sweating.

"Well, you've come to the right place," he said, recognizing that he'd answered too late.

If he hadn't been mesmerized by the gentle sway of her hips in those sinfully perfect-fitting jeans, he might not have tripped over the puppy as it wove around his legs, excited by all the commotion. Jasper lurched forward and bumped into Kayla's back. She juggled her load and readjusted, managing to drop only a bath towel.

He lunged to pick it up and tucked it under his arm. "Sorry."

"Been walking on two legs for a long time?"

She continued into the room without looking back and dumped the linens on the bed next to her bag.

"Not long enough, apparently."

Jasper stopped in the doorway, grateful that she hadn't called him out for paying too much attention to her butt.

"Might want to practice," she said.

They'd bantered almost nonstop since he'd returned to pick her up, as if clever turns of phrase could stop the nervousness inside their bellies. His, at least. He suspected she was uncomfortable, too. She'd slipped out of her living quarters like a teenager running away from home, a duffel strapped across her body one way, her soft rifle carrying case draped the opposite direction. Then she'd worn cowboy boots with her sweats and carried her muck boots in her arms.

Kayla was right about one thing: he hadn't thought through his offer for her to stay at his house. If he had, then he would have considered just how tough it would be for him to get any sleep with a woman who'd dominated most of his thoughts lately, sleeping under the same roof. Already, just the thought of her bare legs sliding beneath those sheets, her hair fanned out across the pillow and a come-hither smile on her lips made his own mouth dry.

He needed to pull himself together. Kayla was staying with him because she might be in danger. That was the only reason. He had to remember that. If they quickly discovered who'd been sending her texts, she would be back at the bunkhouse and avoiding him, just like before. He hated to admit that part of him hoped his siblings wouldn't find the answers too quickly.

"You could have picked the room with the bunks," he said, still standing in the doorway. "The house was originally set up to be a guest cabin, so there's a kids' room."

Jasper glanced around the space she'd chosen instead, suddenly wishing he'd listened to his mother's and Aubrey's suggestions. He should have made the house look like a home. Even if it was only for a few days, he wanted to give her something nicer than the basic shelter the bunkhouse provided. She'd probably picked this room because it was the farthest from his, anyway.

"This will be fine." She unzipped the satchel and started unpacking.

She worked efficiently, tucking flannel shirts and jeans into the empty dresser in the corner. Though he recognized in her quick trips back and forth that she was signaling that the time had come to leave her alone, he couldn't make himself walk away yet.

"Did the guys give you a hard time when you went back to the bunkhouse?"

She stopped and lowered her head. "I live with a bunch of seventh graders."

"They were already waggling their brows?"

"So much that they probably all had headaches."

He couldn't help grinning as he pictured those pained faces. "They deserve some hurt for being so nosy."

"One of them asked if I had something better for dinner at the boss's house. He suggested surf and turf."

He narrowed his gaze. "Was it Hank?"

"No. Charlie."

She grabbed a pile of socks from her bag and carried them to the dresser. "This time Hank kept his mouth shut."

"Small miracles." He leaned his shoulder against the door frame, becoming more comfortable than he should have been while watching Kayla inside her bedroom. At least he wasn't like the dog that had invited itself into the room and trailed after her as she put away her clothes.

"Sorry to be right about everyone already being suspicious. It's just that, well, I'm—"

"A guy?"

"There's that," he said with a chuckle. "I'm also one of *twelve* siblings. You said the ranch is like a small town. I think it's more like a family. And in *my* family, if anyone might be dating somebody, one of them sniffs out the details and spreads the word faster than a brush fire in the lower pasture."

She rested her back against the dresser. "Wait. You're the one who said it wasn't anyone's business that I'm staying here."

"I didn't say they wouldn't make it their business." Jasper tilted his head to the side and studied her. "What did you tell the guys when you left?"

Kayla stared at her folded hands.

"You said *nothing*?"

"I waited until they were asleep." She shrugged. "Never claimed to be brave."

No, she'd only said she could handle her problem all by herself, which was kind of the same thing. "So, you sneaked off in the night like Huckleberry Finn for his adventure heading down the Mississippi? You didn't fake your death, too, did you?"

She crossed her arms, frowning. "You don't have to be so dramatic."

When she sat on the bed, the dog immediately rested its head on her lap. After taking a few seconds to scratch those fluffy ears, she gestured to the doorway. "I'd wondered if all those books in the living room were just for show."

"Those? I keep them in case I need extra napkins when I'm eating cheese puffs."

"At least you think ahead. I like to keep books around, too, but since I get mine from the library, I just eat potato chips."

"Good plan, if you can avoid the grease marks."

Ah, man. He could do this. He could talk to this

woman all night long about everything and nothing. Not just because he was pleased that she'd noticed his lifelong reading habit. He didn't know her well, but he wanted to. Jasper smiled at her until she dampened her lips and then stood to continue unpacking.

Since she'd packed light, he was surprised when she pulled out a bundle wrapped in an impossibly small quilt. She carried it to the dresser and carefully removed the blanket, producing a musical snow globe. Once she'd positioned it on top of the dresser, she folded the cloth and placed it in the top drawer.

"That's beautiful. What's inside it?"

Jasper didn't realize he'd stepped inside the room until she looked over at him, surprised.

"Sorry." He stuffed his hands in his pockets. "I didn't mean to—"

She waved away his apology and carried the globe over to show him. Within the glass, a pair of horses pulled a sleigh through a Christmas scene, a man and a little girl with pigtails sitting inside. Kayla shook it and then held it still, allowing the fluid-suspended glitter that was supposed to be snowflakes to float down on the occupants.

"That's amazing, but it looks delicate. I'm surprised you brought it here with you."

"I take it everywhere. It was a gift."

When Kayla turned the key on the globe's bottom, Jasper expected to hear strains of "Jingle Bells" or another carol with "sleigh" in the lyrics, so the tune of "I'll Be Home for Christmas" didn't seem to match. Then he caught sight of the engraved plate on the front of the base, which read "To Cup-Kay, Love Dad." Emotion thickened in his throat. The globe's unusual tune, its tiny sleigh riders and the reason she packed it for just a few days away all made sense. Those were reminders of why letting himself get too close to Kayla St. James would be a mistake. It had heartbreak written all over it. His.

"Cup-Kay?" he managed to ask.

"An old nickname. A version of *cupcake*, I guess."

Neither mentioned who the gift was from, though the man's presence lingered in the room, a ghost between them in so many ways.

Kayla moved suddenly and returned the globe to the dresser. "It's getting late."

He glanced at his watch as he retreated to the doorway. "More like early."

"And don't count on me to get the horses fed if you oversleep this time. Unlike you, I don't have a pickup here, and I'm not running to the barn."

"Okay, I'll let you get some sleep." He started toward the front door. "Come on, Bandit. Let's go outside."

At the magic word *outside*, the puppy that had refused to leave Kayla's side darted after him. Jasper watched more closely than usual as the puppy sniffed at the brush closest to the house and then crept out farther, becoming more difficult to see, even with all the lights. He sensed Kayla's approach behind him before he heard the creak from the loose floorboard that he kept forgetting to fix.

"Can you still see him out there?" She leaned close to his shoulder and peered out the door's sidelight.

"Barely."

"Are you sure he's okay?"

"He's fine." Still, her words unsettled him, so he

stared harder, trying to separate the black-and-white dog from the all-white covering of new snow.

"There he is."

She pointed just as he caught sight of the pup himself. Bandit ran full force at the house, appearing out of control and unable to stop. Jasper jerked the door open to prevent an accident. It almost worked, though Bandit whacked against his owner's legs, sending a snowy gush through the doorway with him.

"I give you my guard dog."

"You poor boy. Everybody expects so much of you. Ranch dog. Watch dog. Dinner guest." Kayla bent over Bandit, starting to use one of the guest towels to wipe its paws.

"Not that. Use this." He tossed her the old towel he kept behind the coat tree.

When she finished, she returned the towel.

"Don't let the rest of the crew see you do stuff like using the good towels on the dog, or they'll know for certain that there's no way you're here teaching Bandit manners," he said.

"It doesn't matter. As you said, they'll have their own ideas about what's going on at the boss's house, anyway."

Though he hadn't said exactly that, he didn't argue. Before he started wishing again that the assumptions sure to fly about them were true, he headed toward the staircase.

"Come on, Bandit. Let's go to bed."

"Will you be locking him up in the laundry room again?" Kayla called after him.

He stopped at the bottom of the stairs. "No, he's

passed the house-training test. I'll have him sleep in my room."

Luckily, she didn't point out that Bandit couldn't protect anyone without having full run of the house. He didn't have an answer for that. At least Bandit could alert him of noises outside. Halfway up the stairs, after the puppy bounded past him, Jasper turned back again. Kayla still stood there, appearing lost in her thoughts.

"Can I ask you one more question?" he said. "Was the reason you were up so early the other morning because you received another text and couldn't sleep?"

"That's two questions. But yes and yes."

"Then I have one more. If you get another text tonight, will you promise to come and wake me up, too?"

She stared at him for several seconds, as if deciding, and then nodded.

"I promise."

A sound yanked Jasper out of his sleep what felt like only minutes later, his heartbeat pounding a hole in his chest. He sat up in bed, already sweating. Had he really heard something, or had he just dreamed it? Though he tried to blink away the darkness that squeezed in all around him, he couldn't shake the disconcerting sense that something had changed. He shot a look to the space on the floor where he'd piled blankets as a makeshift pet bed while too exhausted to do anything but collapse on top of his own covers. The answer appeared in the gaping doorway.

Bandit was gone.

He threw back his blankets and jumped out of bed. His feet hit the floor in twin thuds. Why had he gone to sleep at all? *How* had he even closed his eyes with

Kayla downstairs, close enough to sense her presence but too far to touch? Or to reach her if she needed him. If someone had come after her while he'd snoozed like a baby, he would never forgive himself. Bandit hadn't missed it. The dog had obviously rushed down to help. Were they both gone now? Or hurt? Or worse?

He hurried to the doorway, racking his brain to recall whether he'd ensured that the latch had engaged when he'd put Bandit to bed. His fingers fumbled along the wall as he moved out of the room. At the top of the stairs, he stopped. He didn't have time to panic. Kayla needed him to think clearly. Maybe they both did.

With a look back to his room, he shot inside and grabbed his phone. He would need the flashlight app. Even though the main outdoor light was always on at night now, he couldn't see it from this part of the house, and the windows didn't help. The downside of those amazing stretches of clear night sky on the ranch was the near complete darkness outside.

He edged his way downstairs, his back to the wall, careful to avoid the squeaky step. At the landing, he paused and listened. No barking. No crying, human or canine. No sounds but the refrigerator, never as quiet as the brochure promised.

With brightness filtering from the sidelights on the front door, he tucked his phone in his pajama-bottom pocket and continued to the room where Kayla slept. This door was closed. Would an intruder have bothered to shut it again? He checked the entry door as well. Bolted from inside. Nothing made sense.

He stared at the bedroom door again, an acidic taste on his tongue, but he had to know. Bracing himself, he grasped the handle and pushed down. More of that darkness greeted him as the door opened. Pulling out his phone, he turned on the flashlight app and aimed it at the bed, holding his breath. Not one but *two* lumps were formed under the comforter. Pillows? He was still trying to make sense of that when one of the shapes moved.

"What's going on?" Kayla whispered as she sat up, using both hands to shield her eyes.

As an afterthought, she lowered one hand and yanked the covers over her chest. Though she still wore the sweatshirt from earlier, she'd clearly removed her bra, and now the material clung in all the right places. Places he shouldn't have been noticing. Nor should he have been wondering what else she'd shed before climbing into bed. She wore her hair down like he'd imagined, but instead of fanned on the pillow, it fell over her shoulders in a riotous mess. And unlike in his fantasy, she wasn't smiling.

"What are you doing in here?"

Jasper turned off the flashlight before hitting the switch that lit the lamp next to her bed. "I thought I heard—"

"Heard what?"

"I don't know. *Something.*" He rushed to yank up the blinds and tested the window. Locked. After crossing the room to open the closet, revealing only boxes, he stepped toward the Jack-and-Jill entrance to the bathroom. Behind that door, he found more darkness.

"What did you hear? And what are you looking for?" Though she'd kept her voice low until now, this time her tone edged up, as if reacting to his panic.

Jasper's pulse still beat furiously as he returned to the safe zone near the door. It seemed silly now that he'd rushed in as if to announce that the sky was falling. Had the danger only been in his dream? Or had the sound been real? That he couldn't describe it made him wonder.

"You didn't hear anything?"

"Not a thing." She tucked the comforter under her armpits and then pushed her hair back from her face with one hand. "And I haven't received any new texts. In fact, for the first time in a week, I was actually sound asleep."

"Oh. Sorry."

She studied him, her brow lifted. "Let me get this straight. You heard something and rushed in on your steed to save the day. Or night. And you did it dressed like *that*?"

Already, he felt ridiculous, but at her question, he glanced down. His chest and his feet bare, he stood there in a pair of flannel pajama pants, slung low on his hips, cartoon cows printed all over them. He'd brought a cell phone in case they wanted to take a selfie with an attacker, but no weapon. And worse, beneath those comical pants, he wore nothing at all.

Kayla studied him for so long that he shifted from one foot to the other on the floor, so cold that it made the bottoms of his feet ache. Then she grinned.

"What did you plan to do, kill my attacker with laughter?"

"It's my secret weapon." He brushed the leg of his pants. "A birthday gift from my twin."

"To make sure that women keep their distance?"

"She said it was to celebrate the Gemini, since the cows are Charolais," he said with a shrug. "But she could have had an ulterior motive."

He hoped her nod indicated she would let the subject drop.

"I really did think I heard something, and since Bandit was gone, too—" He broke off and looked around again. How could he have forgotten that part? "Have you seen him?"

"You probably heard snoring." She tapped the lump at her side. "His."

Something started wiggling, and then Bandit's head emerged from beneath the covers.

"Bandit? How did *you* get in here?"

The puppy tunneled out from beneath the covers on the side of the bed and scampered over to him. When the dog whined for an ear scratch, Jasper obliged, though he couldn't have felt more torn. How could he be relieved that Kayla and Bandit were safe and still be both jealous that the puppy got to cuddle up with her *and* grateful that the animal had been there to protect her? In short, he was a mess.

"I must not have latched the door when I went to bed," Kayla said, still rubbing her eyes.

"We couldn't *both* have forgotten."

"He opened your door, too?"

He nodded. "And remember the laundry room earlier?"

"Guess you're going to have to stop closing him in rooms unless you lock the doors. Or change all your door handles."

"He might be a great escape artist, but he's not much of a guard dog." Jasper frowned at his pet that looked up at him panting. "I came all the way in here, and you slept through the whole thing."

"Poor boy. He was tired."

Jasper's lips lifted, despite his attempt to keep a stern face. "You were having sweet puppy dreams while— wait." He pointed to the open door as pieces of the earlier puzzle fell into place. "That was *closed* when I came downstairs. He didn't do *that*."

A sheepish grin appeared on Kayla's face. "Well, he did *open* the door. Then he hopped up on the bed, so I—"

"Closed him inside," he finished for her.

"Haven't we already established that he won't stay anywhere he doesn't want to unless the door is locked?"

"So, let me get this straight," he said, repeating her words from earlier. "You *let* him sleep with you? What kind of dog trainer are you?"

"The kind that's *not* a dog trainer."

Their smiles spread by increments until they were both chuckling. It felt good to laugh after their stressful evening poured itself into his dreams. He'd probably imagined the sound that had dragged him out of sleep, after all.

"By the time you're done, he'll be making a bed for me on the floor." Jasper shook his head. "I'd better get a little more rest, for the few minutes I have left, anyway."

He pointed to her. "You, too. Sorry, again, for waking you."

Her phone vibrated then, and for a few seconds, both of them stared at it, plugged in and facedown on the bedside table.

"Aren't you going to look?" he asked finally.

"Yeah, but it's probably nothing." She reached for it, took a quick look and returned it to the table, screen-side down.

"What was it?"

"Just junk email." She coughed into her sweatshirt sleeve, the blanket falling away from her chest until she repositioned it. "Can't believe that I get those at all hours of the night. Doesn't anybody respect business hours anymore?"

"Okay. Glad it's nothing."

Jasper already had his hand perched near the light switch when Kayla cleared her throat. He turned back to find her watching him.

"Is it going to be like this every night? With you rushing in every time the house makes a sound?"

"No, it won't." At least he hoped not. But he suspected he would be talking himself out of all kinds of scenarios until they had answers about who was targeting Kayla. "Anyway, I know you'll be safe here."

"How could I not be with that little guy staying in here with me?" She gestured from Bandit to her bed.

He shook his head. "Fine."

Kayla patted the empty side of the bed, and the puppy rushed over and hopped up, folding into a circle of fur on top of the covers. Jasper closed the door and grinned into the darkness as he felt his way back upstairs. If he couldn't be in the room with her, at least to protect her, having Bandit there was the next best thing.

Chapter 6

Kayla waited until Jasper had enough time to get back to his room and into bed, and then held on a few seconds longer, just to be sure he wouldn't return. Then she lunged for the phone and yanked it off the power cord. She fumbled with it and had to reenter her password twice, but finally she opened the screen and stared down at the words.

Don't make me wait.

Her hands shook like they always did when she received one of the messages, but this time her chest felt heavy, too. The person on the other end of that message wasn't the only one who'd done something wrong. She'd lied to Jasper. He'd stood right there, ready to support her, and she couldn't bring herself to tell him.

"Why?" she whispered into the darkness, as she set

the phone next to her. Only there wasn't just one reason, and all of them added up to the truth that she'd made a mistake in agreeing to stay at Jasper's place. She should have known that it was a bad idea when she'd been forced to sneak out of the bunkhouse while the rest of the ranch hands snored.

Didn't Jasper understand? He expected her to immediately go to him when she'd already relied on him more in one day than she'd leaned on any man in years. Since The Liar. No, even before him.

"It was too much," she whispered into the darkness. And far too tempting.

Bandit whimpered on the bed next to her.

"Sorry, buddy. Didn't mean to wake you again."

The dog squirmed until, though still on top of the covers, its back rested firmly against her side. Still a puppy weighted blanket, even in sleep.

Petting the soft fur, Kayla settled back into the center of the pillow and stared at the ceiling. Sleep. That was one of the reasons she'd lied. Though she'd been walking around like a zombie for days, she'd had no trouble sleeping tonight, even before the pup had sneaked into her room for a slumber party. She couldn't tell Jasper that his home, and maybe even his presence in it, felt like a safe haven from all her worries. It would be a mistake to forget that the only person she should rely on looked back at her every morning in the mirror.

That she hadn't minded Jasper's come-to-the-rescue stunt nearly as much as she'd let on counted as a good Reason Number Two. She should have hated the whole thing. It shouted that he found her weak and vulnerable, two things she'd promised herself never to be, but she couldn't help finding comfort in the knowledge that *someone* would come running if she called for help.

But both of those reasons paled when compared to her reaction to having a half-dressed rancher, one she'd sworn off for sound reasons, show up in her bedroom in the middle of the night. How she could still picture him in vivid color, her pulse pounding out a song of betrayal to her family's memory. When she should have been repeating all the reasons she should avoid Jasper, she was busy wondering if anyone in history had ever looked better in a pair of cow-print pajama pants.

Her memory painted that perfectly formed chest and those tight ripples of abs. She'd guessed at their presence before since no T-shirt could fully disguise them, but she'd still been shocked to see them up close. And, whether Jasper had realized it or not, those ridiculous pajama pants had done a poor job of hiding *any* of his secrets.

She smiled into the darkness. Though he'd been embarrassed, and she might have joked that those pants would work as female repellant, she figured that his commando method for wearing them could easily convince more city girls to take up ranching. The heat that pooled in her own secret places, softness preparing to yield, confirmed that even she wasn't immune.

All of this had to stop. She was only staying with Jasper until she could figure out who had been targeting her. No other reason, no matter how tempting, and no matter how long it had been since any man had awakened more in her than disdain. Her focus needed to be on the messages and what, if anything, came after them. Not on the man, who'd offered protection but couldn't guarantee it. She couldn't afford to relax here, couldn't let down her guard with Jasper. It was too much of a risk and telling that even after receiving another text, she could only think about *him*.

Shoving that thought away and the guilt that clung to it, she grabbed the phone off the pillow, tapped the screen and read the words again.

Don't make me wait.

Kayla blinked and read it a third time. *Me?* Not *us*? Had the texter made a mistake by using a singular pronoun this time? Or was it just part of the game he, or they, had formed to confuse her? To terrify her? Even if the messages were from just one person, did it make a difference? Plenty of serial killers had amassed impressive body counts all by themselves.

Finally, she put the phone aside and scooted closer to Bandit. Convincing Jasper to leave the dog with her felt more duplicitous now, even if he probably would have insisted on it if she'd told him the truth. She should do that tomorrow, anyway. At least some version of it. She could even say that she hadn't told him right away for his own sake, since he needed to sleep. But he would only see it as another lie.

She buried her face in Bandit's fur, trying to ignore the biggest irony of all: she wished she was in the arms of the dog's owner instead.

Jasper sat on one of the bar stools in his mother's open kitchen that afternoon, staring out at the view, the scenery layered from the white of last night's snow to the green of the trees to the deep purples of the mountains. Usually, the sky would have completed the painting with rich blues, but today suffocating gray striped the whole landscape. Or maybe that was just his mood. He stirred the orange in his old-fashioned and sipped.

When a beep of the security system announced that he wasn't alone, he turned to the front of the house. Since the alarm didn't blare a few seconds later, he assumed that whoever had entered knew the code and made it to the keypad in time.

After some rustling in the entry, his eldest brother, Caleb, appeared in the kitchen, setting his coat on the island, his scarf still wrapped around his neck over his suit jacket.

"What's the deal with that weather?" He shook snowflakes from his headful of dark brown hair, unraveled the scarf and then hung his suit jacket on the other bar stool. "It's only November."

"Mother Nature's got her speed set on high this year." Jasper jiggled his glass and took another sip.

Under the scrutiny of those observant brown attorney's eyes, Jasper brushed his hands over the front of his flannel.

"A little early for happy hour, isn't it?"

Then they responded together, "It's five o'clock somewhere."

"Care to join me?" He didn't want to drink alone, after spending most of the day wanting exactly that. Kayla had lied to him, and he wasn't ready to pretend it didn't matter.

Caleb glanced at his watch. "Guess one couldn't hurt as long as there's plenty of time before I have to drive home. I already told Nadine I would be a little late. And that I would bring home Chinese for her, her dad and our kids."

"Wow. *Your* kids. That's such a cool thing you and Nadine are doing."

After loosening his tie, Caleb crossed into the living room and made himself a drink at the bar, probably weaker than the one Jasper nursed. "You mean not all couples go through foster-parent training and bring two ten-year-olds and their six-year-old sister into their family during their first year of marriage?"

"I'm thinking no. How's it going? Really."

"It's tough sometimes, but anything that's important is." Caleb stared out the window and then smiled when he looked back again. "We can't wait to introduce Romeo, Juliet and Portia to the whole clan at Thanksgiving. Portia will love playing with Theresa's twins. Three little first graders."

"That was convenient of Ezra to fall for a single mom to give her some ready-made playmates," Jasper said, chuckling.

Caleb carried his drink over, pulled out another bar stool and sat. "But I doubt you called me here to talk about the kids. And are you going to tell me why you made me drive all the way out to Mom's when you could have met me at the office? Or at least your place?"

He glanced from one end of the room to the other. "And for that matter, where's Mom? And what did she say about having him here?"

Caleb pointed to the puppy pressing its nose to the shiny window on one of the French doors.

"She frowned but didn't say anything." When the pup curled up next to the door, Jasper turned back. "Thought I'd kill two birds with one stone by checking in on her after last month's episode."

"That the only reason you wanted to meet here?"

Jasper shrugged and then adjusted his drink on the counter. He also didn't want some of their siblings to know they'd met, but he kept that to himself.

"Mom must be fine," he said. "She practically mowed us down on her way out the door to a meeting with one of her clients. She reminded me to—"

"Clean up after yourself before you go," his brother finished for him. They both laughed.

When his chuckle died down, Caleb leaned his elbow on the counter and rested his head in his hand. "What about the other *bird*?"

Jasper cleared his throat. "I need help finding some answers for Kayla St. James."

"Bet that's a story."

"Two, in fact. There's the one that's true and the one we're telling everyone else."

Caleb sat back and crossed his arms. "Let's start with the truth."

"Someone's after Kayla, and I'm letting her stay at my place to keep her safe."

The oldest Colton brother gestured in a circular motion for him to say more. Jasper filled him in on the details, at least as much as Kayla had shared with him. When he finished, Caleb leaned away from the counter.

"Now tell me why you're getting involved in all of this."

Jasper set his glass down with a clink. "Because someone is threatening a woman I employ, and I'm trying to help."

"You get that these texts qualify as the crime of cyberstalking, right? That's using an electronic means to harass or threaten."

"I get that."

Caleb held his hands wide. "And you already said that you thought she lied to you this morning when she received another message. How do you know you can trust her to tell you what's really going on?"

That was the question Jasper had been asking himself all day. He still didn't have an answer for it, at least one that didn't cause more churning in his gut.

"Maybe she just wasn't ready to tell me. I do believe she's in danger, though. I've seen the texts. I can't turn my back on her. She has no one else."

"You're sure that's all there is to it?"

Jasper pushed back his stool, nearly toppling it as he stood. "Forget I asked."

After rounding the island to the sink on the opposite side, he dumped his drink and then had to fish the orange slice out of the drain.

Caleb planted his elbows on the counter and folded his hands. "If you're finished with whatever that was, please sit. We'll discuss why you've brought this to me."

"Thought you cared about justice, is all," Jasper grumbled, but he did as his brother asked.

"You know I do." Caleb twirled his own drink, which he'd barely touched. "I haven't spent years helping run The Truth Foundation for nothing. But I know what it's like to be so obsessed with making up for the things Dad did that you mess up your own life. Like I messed up a marriage and every relationship I was in until Nadine."

"Your wife is a saint to put up with you."

"I'll agree with you on that, but I have to ask if you're doing what I did. You've already given Kayla a job and a place to live. Are you still trying to make up for our father sending hers to prison?"

Under his brother's scrutiny, Jasper couldn't help but to look away.

"Nothing could make up for her dad dying there."

"That's true, but he also could have been guilty."

"Kayla doesn't think so. And I don't know what to think."

"We didn't want to believe that our dad was guilty, either," Caleb said in a soft voice.

That truth hung heavily between them.

"What I'm saying is you'll be no help to Kayla if you're in this for the wrong reasons."

Jasper shifted in his seat, his brother's words ringing disconcertingly true, even if Caleb had it all wrong. At least part of his desire to help Kayla was more self-serving than noble.

"I know," Jasper said, finally.

"This is also a matter that you should take to the police and not your attorney brother."

"I know that, too."

"You could even take it to the chief of police." He grinned at him conspiratorially. "I'm sure he would do anything for one of Isa Colton's kids."

"I tried to get Kayla to do that, but she's just not ready to go to the authorities. She doesn't think it's serious enough."

"That might change quickly." Caleb folded his hands, signaling that the lecture was over. "So, what type of help do you want from me, little brother?"

"I need you to use some of your friends to help track down whoever is sending Kayla the texts before they escalate to violence."

Caleb put his hand to his chest, all innocence. "I don't know anyone who does that kind of thing."

Jasper waved away his comment with a brush of his hand. "Save it for the judge. I know you have...people."

"I'll have my assistant, Rebekah, look into a few things. Just get me Kayla's number and the list of the numbers the texts have come from. I'll also need a transcript of all the messages."

Jasper pulled out his phone and started a list. "I'll get them to you as soon as possible. Anything else?"

"See if Kayla has any idea what the texter might be looking for. If we know what the suspects want, then it will be easier to identify them."

He looked up from his phone. "She says she has no idea."

"Keep asking." Caleb waited for his nod before he continued. "Is it okay if I share this with Morgan? She's my partner, after all."

"Okay, Morgan and even Dom or Ezra, if you think they'll be able to help." He ticked off the names on his fingers. "But no one else. We're keeping this on a need-to-know basis so that no one accidentally tips off the texter. Especially since we want to rule out the other ranch hands first."

"Are you going to tell Aubrey?"

Jasper shook his head. "She'd be the first to slip up."

"Got it. You said before there were two stories. What are you telling everyone else?"

"That Kayla is staying at my place to help me retrain Bandit, so I can bring him to Thanksgiving dinner."

Having finally taken a sip of his drink, Caleb spewed it on the counter. Jasper frowned at him.

"I'm *not* cleaning that up."

Caleb grabbed the antibacterial wipes from beneath the sink and wiped up the mess.

"That bad, huh? Even if it's kind of the truth?"

"Do you know how little the truth matters in the court of public opinion? Even The Truth Foundation got caught up in that when we petitioned for Ronald Spence's release after Clay Houseman confessed."

Jasper nodded, sharing his brother's pain over that mistake. "You couldn't have known."

"We shouldn't have been so quick to believe without confirmation, either."

"Don't worry. The police will stop him again, and he'll pay for everything he's done."

Caleb stared at the ceiling, holding his head in the basket formed by his laced fingers. Then, with a jerk, he sat up again. "Good attempt at distracting me, but we were talking about *you* and that pitiful cover story. My guess is everyone believes—"

"That I'm sleeping with Kayla St. James." Jasper blew out a frustrated breath.

His brother held out his hands and moved them up and down in an imaginary scale. "Beautiful woman. Eligible guy. Playing house. What's not to believe?"

"But I'm her *boss*." Now he was the one saying it like it was a dirty word. "I can tell how much it bothers her that the others would assume that about us."

"More than it bothers you?"

"Hey, I'm a guy," Jasper said finally.

Caleb shook his head, not buying it. "You're not *that* kind of guy. You're the kind that worries about how news like that makes a woman feel instead of how it makes you look."

Jasper shifted, finding no answer to that.

His brother slid off the stool and pushed it in. "I'd better get home. Nadine, her dad and the kids will be waiting for their chicken lo mein."

"I'd better get back, too. Kayla will need a ride home." He'd already picked up his keys, making a mental note to give her the spare one for the house later. "I mean *to my place*."

"There it begins."

The side of Caleb's mouth lifted as he slid his suit jacket and coat back on and tucked the scarf inside his collar.

"Knock it off, will you?"

Caleb paced away from him, waving over his shoulder, but paused in the kitchen doorway.

"Be careful, little brother. You might be able to keep *her* safe, but one of you just might get hurt."

Chapter 7

"Putting in some overtime?"

Kayla jumped at the voice behind her in the tack room. She whipped her head around so quickly that she dropped her clipboard, but why she stumbled at all, she wasn't sure. Even exhausted, she would have recognized Luke Bishop's disarming Italian accent anywhere.

Her fellow ranch hand stood not twenty feet away, his arms loaded with halters and bits, his heavy, dark eyebrows drawn together in concern.

"Sorry. Didn't mean to startle you."

Though his arms were already full, he stepped closer, as if to pick up the clipboard for her. She nabbed it herself and smoothed down the ruffled pages.

"No problem. I've been a little jumpy today." Jumpier since Jasper had driven off to meet with his attorney brother, but she didn't tell him that.

"I can imagine," he said after a few seconds.

"I bet you could."

The words popped out before she could edit them. She wasn't ready to have this conversation with Aubrey's fiancé, even if Luke might be the only person who could relate to the sly smiles, open curiosity and even awkward questions she'd endured all day from the Gemini staff. Only, unlike his romance with Aubrey, which began last winter, her assumed "relationship" with Jasper wasn't even real. She ignored the unwelcome voice inside suggesting that she didn't mind those assumptions as much as she should have. Except for those who might think she was after Jasper's money. That bothered her a lot.

Why had she even tried to tell them that she was staying with Jasper to help train Bandit? No one had bought the story. Heck, *she* wouldn't have believed it, either, if she'd been one of them.

She braced herself for a witty comment from Luke, so it surprised her when he stepped over to the racks and started hanging items instead.

"I knew you would need these for the inventory count." He readjusted the remaining bridles he carried and kept working. "But I thought you weren't starting until tomorrow."

"I got a head start." Completing the tack room inventory and checking for wear on the stirrups, reins, bridles and other equipment gave her something to do besides standing around waiting for Jasper to return. It hadn't stopped her from worrying that she shouldn't have involved his siblings in figuring out who'd been sending the texts, though.

"I'm sure Aubrey and Jasper will give you a gold

star on your work record." He gestured with his chin toward the racks. "I don't know which of these you've already counted. Where can I hang them? Or would you rather I put them on the floor?"

"Just put them in their regular racks. I've just been checking equipment so far."

"Okay. Good." He distributed the items into their proper places. When he'd finished, he turned back to her. "You're not planning to be here all night, are you?"

She shook her head and automatically tightened her grip on her clipboard. "Just until Jasper gets back."

Her cheeks burned as Luke lifted a brow and waited for her to explain.

"He's my ride." That was just another reason why she shouldn't have agreed to stay at Jasper's place, though she'd felt more comfortable there than she had in weeks. She couldn't even get there without asking him for a ride or borrowing one of the horses and leaving it tied to the hitching post near his garage. He'd already been forced to pick her up at the house after he'd fed the horses that morning. He would tire of that quickly.

"Aubrey or I could drop you by his place if—"

Kayla shook her head. "I'll wait."

When he nodded again, she couldn't help but wonder what he was thinking. That she didn't have a key? He would be right, and maybe it would help him buy their cover story that she was only working at Jasper's home. Somehow, she doubted it.

Luke adjusted his hat and looked over at her again. "We don't choose *amore*," he said, switching easily between Italian and English. "It chooses us. Everyone will be fine once they get used to the idea."

"It's not like—" She stopped herself before she said something she shouldn't.

"Whatever it is…"

He smiled, probably assuming that she and Jasper were only having casual sex. It didn't sit right with her to think that even an imaginary encounter with Jasper Colton would ever be *casual*.

The barn's narrow side door opened then, and Aubrey stepped inside. "Oh. There you are."

Luke looked from his fiancée to his fellow ranch hand. "I was supposed to tell you that Aubrey wanted to see you."

"Thanks." Kayla forced a smile, first at him and then at her boss. After the reactions from the rest of the staff, she'd avoided Aubrey all day, not ready to face not just Jasper's twin but also her co-employer.

Aubrey stomped snow from her boots and pulled off her hat. Luke strode over to her.

"Would you mind waiting for me in the truck?" She continued past him before he had a chance to answer. "I want to chat with Kayla for a minute."

"Sure thing." Behind Aubrey, Luke shot a knowing look at Kayla.

Now his reference to "everyone" made more sense. He'd given her a heads-up that Aubrey wasn't pleased with this new development. The moment her fiancé had left the building, Aubrey turned back to her.

"He's not as tough as he looks."

Kayla pointed in the direction Luke had disappeared. "You mean…"

"You know who I'm talking about. My brother."

The clipboard still in one hand, Kayla raised the other one to ward off any coming verbal affront.

"Look, it's not what—" She stopped herself from revealing too much again, but she wasn't sure what she could say. "I really am helping out with Bandit."

Aubrey crossed her arms over her open coat. "Sure."

Kayla breathed in through her nose to calm herself. Boss or not, it wasn't Aubrey's business whom her brother slept with. Or who he *was not*, as in this case. Her fierce protectiveness over Jasper took Kayla by surprise. Because it wouldn't be in her best interest to analyze that now, she tucked it away to think about later. Or never.

After adjusting her glasses and tucking her hair behind her ear, Aubrey met Kayla's gaze again.

"My brother feels guilty that our dad sentenced yours to time in prison." She straightened her shoulders. "We all do, but—"

"Please, Aubrey," Kayla said to interrupt her and relieve some of her discomfort. "I can promise that my project with your brother is not about *that*."

"I'm glad to hear that."

Aubrey didn't say she supported the project or even believed anything she'd heard, but Kayla didn't know what she'd expected. Without knowing the real story, a sister was looking out for her brother. If their roles were reversed, and Kayla had a brother, she might have been just as protective.

"You'll see. The pup will be a perfect gentleman for Thanksgiving."

Aubrey rolled her eyes. "I'm sure it will be a miraculous transformation."

"So, is that all?" Kayla pointed to the clipboard as if she needed to get back to work, though after this confrontation, she doubted she would be able to count any more pieces of the tack or saddle blankets.

"One more thing." Her boss waited for her to meet her gaze once more.

"If you hurt him, you'll have to answer to me."

With that, Aubrey turned and continued out the barn's small side door. Her warning hadn't made any sense. Why would she worry that Kayla would hurt her brother? Why would she think she had the power to do that? Did Aubrey know something she didn't?

As the image of Jasper in those silly pajama pants appeared in her thoughts, as it had more than a few times that day, she couldn't help but to smile. No, she would never do anything to hurt this kind, compassionate man, who had a soft spot for animals, just like she did. How many bosses would have allowed his employees and his own sister to believe he could be involved with a staff member just to keep her safe? Kayla could name one.

And she'd lied right to his face.

"Why'd you do it?" she repeated aloud the question that she'd asked herself all day. She still couldn't answer it. After accepting his help, was she still so determined to maintain her independence that she'd held just one thing back? In the moment that she'd received the text, that might have made sense, but now she couldn't justify it at all.

Beyond a full day's work, she'd never believed she owed anyone outside her family anything, but she owed Jasper this. She had to tell him tonight. Even if he would never understand why she'd lied to him. Even if he probably wouldn't trust her now and would decide not to waste his time helping her.

With another glance at her watch, she tucked the clipboard in a slot near the racks and crossed the barn to the stall where Dory was enjoying her extra rest. Hopefully, after she spent a few more minutes with the horse on the injured list, Jasper would finally return from his errand, which had taken longer than she'd expected.

She was still petting the mare's mane when her phone rang in her pocket. Pulling it out, she clicked the button to answer and put it to her ear without looking at the screen.

"Finally. I'm starving. Are you outside?"

"Wouldn't you like to know?"

At the sound of the strange male voice, raspy and lower than Jasper's, Kayla froze. Her throat squeezed as though someone was strangling her from the inside out. Her hands were so sweaty that she had to grip one over the other to keep the phone pressed to her ear.

"Are you there, sweetheart?"

"Who is this?" she finally managed, her voice squeaking in her ears. "What do you want from me?"

At his rumble of laughter, as if they were playing a delightful game, a shiver fluttered up her spine. Her gaze shot to the barn door. The main one was closed, as was the narrow secondary entrance, but it wasn't locked. Was he outside that door? He hadn't answered that question, had he?

"Well, I thought we'd made that clear during all our little chats, cup—"

She jerked the phone away from her ear and stared at the screen, part of the word lost in the movement. Had he said "cupcake" or "Cup-*Kay*"? No. That wasn't possible? People used silly endearments all the time.

This caller had done it twice in the span of a few seconds. And neither of those names had anything to do with her dad. She shook her head, trying to clear the doubts, but the gauze net blanketing her thoughts only twisted and tangled.

"I don't have whatever it is you're looking for. I don't know where anything is. I don't *have* anything."

"Of course you do."

"I don't." She ground out the words this time.

"Better give me what's mine, or you'll live to regret it." He chuckled again. "Or not."

The call ended, and she pulled the phone away from her ear and stared down at the number. A different one from the six others she'd already memorized. She swallowed a scream but forced herself to hurry across the barn to where she'd set her rifle in the corner. Grabbing the detachable magazine, she loaded it and waited, listening.

After what felt like forever, with silence filling the vacuum until it swelled and pulsated, the door handle clicked. Kayla pressed the rifle to her shoulder, moved the knob forward to seat the shell in the chamber and aimed.

"I would stop right there, unless you want a hole in your chest," she called out in a loud voice that she could only hope wasn't shaking.

"Kayla, it's Jasper," he called from the other side of the door.

She stopped, blinking repeatedly. Emotions rushed at her from all sides, squeezing, shaking, tormenting. She couldn't breathe. What was she doing?

"Can I come in? Don't shoot, okay."

"All right," she managed. She leaned against the

wall next to the saddle racks and bridle hooks, certain it was the only thing keeping her standing. With trembling hands, she moved the bolt up and back to eject the shell.

The door slowly opened, and Jasper leaned his head inside. Bandit pushed past him and bounded into the barn, running right up to her. As she rested one hand on the dog's head, she was finally able to lower the rifle's butt pad to the floor next to her.

"What happened?" He slowly approached her, his gaze moving from her face to the weapon and back.

"The texter. He just called and threatened me."

His eyes widened, but he came closer on the opposite side from where the puppy rested against her leg. When he was close enough, he reached out for the rifle. He nodded several times until she realized he was waiting for her response. She dipped her chin and lifted it again. His hand closed around the weapon, and he moved it away, resting it in the corner.

Then he returned to stand in front of her, reaching out a hand. "Are you okay?"

She looked from his eyes that reflected her fear to a hand that offered assurance. Then she threw herself into his arms.

Chapter 8

Kayla picked up the last egg roll from a plate on the table and took a big bite. She'd already stuffed her stomach with heaping servings of Mongolian beef, cashew chicken and chop suey, but couldn't resist. She caught Jasper watching her again. His worry, though less obvious than earlier, still showed in the vertical line between his brows. He'd set his fork down on his empty plate, so she wasn't sure how long he'd been observing her.

"Feeling better now?"

She pushed back slightly from the table and rested a hand on her belly. "Maybe. But I might not be later."

Though she recognized that he hadn't been asking about the food, she wasn't ready to talk about *that* yet. She still couldn't make sense of any of it, from the leap her thoughts had taken over her childhood nickname to that intensity of need that made her catapult herself at Jasper. The certainty that he would be there to catch her worried her most of all.

"Well, you answered a couple of my questions."

She set the rest of the egg roll on her plate and waited for him to explain.

"When Caleb mentioned that he was picking up Chinese for his family, I thought it sounded like a good idea, too, since I would be getting back late. But I didn't know, one, if you liked Chinese, and, if you did, which specific dishes." He gestured around the table, where they'd spread several plastic-lidded boxes. Most were close to empty now, the damage primarily hers.

"I can see that you do like it, and you like *everything*," he said with a chuckle. "Much more so than Bandit."

He pointed to the dog that had started out begging but had eventually lost interest and taken a nap in the corner.

Kayla sat back in the chair and crossed her arms. "I was starving. And I'm not one of those dainty ladies who pretends that she doesn't eat."

"Who wants one of those?"

She narrowed her gaze at him. His question didn't necessarily mean he wanted someone like her, no matter what his sister's words tempted her to believe.

Finished with that topic, Jasper carried some plastic containers over to the counter. Kayla grabbed the remaining few, along with her water glass. He started rinsing and set a few items aside for the recycle bin.

They needed to discuss the matter they'd both been avoiding since Jasper had unraveled her arms from their death grip around his back and guided her to the truck. She stalled a little longer, tucking the plates into the dishwasher, but finally she forced the words to come.

"Sorry about earlier."

He gave her a sidelong glance but kept rinsing and stacking. "Which part? When you threatened to shoot me? Or when you threw yourself into my arms like a barmaid in the Old West?"

"I can't believe I could have fired at you." She shuddered at the memory. "That could have been so bad."

"Definitely would have been bad for me. I'm pretty partial to my chest *without* any holes in it."

She frowned at him. "Could you please take this seriously?"

"I was dead serious about the holes," he said with a shrug. "Guess I'd expected a different response after bringing home Chinese. Especially after I'd shielded the box of food from Bandit the whole way back to the ranch."

"Thanks for the food. And sorry I almost shot you."

"Now that's the kind of response I was looking for."

She watched him as he finished rinsing. He wouldn't push her to talk about it until she was ready. Somehow, just knowing that made it easier to start.

"I was really scared."

He swallowed visibly and shut off the water before turning to her. "Me, too. I'm sorry I wasn't there."

"There's no way you could have known when, or even if, he would call." But that he wished he could have been there touched a tender place in her heart.

"You said that the guy called this time and threatened you. But why did you think he was outside?"

"I didn't look at the number when I answered. Since

I was expecting you to pick me up, I asked if you were outside." She stared at her hands, the memory tightening her throat. "He said, 'Wouldn't you like to know?'"

Just repeating his words made her shiver again, her limbs shaking just as they had when the man had spoken them.

"That had to be terrifying."

She didn't miss the way Jasper's jaw tightened on her behalf, as if he were grinding his teeth.

She shook her head. "Let's not talk about *him* anymore. At least for now."

"Okay," he said, watching her as though he wondered if that was the best idea.

"And about the thing in the barn, can we just forget that second part?"

The side of his mouth lifted. "I don't know. Maybe *you* can…"

That was the thing. She couldn't forget any of it, either. Not the truth that despite her training, she'd been inches away from a firearm accident. Not the reality that no matter how determined she was to need no one, in a moment of crisis, she'd reached out to Jasper. Even now, the memory of his strong arms encircling her, offering comforting stability when she'd felt unmoored, drained tension from her shoulders.

"Wait. Why did you say before that I was like a barmaid?"

"They probably knew their way around a rifle, too. Also, I imagine that they were pretty tough like—"

"Me?" She wasn't sure why his compliment made her feel so good, when in the barn she'd felt anything but tough, but it did.

Jasper didn't say more. He pointed to the coffee

maker, where a full pot had greeted her when she'd awakened for work that morning. Without waiting for her answer now, he loaded a filter in the brew basket, added some grounds and flipped the switch.

He gestured toward the machine. "To settle your stomach after all of that food."

"I would say that coffee would keep me up all night, but after today, I don't think anything could."

"It's not decaf, but it will go good with dessert." He crossed to the pantry and returned with a plastic container of brownies, napkins and dessert plates. Without stopping at the dinette, he continued into the living room and rested them on the scarred coffee table.

"Don't tell me you bake, too." Kayla trailed after him, past the woodstove that radiated heat and the scent of crackling oak.

"As I told you before, I like to eat."

She sat on the love seat, and he settled on the sofa, with the end table between them forming an L-shape. She found her immediate comfort surprising, as if the space was one that she'd visited before and to which she would happily return. Already in her socks, she tucked her feet beneath her and settled against a plush pillow. Jasper opened the container and placed a brownie on each plate.

At her first bite, she sighed over the chocolatey richness. "How could I not know these things about you?"

"Even after all this time, I guess we don't really know each other that well."

She pointed to the pile of books still stacked on the end table. "Guess not."

But she found herself wanting to know more about him. Wanting to hear about his favorite reads and the things that made him laugh. After polishing off his brownie, Jasper headed back into the kitchen. He returned carrying two steaming mugs of coffee. He handed one to her and then picked up the container of brownies and offered her another one.

"Just to be polite." She took a smaller one this time and immediately bit off the corner.

Bandit rounded the back of the sofa just as Jasper put another treat on his own plate. When the dog attempted to slip in for a bite, Jasper raised the plate above his head.

"None for you, buddy. No chocolate for dogs."

Kayla had to dodge those pitiful puppy eyes as well. "We definitely have work to do with him before the holiday."

"You really think we can make some improvements in his behavior by then?" Jasper asked over his shoulder as he carried the dishes to the kitchen.

"Now we *have* to."

He returned to the room and lowered himself onto the sofa. "Why is that?"

"Because I promised your sister that he would be a lot better."

"Aubrey?" He leaned forward, planting his hands on his thighs. "Why was she talking to *you* about it?"

Kayla watched him over the rim of the mug that she brought to her lips. "You have to ask?"

"That sister of mine," he said through closed teeth. "Sorry about today."

"Which part?" She grinned as she set her mug on a coaster.

"Well, the call, obviously. But everything before

that as well. Sorry you had to put up with everyone's prying eyes."

"Most of the staff weren't too bad. Well, other than the eye-rolling over my claim that I was helping to train Bandit. And *the looks*." Her cheeks burned at just the memory of those. The ones that said, *I know what you were doing last night*.

"I had my share of the looks, too," he said. "What do you mean that *most* weren't too bad? You mean except Aubrey?"

She answered with a shrug. "She was just being a good sister, looking after her brother and business partner, worried that some ranch hand was taking advantage of him."

Though Kayla had intended it as a joke, when he grinned back at her, something fluttered in her belly. She grabbed her coffee and took another sip that she had to choke down.

"Twins." He shook his head, frowning. "Can't live with them. Can't celebrate a birthday without the other one. Glad none of my other four sisters are as into my business as Aubrey is."

"You complain about them, but do you realize how lucky you are to have siblings who care about you? Do you know what some of us would give—" She stopped as her voice cracked.

He studied her for several seconds and then nodded. "Yeah, I'm lucky. Sorry. That was pretty insensitive."

"And it was *too* sensitive of me."

"For the record, my brother Caleb was curious, too, when I spoke to him. He promised to do some checking into the texts. We'll have to let him know that the texter has escalated to making calls. He told me the texts qualify as cyberstalking. He'll probably try again to get us to go to the police."

"We already agreed it wasn't necessary."

"But things have changed now." He lifted a hand as if to ward off her next argument. "Either way, he said he'll check out the texts once we give him access to your number. He may ask for help from a few of my other siblings, but he'll keep it only to those who need to know."

"Like Luke and Aubrey?"

"Why would we tell them?"

"You're not going to?" She lowered her feet to the floor. "Well, for one thing, they live here with us on the ranch. And, for another, because Aubrey seems to think I'm a gold digger chasing after her brother's money. And, equally bad, Luke wants to be my ally as a Colton plus-one."

"That is rough, but I don't think we should tell them. At least until we know for certain that the person targeting you doesn't work here. We don't want them to accidentally give something away." He rubbed his chin between his thumb and forefinger, thinking.

"Would you want me to speak to Aubrey? Without telling her about the investigation, I can assure her that you're only helping with Bandit, and there's nothing going on between us."

"That'll just convince her more that you're trying to protect your favorite employee."

Jasper glanced at her but quickly looked away. "Probably."

"I get why we should keep it to ourselves," Kayla admitted, "but it still doesn't seem right, lying to them."

Jasper slowly turned back to her again, but this time

he didn't look away. The stark look in his eyes grabbed ahold of something inside her chest and squeezed. He knew she'd lied. He'd probably known it all along, but her own discovery of this was new. She couldn't have felt more ashamed.

She stared at her folded hands. "Say whatever you need to. I deserve it."

He blinked away that raw look. "You lied to—"

"I'm sorry," she blurted before he could finish. Somehow, she needed to explain. She licked her lips. Her mouth had never felt so dry. "I just didn't want to worry you. And I knew you needed to get some sleep, so—"

"It doesn't matter *why* you did it," he said, interrupting her this time. He turned his body to face her, his knees brushing the corner of the end table. "If we hope to figure this out together, to find a way to keep you safe, we need to be able to trust each other."

She winced at that word again. *Trust.* If she'd really believed in him, she would have just told him rather than to hold something back, a bit of information that was hers alone.

"That's why you let Bandit stay with me until you went to feed the horses, isn't it? Because you knew?"

"I would have left him with you then, too, but after I let him out, he was raring to go, and I thought you might want to sleep a little longer."

Kayla had lifted her cup to take another drink, but her hand jerked over his admission, sending a trickle of lukewarm coffee over the back of her hand. She dabbed at the drip with her napkin, but she couldn't wipe the realization from her mind that not only had she slept more peacefully in Jasper's home than she had in weeks, but also he might have watched her sleeping. That notion should have creeped her out, but it comforted her instead.

"No more lies or omissions, okay?"

He was watching her now, his eyes narrowed, as if wondering just where she'd traveled in her thoughts. That she planned to keep to herself.

"No more lies or omissions," she repeated, hoping she could keep that promise.

"Good." He nodded, as though the matter were settled.

"Caleb also cautioned me about ruling out anyone too soon, even if it doesn't seem to fit. Since you're living on land a couple of Coltons own, and my family has had so much trouble this year with one of the men my father sentenced to prison, you don't think it could have anything to do with *him*, do you?"

"I don't think so." She braced herself for him to ask about her father again, but he only stared at the flames dancing behind the glass door on the woodstove. "If that guy, Spence, wanted to scare a Colton woman, wouldn't he have sent the texts to your sister and not me?"

"Fair point."

"Also, what would Judge Colton have been hiding that someone wanted?"

He chuckled, but the sound held no real laughter.

"Any number of things, unfortunately. You've read the articles about him, haven't you?"

She shook her head, needing to convince him that his concerns about his father were unfounded this time. "That doesn't add up. Like I said, why me? Why would the texter think I knew anything your dad did, anyway?"

"You knew him about as well as I did."

"You mean not at all?" she asked.

"I couldn't have known my father if the guy I thought walked on water was also the puppet master who accepted bribes and kickbacks and then controlled so many people's lives, sending some to certain private prisons and falsely imprisoning others. Aubrey and I were just ten when he died. Gavin was eight, and the two youngest, Alexa and Naomi, were only six." He'd been watching the fire again, but now he met her gaze directly. "I'm sorry for what he did to your dad."

"I know you are." She stared into those same flames, now seeing a time machine of her past with too many voids that crowded out even the brightest moments. She couldn't help wondering if Jasper had experienced a similar collection of memories, the darkness squeezing out the light.

"You and I have more in common than I thought."

"How's that?" he asked.

"We both lost our fathers, and neither of us really knew them. I mean, sure, though mine was wrongly convicted, I still didn't get the chance to really know him."

He shook his head, not buying her argument.

"Our situations weren't close to the same. Ben Colton was this larger-than-life alleged hero for justice, wearing a black robe and wielding a gavel. He turned out to be just another grifter, but he died before he could be convicted of his crimes. Your dad died without getting the chance to prove his innocence."

Her heart squeezed as she considered his pain.

Jasper tilted his head to the side. "What did your father die of? I don't think you ever said."

"The way I heard it, one of his fellow inmates started a fight with him in the cafeteria, and he gashed his leg on a metal folding chair. The wound kept festering, and without proper medical care, he developed sepsis." She shrugged. "That was it."

"And how old were you when your dad passed away?" he asked after a long stretch of quiet.

"Sixteen. But, like your twin sisters, I was just six when he was effectively taken from my life. He missed ten years of my childhood."

"Because of what my father did."

She couldn't argue with that, so she gave him a sad smile. His lips formed a thin line as he lowered his gaze to his hands.

"That doesn't mean that I knew him any better than you knew yours. To me, he was the guy in photographs. Most of them pictures I wasn't even in," she said. "The guy who bought me candy bars on family visitation days at the prison."

"I get the picture part. There's a photo wall at my mom's house with individual shots of each of us and then a large family photo with my father and mother in the center. It feels like a lie. I wish she would just take it down and burn it."

"So you wouldn't have to remember him?"

"No, so I wouldn't have to be ashamed of him."

Her chest squeezed again. She hoped he had some positive memories to balance the difficult ones. Even she had some of those.

"Want to know something funny? I carry an old Remington like my dad's, but it wasn't even his. I saved up money and bought it myself from a gun dealer years after he died." She lifted her shoulder and lowered it.

"He had to give his weapons up when he was convicted of a felony."

"That's not a funny story. It's sad." He shook his head. "You still wanted to be like him. I can tell you one thing—there's no way I would ever want a gavel like my father's. I was a kid who was supposed to be mourning my dad's loss, and all I could do at the funeral was promise myself I would never do anything that would make my child feel the shame I felt."

He blinked several times as if surprised he'd revealed so much. She couldn't help feeling honored that he'd trusted her with that story. She considered that for a few seconds, feeling his pain in a way she never had before. Finally, she spoke the words that he probably needed to hear.

"Our situations are different. I get that. But the scars from losing a parent when we were so young, the inherent injustice of it, are the same." She paused, meeting his gaze directly. "And I don't need to have met the judge to know this—you're nothing like your father."

Chapter 9

Jasper rustled around in the kitchen, needing to do something with his hands and take a break from the emotions that Kayla had just forced to the surface. How could she tell him, having never met his dad, that he was nothing like him, even if Jasper had focused his life on proving exactly that? And how could Kayla believe, even for a moment, that their situations were the same?

Pain that he'd buried so well he couldn't feel it sometimes broke through, long scarred-over wounds seeping at the edges. But he wanted to know *her* story, craved hearing it, no matter how painful, with an intensity he hadn't felt in a long time. And if he wanted her to truly trust him with hers, he had to be willing to share his, even if it had been locked in the past for so long that he wasn't sure himself what it contained.

When he could stall no longer, he grabbed stemmed wineglasses from the rack beneath the cabinet, stuck a corkscrew in his pocket and pulled a bottle of Cabernet from the wine rack. He didn't bother starting with two conservative pours. He would need the whole bottle.

Kayla stared at him as he crossed back into the living room, her nearly empty coffee mug nestled between her hands. She looked from that to the glasses dangling by their stems from his fingers and smiled. He waited for her to make a joke about him moving on to something stronger. She didn't.

"I forgot to ask if you like wine." He lifted the bottle in his other hand.

"I do."

"Guess we'll no longer need those." After setting his items down, he carried the mugs to the dishwasher.

When he returned, he uncorked the wine and poured. He lifted his glass to offer a toast and then searched for something appropriate to say. "To…"

"Being partners?" Her voice lifted, making the phrase a question.

"Being partners," he repeated, clinking his glass against hers.

They sipped in companionable silence for several seconds, the wine warming his insides as the fire heated his skin. Finally, he set the wine aside.

"Tell me about the snow globe."

She'd already been preparing herself for his questions, if the way she sat, elbows pressed against her sides, offered any clue. But at the one he chose, Kayla's tight expression softened into a smile that started at her lips and ended with eyes crinkling at the corners. In a reflex, she gestured to the closed door of the guest room where she'd left the globe.

"I was eight," she said after several seconds. "I wasn't expecting much for Christmas that year. Just those few packages from the charity that provides Angel Tree gifts to children of convicts. Plus, that little doll quilt that Mom thought I didn't know she'd been stitching for me every night after I went to bed."

"The one you wrapped around the globe?" At her nod, he added, "That's a special gift, too."

"Yes, it is. More precious than I realized at the time. I was a tomboy with no real interest in dolls, no matter how many times Mom tried to convince me it was okay to play with them *and* ride horses."

Kayla finally took a sip of her wine and then held it between her hands.

"But when I opened the snow globe, I could have sworn that Christmas had just shown up in my living room, all snowy and perfect."

She'd been staring into the deep red liquid in the glass, but now she looked up. "The father, the little girl and the horses were supposed to represent Dad's new business raising Thoroughbreds on The Rock Solid. He wanted me to be his partner someday. He said we'd make western Colorado a new center for raising race-horses."

Though he suspected that her father had been a dreamer to suggest that plan, Jasper nodded, picturing the decayed ranch that the bank had claimed but never bothered to sell. He ached for the little girl, who'd shared those dreams, only to be left there to watch them die.

"The song the globe played seemed unusual," he said.

"Dad special ordered it. Before he ever went to prison,

from what Mom said. But he wanted her to wait to give it to me when I was a little older. I guess he knew someone who made music boxes and wanted it to play 'I'll Be Home for Christmas.'"

"Why that song?" Though the answer was obvious, he couldn't help asking, as if he needed to hear the grave truth spoken aloud.

"It was his promise to me. He said the same thing every year. Only he never made it home at all."

She blinked hard, her eyes suddenly shining. A knot formed in Jasper's throat as well, and he had to grip the sofa cushion to keep from going to her and pulling her into his arms.

"It was a lovely promise, even if he was *unable* to keep it." His voice cracked on the word since it suggested that the man had been given a choice.

Kayla's gaze flitted to his and then away. "It was."

She took another drink and then swirled the glass, watching the liquid cling to the sides and then fall in waves. "Who'd have thought that a money laundering conviction could turn out to be a death sentence?"

"Money laundering? That's what he was convicted of?"

"I guess you didn't know all the details. He was just a rancher looking for investors for his new horse project. Some drug traffickers needed businesses to legitimize large sums of money. Dad didn't realize what was going on, but he was convicted, anyway," she said with a sigh. "He would have been exonerated, but he didn't live long enough for the appeal."

"Ten years? Isn't that a long time to get an appeal?"

She set her glass aside and crossed her arms. "Not when your family isn't loaded like the Coltons. We had to raise the money for an attorney to even *file* the appeal."

"We weren't loaded," he said automatically, and then frowned when she rolled her eyes.

Her explanation didn't sit right with him. Nor did her story about how her father died. But he didn't bother asking her more about either. She'd only repeated what she'd been told, so she wouldn't appreciate him challenging a story she'd embraced for so long. He, however, wasn't honor bound to believe it. Just as Caleb had suggested, he needed to consider the possibility that Mike St. James could have been guilty.

He chose another approach. "How did you and your mom make it all those years without him?"

Kayla drew her brows together and studied him. "You mean you don't want to know more? All the gritty details?"

"Why would I? That's not *your* story."

"Well, The Li—I mean, someone I knew—always wanted more information. Kept coming up with questions I had no answers for, as if we were watching a cold-case TV show."

She glanced from the window to the woodstove and then to the kitchen in the distance, never lingering on any space and clearly avoiding looking at him.

"Sounds like a jerk," he spat before he could stop himself. His own discomfort told him that whoever she'd spoken about had hurt her.

"He was."

Why he hoped she would tell him more, he wasn't sure. Already, his jaw clenched at the idea of any man who'd had the privilege of getting close to Kayla and failed to cherish that gift.

"Clearly, we didn't."

He blinked, trying to retrace the conversation, unsure if they were still talking about the guy who'd hurt her.

"You asked about my mom and me," she explained. "Ultimately, we didn't make it. As you know, I lost the ranch after she died. But for years, we sure tried to hold on. That wasn't easy since all the investors in Dad's business vanished the moment he was arrested."

"How did your mom pay the bills?"

"At first, by selling off most of the horses that we didn't already lose in the criminal seizure. The cattle still brought in money then." She twirled her finger as a sign of time passing. "Later, we had to sell off most of the other livestock."

Jasper sat straighter. Though he'd wanted to know her story, each part made him feel more helpless as he could do nothing to change it. "Did you get any help from community services? Charities?"

"Sometimes. Like the Angel Tree gifts for Christmas. Mostly, we limped along on our own. Because of the land, our financial shape was still too good for us to receive public services." She held her hands wide. "You know, land rich and life poor. Mom always made sure I had decent clothes for school, but other than that, we learned to live simply and eat and entertain ourselves on a budget."

"That had to be hard."

"It wasn't all bad. And I learned valuable skills. Like frugal cooking. You'd be impressed by how many meals I can make from one chicken."

"I'd like to try some of your low-cost cooking sometime."

She blinked as if his comment had surprised her and then smiled so wide that he could have sworn he'd given her a gift.

"Maybe one day. Mom also did her best to make my childhood fun."

He recalled their conversation from the day before. "Is that when you became a public library fan?"

"My library card was among my most prized possessions. Still is, though I have to borrow one of the guys' trucks to check out new titles every few weeks. In books, I could travel anywhere, and I could learn about other families who had big, loud meals together or went to the beach or played ball in the park."

"What about friends?" He suddenly needed to know that she and her mother had others in their lives. Even if he and his siblings hadn't been getting birthday party invitations, they'd always had each other for those loud family meals that Kayla had never known. He suspected that other than her mother, who'd focused on keeping the family's ranch, Kayla had been alone.

"A few."

Her simple words made him wonder what she hadn't said. Then she spoke up again, filling in the blanks.

"Parents don't often want their kids to become besties with a convict's child."

"Yeah, I know what that's like. You said your dad died when you were sixteen?"

She nodded. "After that, Mom just gave up. She passed away as well just after my twenty-first birthday. Supposedly leukemia, but I always thought it was from a broken heart."

His chest squeezed as he considered the lonely widow who'd tried to hold down the fort until her husband returned. Then, like always, his heart ached for the little girl who'd lost both parents and then her home. If only he had a way to return it to her.

"After Mom was gone, I learned about the second mortgage on the ranch. She'd always said things were tight, but I'd had no idea just how bad they were."

"You just couldn't turn the place around?"

"I tried. The bank refused to work with me. Said it was too late."

"So they foreclosed." Jasper didn't pose it as a question. He'd been around for this part of the story.

"I refused to leave, but the police removed me forcibly, threatening me with trespassing charges if I returned." She studied him for several seconds before adding, "But you already knew that."

He gave her a guilty look and then nodded. "The cop was a friend of mine. He reached out to Aubrey and me to see if we could help."

"I'm going to buy it back someday. It might be a while, but someday." She straightened on the love seat, as if realizing she'd told him more than she'd intended.

"So, that's my story. Sadder than some. Brighter than others." Kayla settled back into the sofa cushion and crossed her legs. "Your family had a rough time after your dad died, too, right?"

Automatically, he shook his head. "Not compared to what you and your mom went through. We lived in a pretty big house."

"It was probably a mansion."

He knew she was waiting for him to deny it. When he didn't, she grinned.

"I didn't ask you to compare your story to mine. I just asked if you had it rough." She lifted her glass off the coaster, emptied it and set it aside. "Also, I'm tired of doing all the talking."

Jasper gestured to the bottle to ask if she wanted a refill. When she shook her head, he poured himself another glass. After hearing her story, he found it tougher to talk about his past, which seemed like a series of holidays by comparison. Before tonight, he couldn't remember the last time he'd spoken about those lonely, painfully awkward days.

"Rough in an upscale, totally-not-desperate way, I guess. There were a lot of us. And Dad's life insurance policy went to pay off all the civil suits against the estate." He shot a look her way. "I guess your family didn't file one."

"Guess not."

He hadn't thought about that. Whether or not the St. James family had the money to start an appeal, attorneys would have swarmed around them to offer their services and agreements to take part of the proceeds if they won. He couldn't help wondering why Kayla's mother had never filed one if she thought they had a good case.

When he didn't say more, Kayla gestured in a circular motion for him to continue his story.

"The house was paid off, so at least we didn't lose it." He took another drink, not looking at the woman who hadn't been as fortunate. "Mom also had a little inheritance from her own family. If not for that, I'm not sure what she would have done with twelve kids, at least until her graphic design business took off."

She seemed to take that in, and then she studied him. "That's it? Aren't you going to tell me the rest?"

"What do you mean?"

"You were *the Coltons*. Well-known family in the center of Blue Larkspur society. Don't try to tell me it wasn't a huge scandal."

"I won't." He closed his eyes as those cloudy memories shimmied before him, the slight nausea he always felt when recalling those days reappearing right on time. "It was humiliating for us. The worst part? He did it for money. He made a good salary, but it was never enough to keep up with his need for finer things."

"Most situations come down to money, don't they?"

Her nonjudgmental words surprised him, since her dad might have been one of those who paid for his father's need for luxuries.

"We just have to hope that greed like his isn't an inherited trait."

As she stared back at him, Jasper realized he'd revealed too much. Nothing like laying his biggest fear right out in front of her. He rushed on before she had a chance to say one of those platitudes people used to relieve him of his guilt.

"You mentioned we were part of Blue Larkspur society. Well, our whole family became social pariahs. Not that we kids cared much about all that, but Mom had always been involved in the social stuff. She'd chaired a bunch of charity events. Suddenly, no one wanted her to volunteer."

"That must have been hard for her."

He reached for the wine bottle again, and this time, she extended her glass for a refill.

"There was one thing I missed," he admitted. "We used to have this annual Colton Christmas party. It was kind of a big deal. People called it Blue Larkspur's party of the year. Everyone wanted an invitation."

"I take it the parties stopped."

He nodded. "Mom couldn't afford to have them anymore. But after everything came out about my father, even if she could have, no amount of free food or music and dancing could have enticed the community's elite to risk being seen at a Colton soiree."

"How good *was* the food?"

Kayla grinned as she asked, so Jasper closed his eyes, remembering. "So good. You know, cocktail-party stuff like mini quiches, meatballs and those perfect tiny cheesecakes, but also there'd be a roasted pig and mozzarella-beef sliders. Plus, grown-up drinks of every color. We kids were forbidden to go near those, even if they did look like fruit cocktail."

"Sounds amazing. Now I'm hungry again."

Her eyes were closed when he opened his, a sweet smile on those lips that looked more appealing than anything that ever appeared on that menu.

"You had stuff like that, and you *still* couldn't draw a crowd?" She opened her eyes again, catching him watching. "Maybe you were just inviting the wrong people."

"Maybe." Instead of looking away, he kept on watching her. "I would have liked it if you'd come."

"Me? Why me?"

"I'm just so impressed. If you can still be hungry after eating half a Chinese restaurant's menu, plus brownies, I can just imagine the damage you would have done to my mom's party spread. It would have been legendary."

"I wouldn't have been a great party guest."

"Why do you say that?"

"Let me think. I would have been just out of first

grade. Hated dancing. And you couldn't have paid me enough to put a dress on, even for a party."

"Well, good thing I was just a smart-ass ten-year-old who wasn't big on baths, hated girls and did no dancing unless it involved imitating Frankenstein."

As he stared at her smile, the room grew more intimate, the sloping ceiling appearing closer to them now, the stove reaching out to envelop them in its warmth.

"We would have had a great time and probably would have become great—"

Kayla stopped herself, her eyes going wide. She'd almost said *friends*. A St. James daughter and Judge Ben Colton's son. She must have recognized how impossible that would have been back then, even in a world of pretend. Twenty years later, it remained just as improbable for them to have formed a connection, but no matter how hard he'd tried to resist it, something tugged Jasper to her like a fine but rugged string. Did Kayla feel it, too? Did she feel just as torn by the calamitous results of other people's decisions that still ruled theirs?

She leaped up from the love seat and set her empty glass aside so quickly that it toppled over. Though a sharp sound escaped her, the glass only clinked on the wood but didn't break.

"Sorry," she said, anyway, and righted it.

"No big deal. It's just a glass."

"I'd better—" She didn't finish as she shot around the coffee table on the way to her room, but as she passed him, Jasper rested a hand on her forearm, where she'd pushed up her sleeve. Not stopping. Just delaying.

"Are you okay?" he asked, seeing that she wasn't. What was she running from? Him? Why would she…

He blinked as the realization dawned. Was it possible that she, too, felt the connection between them? Did the tenacious tug of that string confuse her as much as it did him?

"I'm fine."

She didn't pull away but stared at his hand on her arm. Though he knew he should remove his fingers from her skin, either the message from his brain wasn't reaching his extremities, or they'd chosen to ignore it.

She cleared her throat, still not looking at him. "Thanks for everything tonight. The food. The conversation. Even the barn. I don't know what I would have done if—"

So quickly that Jasper didn't have time to brace himself for it, she tilted her chin up and pressed a kiss to his cheekbone. They both froze. His skin tingled, first on the cheek her lips had brushed and then on his fingertips that still gently held her arm, each of his nerve endings yearning for her touch.

He could feel her pulling away from him before she moved, her halting breath signaling fear and retreat. So he did the only thing he could think of to keep her near. He shifted so that she faced him and slid both hands beneath her bent elbows, offering a steadying support, if she would only accept it.

"Kayla, I—"

Jasper stopped as both too many and too few words lay suspended in the weighted air between them. She stared at him, just shy of straight in the eye, so many questions in her expressive green gaze. He had only one. But he couldn't say it aloud, couldn't ask for permission to kiss her—the one thing he'd craved first in his body and now in his soul. He feared it would break the spell, and these ticking seconds of possibility might turn out to have been a misplaced moment, lost to chance.

So he bent his head closer to her in halting movements, requesting consent in acquiescence, liberty in absence of rebuff. When their lips were so close that her breath whispered across his skin, she nodded in a way that would have been imperceptible if every hope inside him hadn't been searching for it. Waiting and yearning.

She didn't have to tell him twice.

He crushed his lips to hers in a kiss formed of too much longing and precious little finesse. But from his first taste as he sank into the plushness of her lips, just the tiniest bit chapped from the wind that marked their lives, Jasper recognized that kissing Kayla St. James once would never be enough. Giving in to this need, he adored her lips again and again. He couldn't stop. Didn't want to. When she opened for him, inviting him close, he claimed her mouth in a discovery that already felt like his most precious memory. She kissed him back too, first with just lips as she indulged his lead before joining him in fervent exploration.

As he recognized that she had rested her weight in his palms, leaning into him so that her breasts molded to his chest, Jasper glided his hands to the small of her back. Her fingers slid over his arms and clasped behind his neck, the work-roughened texture of her fingertips igniting his skin everywhere she touched.

When their position on her back was no longer enough, his fingers dipped lower and traced over the curves of her behind, drawing her against him and letting her know just how much he wanted her. Had always wanted her. She wiggled her hips against his in just a flick of a movement, and he nearly lost control and embarrassed himself then and there.

Jasper shifted his mouth away from hers so that his lips rested on her satiny cheek. "Wait."

Since he could hear the desperation in his voice, he didn't try to convince himself that she wouldn't notice. He only needed a moment, a chance to take a few breaths and slow down his body, so he could make love to her with the attention to glorious detail that she deserved. If only she gave him her blessing.

Kayla jerked back her head and stared at him with wide eyes, her lips swollen, the skin on her chin and just above the bow of her top lip abraded from his whiskers.

"What am I—"

Her hands slid back from his neck, and she planted them at the center of his chest. Just as she pushed him back, one sharp bark drew their attention to the area in front of the woodstove, where Bandit had been sleeping peacefully only moments before. The dog sat on its haunches, looking back and forth between them and then whining.

"I can't—"

Kayla stepped back from Jasper until her legs bumped the coffee table just as the puppy rushed up to them, its body closing off the exit and pinning them between the sofa and the table. A whimper and familiar dance announced the pup's need for a potty break.

"I should let him out."

Still, Jasper didn't move. He couldn't look away from the woman whose warmth had just touched him everywhere but had now turned to ice. This was a lousy time to have to walk away from her. But the next whine was sharper, more needy.

He gave Kayla an apologetic look as Bandit pawed his leg. "I have to do this. Just give me a minute. We need to talk about this."

"There's nothing to talk about."

She turned and escaped around the other side of the coffee table, past the love seat. Once out of the maze, she headed straight to the guest room. She closed the door with a final-sounding click, and this time Jasper was certain that he heard her flip the lock.

Chapter 10

Kayla rushed through the bedroom and into the bathroom, locking the door on the other end before coming to a stop in front of the mirror. What had she done? The answer to the question was written all over her face, from the tender places that had rubbed against his scruff to her puffy lips. Those told the story all by themselves. She didn't even want to think about her feminine places, which had all but rolled out the welcome mat for him. Or admit that they still ached with an uncomfortable void.

She'd kissed Jasper Colton. Apparently, working for the man whose father had destroyed her family and then accepting his help hadn't been enough for her. She'd had to put her lips on Ben Colton's son, too. What kind of daughter was she? Though she'd listened to Jasper's story, convinced that he'd been just as much a victim of circumstances as she was, she doubted that her father and mother would have seen it that way.

If it had been *just a kiss*, an accidental bounce of lips off another pair in an unfortunate pucker, that would have been bad enough. This was worse. She'd started the whole thing. Now, when she should have been bathing in guilt, all she could think about was the pressure of Jasper's mouth on hers. How she'd felt his kiss everywhere. And how the strength of his arms around her had made her feel both safe and a little dangerous.

"What were you thinking?" she whispered to the woman in the mirror, the person she barely recognized with pupils still nearly covering the green of her eyes, her lids halfway closed.

Bracing her hands on the edge of the bathroom counter, Kayla lowered her head in shame. If she'd been thinking at all, she would have dodged the kiss she'd known was coming, or at least ended it before the smoldering embers set her hair on fire. She hated to admit that she would have done a lot more than kiss, proving the rest of the staff right, had Jasper not called for a time-out. Or had Bandit not popped in on the conversation.

Kayla was grateful to both of them, though she wasn't certain how Jasper had easily hit the brakes when his body had been on board for whatever joyride she had in mind. She'd been planning a lovely one, too. She would thank the puppy for its interference with extra dog treats, but she was too humiliated to talk to Jasper about it at all. Not when she should have been the one placing roadblocks around whatever was happening between them.

After giving her reflection a mean look, she grabbed

a towel and turned on the shower. She kept the temperature cool and ducked her head under the spray. Her teeth were chattering when she finally turned off the water, which had done a lousy job of washing away thoughts working their way beneath her skin.

She went through the motions of drying off, donning fresh sweats, combing her hair and brushing her teeth, while trying not to picture herself on the other side of her flimsy fortress of a locked interior door. With him. That had to stop.

Back in the bedroom, she flipped two pillows on their ends, stacked them against the headboard and sat on top of the covers. If this were only about kissing, or even sex, she wouldn't be as worried. She worked on a ranch, for goodness' sake. She had a good understanding of livestock breeding and instinctual drives, even if it had been an awfully long time since she'd done any *driving*. But this thing with Jasper was more than that. She was starting to *like* him. In a way that was real and adult and dangerous.

And impossible, she reminded herself. They were boss and employee, and their families had the kind of history that should have sent her running in the opposite direction. It couldn't matter that she felt safe with him in a way that she hadn't with anyone, not just in recent weeks, but maybe ever. Jasper tempted her to trust, to give another person a chance to hurt her. That was a risk she couldn't take.

Just as she pulled back the covers and flipped off the lamp, her phone vibrated on the table again.

"Just leave me alone, will you?" She couldn't help reaching for it anyway.

So nice to hear your voice, sweetheart! You sounded so scared. Give me what I want, or you might not get the chance to scream.

Kayla shivered in the dark, and not just because of the words on the screen. For most of the night, while she and Jasper had shared food, laughter and then that kiss, she had forgotten about the texter—the cyber stalker—altogether. She couldn't afford another distraction like that. If she wasn't diligent, didn't pay attention, how would she stop them when they really came after her?

The man had called her "sweetheart" this time. Maybe she'd just imagined that he'd used her father's endearment rather than "cupcake" when he'd called earlier. While looking so hard for answers, she could have created some where none existed.

She set the phone on the table and rolled onto her back. For a moment, she considered keeping it to herself, at least until morning. But she'd promised to tell Jasper before, and tonight she'd sworn she wouldn't lie to him again. No matter what else had happened between them, she intended to keep her word this time.

Throwing back the covers, she climbed out of bed and stuffed her phone in her pocket. As an afterthought, she yanked her sweatshirt over her head, snapped on a bra and then pulled the shirt back on. The last thing she needed was for him to focus on her body rather than her words and risk allowing herself to react to his attention. Prepared for the humiliation of facing him after the kiss, she would march up to his room, knock on the door and tell him not only about the most recent text but also that whatever had happened tonight was a onetime thing.

When she turned the lock and opened the door, she was surprised to find that Jasper had left the lamp on in the living room. But as she crossed the open area to the grouping of furniture, she discovered why. Jasper lay sleeping on the sofa, a comforter covering him except for a foot that poked out from one side. A book laid open on his chest.

Bandit heard her first, popping up from its spot near Jasper's toes. When the dog bolted over to her, Jasper sat up with a jolt, his book plopping to the floor.

"Is everything okay?"

He threw back the blankets and leaped to his feet so quickly that he had to stretch his arms to the sides to regain his balance. The pup barked over the commotion and then squealed until Kayla patted its head.

In his rush, Jasper stubbed his toe on the coffee table. He cursed under his breath when he reached her, dressed in sweatpants like she was, but he'd paired his with a well-loved Johnny Cash T-shirt.

"I'm fine," she said, fighting a smile. Well, this was one way to get past the awkwardness of their groping session earlier.

He winced, staring down at his injured toe. "You could have led with that."

"I didn't get a chance. Why were you sleeping out here?" She gestured to the pillow and blanket on the couch. The thought that he'd been right outside her door while she'd been in the bedroom thinking about him unsettled her more than she cared to admit.

Jasper dabbed his lips with his tongue as he followed her gaze to the sofa. Then he hurried back to it, limping.

"Just wanted to make sure you were—" He stopped and glanced down at the dog that had trailed after him. "She's okay, buddy. Now go lie down."

Kayla didn't miss that he hadn't said "it's okay" or even "everything's okay." He'd said "she." As much as she hated to admit it, his words soothed her insides.

Bandit followed his instructions, curling up in front of the woodstove.

"It's not because of, you know, uh, *earlier*, is it?" she couldn't help but ask.

Her face had to be as red as the decorative pillow on the love seat, and her pulse pounded as if she'd been running stair laps in his house, but she forced herself not to look away when Jasper glanced back.

"No. Not entirely. It also had to do with that other thing, too. The stalker."

"Right."

Great. She was the only one who'd lain awake thinking about that explosive kiss, reliving every sigh, every nuance. As if her humiliation hadn't already eclipsed any she'd experienced before, his reminder of why she was in his house in the first place made her wish the hardwood floor would slurp her in between its slats. Still, there was something sweet about his standing guard over her bedroom door from a lumpy sofa, despite what had taken place earlier.

"At first, I couldn't sleep, either." He pointed to his book.

"From where I stood, it looked like you were doing a fine job of it."

"I said, at first. Since you brought it up, we probably should talk about what happened earlier."

For all the emphasis he placed on those words, he could have been describing a wine spill on the table or a puppy accident on the rug. There was no way she would let him see how it had shaken *her*.

"No need to talk about it since it was a onetime thing. A mistake after an emotional event and probably too much wine."

"Probably?" He pinched the bridge of his nose between his thumb and forefinger, as if fighting a headache.

"It can't be repeated, so there's nothing else to say."

"Good. Then that's settled," he said, his expression unreadable.

Kayla waited. Why hadn't he called her on the fact that she'd kissed *him* first? He could have refused to accept part of the blame. She wanted to shout at him to stop being the good guy when she didn't deserve someone like him tonight.

"Then why did you...?" Jasper gestured from her to the open bedroom door.

She pulled the phone from her pocket and jiggled it in her hand.

"You received another text? So soon?" At her nod, he added, "Again, you could have led with that."

"I promised to tell you if I did."

Neither mentioned that she hadn't kept that promise before.

"Thanks."

He crossed back to her and extended his hand, waiting while she typed in her passcode and opened the text. Then she gave it to him.

As Jasper read, he pressed his lips together. He frowned when he looked up again. "To him, this is all a game. He's having fun."

"I know. Especially on the call." She shivered as the man's words repeated in her thoughts. *I thought we'd made that clear during all our little chats, cup—* Having replayed it so many times now, she was even less certain which endearment he'd tacked on to the end. If he had used her father's name for her, what did it mean? Whether she was sure or not, she worried she should have told Jasper about it since she'd promised no lies and no omissions.

"I don't like this at all." Jasper stared down at the phone, his grip so tight that his fingertips turned red. "Forget that I agreed not to before. We should go to the police like Caleb said."

"We will. Soon. But let's get some answers first. Your brother also said he could help us find those."

He shook his head, appearing unwilling to concede. "Cyberstalking might seem like a small crime to you, but you don't know how quickly threats of violence can escalate to the real thing. After all that has happened to my family this year, I do."

"I know. And I'm sorry to put you in this position."

Kayla started to lay a hand on his arm but managed to stop herself before touching him. He returned the phone to her without brushing her hand at all.

"I hope we're not making a big mistake."

"We're not." Her smile contained more confidence than she felt.

"He's getting closer."

"I know." Somehow, she resisted the urge to shiver. Jasper shoved his hand through his hair and then gripped the back of his neck, lowering his head. "This is your life we're talking about," he said in a low voice. "I can't—I mean—we can't let him *hurt* you."

That his voice caught on the word surprised her, and emotion swelled in her throat. She couldn't remember the last time that anyone cared so much, or at least said so out loud.

"We'll find him. Everything will be all right."

The empty promises were similar to the ones he'd made when insisting that she should stay at his house, convinced he could protect her. A guarantee he shouldn't have offered. A safety net punctured with holes.

He nodded, anyway, clearly wanting to believe it as much as she did.

"Thanks again for telling me."

"I'm glad I did." She glanced over at the sofa with a blanket tossed over the cushions. "You're not going to sleep there all night, are you?"

The worry on his face told her he wanted to, but he shook his head. "My neck's already killing me. If I stay there, I won't be able to sit a saddle tomorrow. Do me one favor though, okay?"

"Okay?" She said it as a question, though she would have agreed to almost anything to smooth the wrinkle in his brow and still the worry in his fidgeting hands.

"Could you take Bandit with you?" He offered a close-lipped smile as he gathered the blanket and pillow.

"Now that's a wish I can grant." It also relieved her to know she wouldn't be alone. She whistled. The dog looked back and forth between its owner and the guest before scampering over to her. "Let's go to bed, boy."

"Some loyal friend you are." Jasper gave a fake frown.

"Man's best friend," they said together.

Knowing there was no more to say and yet tempted to linger, Kayla waved and started toward her bedroom door. She clicked her tongue for Bandit to follow. "Good night."

"Sleep well," he called from the bottom of the stairs.

She closed the door, without locking it, and smiled into the lamplit space, hopeful that she would.

Jasper looked up from his computer a week later as six thirtysomething guys passed through the doors into the main lodge. Not for the first time that day, he wished that only female guests would visit until he had answers for Kayla. Or, at least, only couples coming for the romance package in one of the cabins, though that didn't sound so great, either.

"Welcome to the Gemini Ranch," he managed.

Bandit made up for Jasper's lack of enthusiasm by emerging from behind the desk, greeting each of them with a grand puppy hello.

"Look, it's a real ranch dog. Like in the movies," one of them said.

Still not much of a guard dog, Jasper decided. If someone really did break into his house and attempt to abduct Kayla, the pup would be so busy trying to make friends that it wouldn't notice until she was gone.

"This place is amazing," a different man called out. "Even the walls have horns."

Jasper pointed to the mounted bullhorns on the wall opposite the main desk. "We keep sawing them off in the fall, but they grow right back every spring."

The guy, who wore a beanie and holey jeans that didn't look as if they gained those marks through a good day's work, squinted at him. When he got the joke, he grinned.

"Funny."

The man was the kind of city slicker that the Gemini staff introduced to ranch life hundreds of times a year, yet Jasper found this one annoying. In fact, everything had bugged him for the past week. He could trace every bit of it back to that kiss he and Kayla had shared, the one that rocked his world, before she told him it couldn't be repeated.

Didn't she understand that even if it never happened again, that kiss would hold a hall-of-fame position in his memory until the day he died? He didn't doubt that he would still want her until that same day, even if she'd made it clear by her words that night and her distance ever since that the feeling wasn't mutual. Strange, though, for a minute or two, with the way she'd pressed against him and kissed him back, he'd been sure that at least the wanting part they'd had in common.

Jasper shook off the memory just as he'd been doing for days. He glanced down at his notes from his conversation with a local Realtor representing a certain property he wanted to purchase. At least that call had provided a welcome distraction. But he had no time to think about that deal, either, when he needed to offer superior hospitality to this group of guests. He even managed not to roll his eyes as the guys took turns making manly ranch jokes about the rugged decor, variations of which he'd heard many times before. Finally, he stepped around the desk.

"Hi. I'm Jasper Colton, co-owner of the Gemini

with my sister, Aubrey. I'm sure you'll meet her by dinnertime, if not before. We have all kinds of activities planned for you during your stay." He stepped behind the desk again to pull out maps and other printed information. "Horseback riding, hiking, roping practice, you'll have opportunities to enjoy them all this week. You'll work hard, play hard and create lifetime memories."

Jasper delivered his rehearsed welcome speech, hoping to insert animation in the right parts. He should have been a better actor by now after being forced to keep the details of Kayla's stay at his house from his sister and the staff.

"Are there any ladies on the guest list?"

Jasper shot a look to the man who'd spoken. This one wore a dress cowboy hat so new that he probably broke it out of the box to board the flight from East Coast, USA.

"Groups are pretty sparse this time of year," Jasper answered vaguely. "But there will be others here this week."

A guest with a mustache and premature gray at his sideburns stepped to the front of the group, clearly their leader. He gestured to the guy in the back. "Pardon my friend here. We don't let him out of his cage much, but he's all talk."

"We have plenty of corrals if you need one," Jasper said.

He was tempted to share with Hat Guy that he would really have something to talk about after an afternoon spent in the saddle on a trail ride, but he decided to let the man learn for himself about that kind of pain to his sensitive parts.

"You didn't say anything about horseback riding lessons," Beanie Dude said.

"Yes, we offer those as well."

"Well, if that pretty little filly in the corral we passed—and her horse—have anything to do with them, sign me up," the guy said to laughs all around.

For the first time since he and Aubrey had purchased the ranch and started hosting guests, Jasper considered punching one of them. There was no way in hell that dude would be taking riding lessons from Kayla. If he did sign up, Jasper would make sure his teacher was a capable rider and *male*, with the last name Colton.

Their leader must have caught Jasper's death stare as he started tapping his computer keys, heavy on the space bar. The man identified in the reservation as "Marcus Wilde" quickly produced a credit card to complete the check-in procedure. Afterward, he leaned forward so that only Jasper could hear him.

"Don't worry about those two," Marcus said. "I'll keep them in line. Promise."

Jasper nodded and then pulled a copy of the ranch rules agreement from the stacked letter tray and slid it toward him.

"You'll need to read and sign this and then initial it here and here." He pointed to two spots on the document. "You might want to have the rest of your guests read it, too."

Marcus looked up from the paper. "Really. You have nothing to worry about." He shot a look over his shoulder and lowered his voice. "They're both newly divorced. We're here to cheer them up. They're blowing off steam and trying not to look heartbroken."

When Jasper nodded this time, he even looked at

the guy, who smiled. How was it possible that a second man had spoken to him about heartbreak in the same week? Caleb had mentioned the prospect of it again when Jasper had phoned him with the update about Kayla's texts escalating to calls. Though he'd listened to Jasper's flimsy arguments for still not going to the police, Caleb didn't buy his reasons for wanting to be Kayla's self-proclaimed bodyguard.

"I hope you all have a great time on the ranch." He paused, then added, "And leave feeling better than when you arrived."

"Hope so, too."

Marcus gathered up his paperwork and the ranch map where Jasper circled the location of their cabin in red marker. He started away from the desk and then leaned back in again.

"I also won't be letting Bob take any riding lessons from the lady," Marcus said. "Yours?"

Jasper's shock must have given him away as the guy grinned.

"Well, maybe someday," the man said.

Then Marcus turned back to the others. "Who's ready to get this party started?"

Jasper frowned as he watched them go. Could everyone see through him when it came to Kayla St. James? Well, that had to stop right now. If she only wanted friendship from him, that's what he would give her, without asking for more. And if he was able to help protect her life in the process, he would let that be enough for him.

Chapter 11

On the day before Thanksgiving, Jasper waved as the last of the guests piled inside their SUVs after checking out. As promised, the six men had been exemplary guests. They'd also gotten along famously with a group of seven ladies on a girls' trip, though the women were all married and at least a decade older. Still, Jasper was relieved to see them all go. He'd been so busy observing those men and all the male employees, while dealing with the paperwork for his planned surprise, that he'd barely finished his regular duties. And with the weather turning, the last thing they needed to worry about was guests stranded in their cabins.

"Was that the last of them?" Aubrey asked as she appeared beside him, waving at the departing vehicle.

He startled, having missed her approach from behind him.

"Jumpy, aren't we?" She elbowed him in the side.

"Yeah. That's the last group."

"Good thing."

Jasper waved once more and started back up the walk to the lodge. "Why do you say that?"

"Because, brother dear, you really seem to need a vacation from our guests." She met him at the door and glanced sidelong at him as he opened it for her.

"Thanks so much for saying so." He followed her inside.

"Even while they were freezing by the campfire, making s'mores and singing 'Home on the Range,' you were a gracious host. Too gracious. You never let a beer mug or snack bowl stay empty for long."

"Had to find some way to shut them up after someone convinced them to start campfire karaoke," he said.

"Well, one of the waitresses complained she was getting bored while you did all the work."

Okay, he might have been over the top, but he couldn't help it. Every man who came anywhere near the Gemini became a suspect in his mind. Someone was trying to get to Kayla, possibly even in person. Today he'd even tried to avoid assigning her to ride the fences, telling her she was too exposed while alone in those open spaces. She'd threatened to move back to the bunkhouse if he didn't let her take her turn at the job. She'd kept her other promises lately, showing him texts every time she received them. He chose not to test her resolve about moving out. She was right that he couldn't watch out for her every minute, anyway. That truth was killing him.

He and Aubrey approached the front desk, where he would spend the next few hours going over invoices.

He'd hoped she would head off to tackle her own responsibilities, checking in on the preparation in the kitchen and the dining room for the next day's gorge-fest, but no such luck.

"Why are you here anyway? Don't you have things to do?"

"I'll get to them."

Jasper sensed her gaze on him and tried not to squirm.

"There's definitely something going on with you." She pointed at him when he looked over. "I'm your twin. I know you better than anybody."

"Glad you think so."

"I *know* so."

Jasper sighed as he signed into the desktop computer. Keeping Kayla's secret from the sister closest to him in both age and life was proving more difficult than he'd expected. It didn't help that his brothers were searching for answers with the apparent urgency of a turtle enjoying an afternoon sunbath.

What was taking them so long to figure out who was behind this? Already, Kayla had received two more calls, and both times he hadn't been around to listen to the voice with her, to yell at the person on the other end or at least to hold her after the guy hung up. But with his sister still watching him now, he tried to come up with an excuse she would accept.

"Then maybe I'm just getting nervous for our big holiday celebration tomorrow. Don't you feel the pressure?" It was his turn to watch her with suspicion. "This is the first big holiday since Caleb and Nadine's wedding, and Gideon and Sophia's Las Vegas elopement. Plus, we have *five* engagements, including yours and Luke's, and a few upcoming births. It's also our first major family event since the renovation. So it's a big deal all around."

He stretched his arms and looked up at the vaulted wood ceiling and all the new lighting fixtures.

"Not to mention," he continued as he lowered his arms, "if everyone comes, there'll be over a dozen more guests along our massive Thanksgiving table than there were even last year."

"Okay, I'm nervous." She chuckled. "I helped the staff set up the table right after we cleared away the breakfast buffet. I was worried we wouldn't have enough of those holiday runners to pair with the white table-cloths and cover the whole thing, but, luckily, we had a few spares still in the package."

"I saw the room. Everything looks great." Jasper grinned, pleased to have his twin on a safe subject. He needed to keep it that way since lately she'd tried to veer every conversation to a mention of his house-guest. And he definitely didn't need more reasons to think about Kayla and worry if she was all right back at the house. At least he'd left Bandit with her this time, though he wished he were with her as well.

Aubrey crossed to the wall comprised of three sets of French doors that opened to the massive dining room and stood admiring their work. "If our family keeps expanding like this, that table will stretch from the windows all the way through the dining room exit."

She whirled in front of the doors and looked over at him, pushing up her glasses. "Wait. You said *if* everyone comes. Not *when*."

"I just figured with the weather—"

"But everyone already said—"

"Aubrey, have you *looked* at the forecast?" He lifted

his hands in front of him. "Did you *hear* about the blizzard?"

She scoffed at that. "Of course I've heard about it. It's not even supposed to reach western Colorado until this weekend."

"You know weather prediction isn't an exact science. What if it's a little early? Do you think it makes sense for Dom and Sami to come in from Denver or Philip and Naomi to make the drive over from Boulder? Both of those are extended drives to Blue Larkspur, even in good weather."

He shook his head, making his own opinion clear. "Anyway, if they did come, don't you think they would be planning to spend the whole weekend at Mom's?"

"So they're *not* coming?"

From her crestfallen expression, he would have sworn that he'd just said he'd canceled Thanksgiving nationwide. "I don't know what they're going to do. That's up to them. All I'm saying is we might have a slightly smaller crowd. No big deal."

"And what if Snowmageddon turns out to be a dud like last Christmas?"

"Or not a dud, like the storm in February?"

Her eyes took on a faraway look as though recalling that last big snowstorm to hit the area. She and Luke were lucky to have escaped a hit man then, and even luckier to have fallen in love before the snow melted.

"You wouldn't want any of our family members to put themselves in danger just so they can attend a holiday gathering, would you?"

"Of course not. It's just that we already have everything planned. Three twenty-pound turkeys ready to go in the oven, plus smaller ones for each of the staff to take to their own family celebrations."

"I checked in with the kitchen earlier," he said. "Everything's rolling forward like a well-oiled machine. You've done a great job in planning this event."

"Our brothers and sisters all have their assignments for side dishes and desserts, too. Even Mom. She said she's feeling fine and will be bringing her pumpkin bars with cream cheese icing. Like always."

"The holiday wouldn't be the same without those." Or without their mom, but he didn't want to add audio to those worries.

"Do you think she'll bring Chief Lawson?" she asked, wiggling her eyebrows.

"Probably. She'll say something like he doesn't have any family, and we have so much extra food."

"Good. I already included him in the count. Just in case." She considered for a few seconds and added, "But if the others don't come, we'll be missing the dishes they were supposed to bring."

"Something tells me that we'll survive without extra bowls of corn casserole or green bean casserole."

"Yuck!" they called out together and grinned.

"As long as we don't lose the sweet potato thing with the marshmallows on top, I'll be fine."

"I'm bringing one of those, so you're all set." Aubrey crossed back to the main desk and rested her elbows on the counter. "You don't get it. Tomorrow was supposed to be perfect."

"Since when are you worried about perfection? You're the practical twin. I'm supposed to be the dreamer. When did our roles get reversed?"

Even as he said it, he moved his weight from one

foot to the other. Aubrey's change had clearly come from her engagement to Luke. On the other hand, if Jasper still believed he could be Kayla's warrior and protector, then he was as much a dreamer as he'd ever been. But since he'd gotten in the business of surprises lately, maybe he could help his twin make up for the loss of her full-family celebration, too. And it might be time for an old family tradition to be revived.

"Speaking of dreams, you haven't mentioned your plus-one at all."

Jasper frowned. They'd avoided talking about Kayla for a good ten minutes. He tucked his chin and watched her from beneath his lashes.

"I'm bringing *him*, but he won't need a chair. In fact, I would prefer that no one feed him from the table. Kayla has been working so hard with him on his begging."

He didn't want to think about how difficult it would be to leave her at the house and spend the whole day with his family. Without a vehicle, she would be trapped there if someone came after her. She could call him for help, but would he hear his phone at the noisy dinner? Even if he could hear it, would he reach her quickly enough if she needed him?

"You know who I'm talking about."

Her close-lipped smile only annoyed him more.

"You know, your *housemate*? The one with that long dark hair and those pretty green eyes?"

Jasper tapped his pen on the countertop and leveled a glare at her.

"Hey, where is Bandit, anyway?" Aubrey stretched over the counter to look behind it. "I've been carrying around treats all morning, but I haven't seen him."

"Where do you think he is?"

Her eyes widened, signaling that his tone had surprised her as much as it had him.

"Kayla is working with him at the house," Jasper said, trying again.

"So that's where your truck is."

"Is there anything else you need to inventory in my life?" He shook his head and then held his hands wide. "It's crunch time in his training since the holiday is tomorrow."

With as much time as Kayla spent each night focused on Bandit's training for the past two weeks, the pup should have been off to canine university. Unfortunately, he recognized her efforts for what they were: ways to keep her distance from him.

As his twin continued to stare at him, he found himself filling in more blanks.

"I might have mentioned that she's staying at my place and helping me retrain the puppy."

This time, she nodded. "Yeah, you've mentioned it about a thousand times in the past week alone. To anyone who asked. Some who didn't."

"Then why are *you* still asking?"

"Because I'm your sister, and I love you." She paused, shrugging. "And because the gentleman 'doth protest too much, methinks.'"

"If you believe that quoting *Hamlet* will make me less annoyed with you, then you don't know me as well as you think."

"I know there's something going on between you and Kayla."

His memory flashed to the kiss that felt like ancient history now.

"Not that it's any of your business, but there isn't." He blew out an exasperated breath, both because she'd stated it as fact and because he still wished it were true. "But if there *were* something between us, it wouldn't be anyone's business. Even yours."

"Come on, Jasper. This is Kayla we're talking about. I've seen how you look at her when you think no one's watching."

"That's ridiculous." He started typing again.

"You know all the reasons you shouldn't get involved with her."

"Yes, I do. And I'm not." Still, he didn't look up, but he couldn't help striking the keys harder.

"You're going to get hurt."

Jasper slammed his hands down on the keyboard. "Why does everyone keep saying that? So what if I get hurt? Would I be the first person in the world, or even in this family, to get my heart stomped on—"

He stopped as his sister stared back at him with wide eyes. Though he'd kept Kayla's secret, he'd given away his own. So much for neither confirm nor deny.

"I've had about enough fun for one day. Unless you have anything else to say, we both have work to do."

"Right. What I came to tell you in the first place."

He frowned at her and waited.

"I saw Caleb and Ezra out by the barn. They were looking for you and Kayla. Since your truck was gone, I told them to check your house."

"And you couldn't share that with me when you first came in? Glad you enjoyed your little game."

She shrugged, unapologetic. "Guess we've all been keeping secrets around here. I'll drive you over to the house, and then maybe you can tell me what's really going on."

"No, thanks." He grabbed his coat and hat and rounded the desk. "I'll take it from here."

Aubrey trailed after him. "But how are you going to get there?"

"This is the Gemini. We have plenty of horses here. I'll ride."

Chapter 12

Kayla sprung up from the kitchen table as Jasper opened the front door and stomped inside. Too anxious to just stand there, she followed when the dog raced over to greet him. Though she managed to think better of the move and stop, that left her halfway across the room, next to the woodstove. She looked back and forth between two older Colton brothers who were already sipping coffee at the table and their younger sibling by the door.

Jasper tramped toward her. "What did they—"

He stopped, shooting a look at his brothers and then to his own boots, which he'd forgotten to remove. After returning to the doorway to set them aside, he hung up his jacket and grabbed the old towel to wipe up the damp prints on the hardwood.

"What took you so long?" Kayla asked when she couldn't wait any longer.

Ezra crossed the room to stand next to her.

"Yeah, we've been waiting here forty-five minutes." He pointed to the table. "*Two* cups of coffee."

"Sorry." Jasper pushed his damp hair from his eyes as he crossed into the living room. "Waylaid by a nosy sister."

He shot a strange look Kayla's way, his obvious unease making the skin prickle on the top of her head. She couldn't help wondering what his sister had said to him.

"Yeah, she was pressing us for information when we saw her at the barn, too." Ezra, who'd introduced himself as one of the triplets, stepped around her and crossed to Jasper for a hug. "She's persistent. But that's a Colton for you."

"She's something, all right," Jasper ground out.

Ezra gestured to the front door. "Did she drop you off? I saw your truck outside when we got here."

"I rode. Shadow hadn't stretched his legs in a few days. He's hitched up outside."

Ezra and Caleb exchanged a look.

"Sounds like drama's going to be on the menu for Thanksgiving tomorrow," Ezra said.

Jasper glowered at him. "Can we just not talk about—"

Kayla cleared her throat. "As much as I'd love to hear more stories of Colton family tension, can we talk about what you guys found out? You know, about the cyber stalker?"

Jasper shot a look at his brothers. "You mean you haven't told her anything yet?"

Still in a suit but with his tie loosened, Caleb stood up from his seat. The file he'd brought with him lay closed, next to his empty coffee mug. "She wanted to wait for you."

Ezra cleared his throat. "It was probably best to wait until you could both hear it."

Jasper continued into the kitchen and then glanced around until his gaze landed on the stock pot on the stove. "What's that wonderful smell?"

"Chicken soup," Caleb called out before Kayla had the chance to answer.

"Kayla wanted to make dinner for you since you've been so nice to let her stay here," Ezra said. "She invited us to join you, but I promised to get home to Theresa and the twins."

Caleb fought back a smile. "Nadine's cooking tonight, so I had to decline, too."

When Jasper finally looked her way, Kayla rolled her eyes. "What they said."

Maybe being an only child wasn't so bad, after all.

"We're all here now, so what did you find out?" Jasper asked when they were all seated.

Instead of answering, Caleb leveled a look at Kayla so intense that she squirmed in the chair. Why was he treating her like she'd done something wrong?

"What do you know about a man named Jed Presley?" he asked.

Kayla tried out the name on her tongue. "Doesn't sound familiar. Should I know it?"

From the folder, Caleb produced a piece of paper with a grainy arrest photo printed on it. He slid it across the table to her. A middle-aged man with a crop of longish gray hair smiled for the camera. The name he'd mentioned was printed on the sheet.

"Recognize him?"

She studied it and then shook her head.

Caleb crossed his arms, waiting.

She pressed her elbows to her sides, her jaw tightening. "Well, I don't. And I don't know what you're trying to get from me. Who is he?"

Jasper gripped the edge of the table. "Why don't you just tell her instead of questioning her like she's a defense witness?"

Another day, it would have offended her to have a man stick up for her, but she couldn't help being relieved that he'd challenged his own brother on her behalf.

Caleb's gaze flicked to Jasper. "I just had to check something first."

"I'm not sending the texts to myself, if that's what you're thinking," she said.

The attorney opened the folder flat on the table. "Jedediah Presley. Birthdate May 3, 1970."

Jasper strummed his fingers on the wood in front of him. "Can we cut to the chase here?"

Caleb glanced up from the paperwork. "Fine. Jed is an ex-con who served time at Delta Correctional Center. With your father." He watched her as he said the last part.

"I don't understand." The words were as automatic as the thoughts that swirled in her brain. Texts and spoken words circled in that opaque pool until the first shots of light invaded. *We know you know where it is!* What was he looking for? *Tell us or else!* What would he do if she couldn't tell him?

"Why would he want something from me?" she asked even as dread settled deep inside her.

Caleb held up an index finger, asking her to wait.

"Presley was convicted of grand felony theft and served five years." He paused, glancing down at the folder. "It says here he was released six months ago."

"I said I don't understand." She raised her voice this time.

Of course you do. The caller's words from that first conversation chilled her now.

"There were hundreds of inmates at Delta Correctional Center then. That guy and my dad might not even have known each other. Or been in the same cell block."

"We're still looking into that part. Those records aren't easy to access," Caleb said.

She shook her head, none of it making sense. And then it did. Nausea that had started in her stomach backed up into her throat. *Cup-Kay.*

Kayla crossed her arms over her chest, suddenly freezing. Jasper looked back at her, stricken. It was like staring into all those fuzzy faces at the funeral home. People who feigned understanding when no one could have comprehended the quicksand of grief that had threatened to pull her under. Not once but twice. Just like those mourners, Jasper could do nothing for her now.

"You all think my dad was guilty." She pinned Caleb with her stare. Though trying to hold her voice steady, she still heard the tremor.

The attorney closed the file. "We don't have enough evidence to make any statement yet."

The three men looked at each other uncomfortably. At least so far, Caleb hadn't accused her father of anything. She'd come up with that premise all on her own.

"Look, we're not trying to draw any conclusions at

this point," he said with the diplomacy of a man who made his living practicing law. "But we are fairly certain that Presley is the person who's been threatening you."

Why? She wanted to shout it, but she wasn't ready to hear the answer. Would it involve her father? She refused to allow herself to suspect her own dad.

"How are you sure Presley sent the texts?" Jasper asked, looking back and forth between his brothers.

Ezra leaned back in his seat and crossed his arms in a self-satisfied pose. "He must have thought he was a genius, buying burner phones. But he wasn't much of a brainiac, after all. He used his mother's credit card to do it."

"And you were able to track this down how?" Kayla asked, finally finding her voice again. She needed to stay focused on the part of the situation that made sense. The answers she could accept.

Caleb answered with a shrug. "It's amazing the things you can find on the internet."

Jasper started peppering his brothers with questions.

"Do you know if Presley also made the calls? And are you sure he acted alone? And his whereabouts? Has he been sighted in Blue Larkspur? Or on the Gemini?"

Kayla couldn't help smiling at the cowboy, who was out-questioning the attorney, but Caleb gestured downward with both hands to stop the onslaught.

"Slow down, little brother. We're just beginning to find some answers. We still don't know why Jed is threatening Kayla or what he thinks she has. We wanted to let you know what we've found out already so you can keep your eyes and ears open."

Caleb slid a glance from Jasper on one end of the table to Kayla on the other.

"That is, unless you're ready to take this to the police, which you really should do. Chief Lawson will be on the guest list tomorrow and—"

"Can't we wait?" Kayla blurted. "I mean, the guy still hasn't really done anything except—"

"Commit cyberstalking?" Caleb returned the interruption.

"But tomorrow's Thanksgiving. Do we really need to interrupt Chief Lawson's holiday?"

"Police are used to working overtime on holidays," Caleb pointed out. "Also, my brother thought it was a big enough deal to ask for my help. And you thought it was important enough to stay at Jasper's until you could rule out your coworkers."

Kayla didn't miss his unspoken question. Now that her fellow ranch hands were no longer considered threats, would she return to the bunkhouse? To escape their curiosity and her own uncertainty, she popped up from her seat and crossed over to the stove. She took her time lifting the pot lid and checking on the chicken.

She turned back to the men just as Jasper leaned across the table and slid the photo of Presley toward himself. He sat again and studied it, his grip on the paper tighter than necessary. Though she still believed she didn't need a protector, she felt safer just knowing that he would be there to support her if she needed him.

Finally, she returned to the table. "I didn't say I would *never* go to the police. I will. But first, let's try to figure out what this guy thinks I have."

Ezra planted his elbows on the table and folded his hands. "Dom and I can help out there."

"How's that?" she asked.

"While we agree that there isn't much that can be done, even about the vocal threats since they aren't specific, we can use our contacts to gather more information about what Presley might want," he said. "Dom's with the FBI, and I started a security company recently."

"That would be great. Thank you both so much for everything you've done."

"Yeah, thanks, both of you," Jasper added.

Kayla chewed the corner of her lip. "I don't know how I can repay you,"

"Just keep yourself safe," Caleb said as he pushed back his chair. "That will be enough. Wouldn't want Jasper here to lose one of his favorite ranch hands. Aubrey's, too, of course."

She forced herself not to peek at Jasper as the other two Colton men stood, but her face felt hot. Caleb handed the whole folder to her.

"Better get home," Ezra said. "Theresa's making hamburgers tonight."

Caleb glanced at his watch. "I can't be late, either. With three growing kids, food disappears quickly."

As Jasper walked them to the door, Ezra turned and gestured to Kayla. "Will we see you at Thanksgiving dinner tomorrow?"

Immediately, she shook her head. "No. That's for family."

"Are you sure?" Ezra asked. "It's a big group. No one would notice if an extra person popped in, especially since a few might not make it because of the weather."

"Oh. They'd notice, all right," Jasper said, his neck turning red.

"That's your fault for never bringing a date to any holiday gatherings all these years." Caleb shook his head, chuckling. "I'm not even sure you've ever brought a girl home to meet Mom."

"There wasn't anyone special." Appearing uncomfortable with that revelation, Jasper ushered his older brothers out the door. When he turned back, he hurried to the kitchen.

"How much longer will the soup take to cook?"

Kayla followed him, each step feeling heavier than the one before.

"About an hour. Why? In a hurry to get me out of here?"

She swallowed as Jasper's gaze flicked to hers and then away. Of course, he would want her to return to her home now that it seemed safe to do so, but the thought of it made her uneasy.

He pointed to the front door without looking at her again. "There's a horse out there waiting for me to unsaddle him and take him back to the pasture. Then, if you don't mind driving, I'm going to need a ride."

Putting aside her discomfort, she gathered her coat and followed him outside. But as Jasper mounted the horse, and Kayla climbed behind the wheel of the truck, Bandit riding shotgun, another part of that earlier conversation tugged at her thoughts. She couldn't call it an *invitation* to Thanksgiving dinner exactly. Jasper hadn't offered one, even as a courtesy, after Ezra mentioned it. Still, she couldn't resist. Just for a minute, she allowed herself to fantasize about what it would be like to attend that loud, boisterous holiday dinner, surrounded by family, as Jasper's date. She wasn't even sure if she wanted all of that. But one surprising, confusing possibility seemed to be emerging from the fog of her life: she just might be falling for Jasper Colton.

Chapter 13

Kayla couldn't help but grin as Jasper pushed back from the table that evening and rested his hands on his full belly.

"That was amazing." He closed his eyes and leaned his head against the back of the chair.

"You mean you liked my chicken soup?" She chuckled, resting a spoon in her bowl. "I couldn't tell, what with you eating two full servings and slurping like you've never had soup before."

Jasper opened his eyes, still smiling. "Man, you make me sound like an ill-mannered lout."

"You? A roughneck, maybe, but never a lout."

"You're splitting hairs worse than a bottle of lye shampoo."

They'd been volleying words like a sport ever since they'd driven back from turning out Shadow in the pasture, and though they'd laughed together like this every night for the past week, tonight was different. As if a tiny seed of uncertainty had creeped into each clever comeback. So, Kayla kept clowning, knowing that sometime in the next few hours, he would ask her to pack her things and drive her back to the bunkhouse.

She didn't bother trying to convince herself that the ennui closing in around her had only to do with the reverse walk from first class to coach. Or even losing the bright, easily trained puppy that slept with her every night. The truth remained that she'd become too comfortable, not just in the big house, but with the kind, intelligent and funny man who lived in it. For now, she refused to think about the whys or the recriminations she would tie to her reluctance to leave Jasper's place. She wanted to be there. With him.

"So, this was what eating on a budget tasted like?" Jasper gestured to his bowl, empty but for a soup spoon and the speckles of fresh-ground pepper stuck on the bottom. "Doesn't seem so bad to me."

"Mom and I made it fun." She smiled at the memory as she crossed to the stove to strain the remaining broth into canning jars she'd picked up at the store. "But I doubt you'll say it's not bad after I assign you to pick the chicken."

She pointed to the demolished bird on a platter next to the stove, its bones so soft from simmering that it had come apart when she'd lifted it from the stock.

"You can't scare me. I run a ranch. We deal with occasional messiness ourselves."

"Good point."

Chuckling, Jasper carried their bowls to the sink. The awkwardness following their kiss a distant memory now, they'd fallen into an easy domestic schedule.

Shared meals and clean-up each evening transitioned to companionable television on separate couches. Colorado Avalanche hockey for her and renovation shows for him. Even Bandit's daily training time had become a chance to work together and no longer an excuse for her to avoid Jasper.

Each time they said good-night Kayla would go to her room, thinking of what-ifs she would never act on. Their time together was comfortable and safe, and she would miss it more than she could have imagined.

"When did you have time to do all this, anyway?" He returned to the stove with their partially filled glasses.

She took a long drink of her ice water and then set it aside. No wine for her tonight. She needed a clear mind, so she wouldn't do something stupid when he said it was time for her to go. Like beg him to let her stay.

"You obviously hit the grocery store," Jasper noted. "I don't keep whole chickens in the freezer. Not to mention, *vegetables*?"

Kayla grabbed a zipper storage bag and moved to the chicken, taking the messy job she'd threatened to give him.

"I hope you don't mind that Bandit and I took the truck on an adventure to the grocery store when we should have been training. He guarded it for me while I ran inside. You and I both know he didn't need any major retraining, anyway. Just a little refresher."

"I know that Bandit's going to be just fine tomorrow. And of course I don't mind you borrowing the truck. I would have told you so if you'd asked."

"I was trying to keep dinner a surprise." She gave her best sheepish grin. "I did go to the closest grocery store I could find. I got the stuff to make chocolate chip cookies, too, but I didn't get to bake them since your brothers showed up."

She wished she could stop prattling on, but her nervousness spilled in words and phrases.

"Why the surprise?" he asked when she finally took a breath. "My birthday isn't today."

"Like I said to your brothers, I wanted to pay you back, at least a little. For all you've done."

He didn't answer for so long that she couldn't resist peeking over at him. His smile was gone, and the mirth had vanished from his eyes.

"You owe me nothing."

"But—"

"I'm serious, Kayla. *Nothing*." He stared out the window into the darkness. "No one needs to be rewarded for doing the right thing."

Jasper made it sound so easy, but for him, being the good guy really did come naturally. It amazed her that a man like him, one who always put others' needs before his own, could ever worry that he was like his self-centered father.

Instead of waiting for her to acknowledge his selfless words, Jasper grabbed the empty stock pot off the stove and filled it with hot water in the sink. Without her ever saying it, he seemed to understand how much it bothered her to be indebted to anyone. He never made her feel that way. After sharing his home, the help of his siblings and even Bandit with her, he'd never once hinted that she should feel beholden to him. He had no idea what a gift that was.

After they finished cleaning up, Jasper glanced over at her. "Did you mention chocolate chip cookies?"

She turned to face him, leaning against the counter. "But as I said, I didn't get the chance to make them."

"We're two intelligent adults. I'm sure we can figure it out. Because, as I've told you before, I—"

"Like to eat," she finished for him. But her smile faded as she glanced at the wall clock. "It's almost eight. Are you sure you have enough time to do that before you—"

Kayla cut off her own words. She hadn't planned to bring up returning to the bunkhouse again, even if it weighed on her mind. Jasper had been moving deftly around the kitchen, collecting a bowl, hand mixer and rubber spatula, but at her words, he stopped.

"Before I what?"

"I mean, after what your brothers said earlier, that the cyber stalker isn't anyone working on the Gemini, well, I figured—"

"That I would want you to move back with the other ranch hands?" He unloaded the equipment on the counter. "I thought you were joking earlier. No, I don't want you to go back there."

Even as relief filled her, she couldn't help but to argue, maybe to make the case his siblings would have if they'd still been there. "But we know that it isn't one of my coworkers, so it would probably be easier on everyone…"

"Easier for whom?" He moved his hand back and forth as if erasing his own question from a white board. "None of that matters. There's still some guy out there who's frightened you, who's threatened you. In texts *and* in calls. You think he'll stop there?"

Kayla shook her head, her knees wobbly. She reached

behind her and rested her hand on the countertop for stability. "I don't know what he's going to do."

"Precisely. *We* don't."

She didn't miss that Jasper had included himself in the statement in the same way that he'd taken on her problem as his all along.

"At some point, he's going to come after you. I feel it here."

He touched his stomach, and her free hand automatically pressed against her own, where that same instinct squeezed inside her. His gaze lowered to her hand before looking up again.

"And just because we think we know who he is now—and who he isn't—that doesn't change anything. We still don't know what Presley wants." He glanced out the window again, his Adam's apple shifting visibly. "Or what he's willing to do to get it."

Even as his last words made her shiver, Kayla couldn't help trying again, no longer sure why she was arguing. "But now that you have a suspect, you can finally tell everyone why I've been staying here."

"You mean Aubrey and Luke?"

"Them and the other staff."

"Let me worry about everyone else. I'll finally be able to tell them the truth."

"Which is?" Even she was losing track.

"That with everything going on, we agree you'll be safer here with Bandit and me. We can also ask the rest of the staff to watch for unexpected visitors."

"As long as you're sure."

He rolled his eyes. "I'm sure. In fact, I would consider it a personal favor if you would agree to stay here until we figure all of this out."

"Another favor?" She grinned since he'd said the same thing when he'd first asked her to stay. "If you insist, I'll stay, but remember I'm only doing it for you."

She didn't know what to make of the warmth spreading in her chest. Was it relief or something more? That she suspected the second worried her. Yes, she'd agreed to stay, but she couldn't make herself too vulnerable, when they still hadn't discussed whether he believed her father was guilty. Because she worried that he might confirm her own disloyal thoughts, she was relieved to delay questions with impossible answers.

Jasper sighed. "Now that we have that settled, can we move on to more important matters? Like those cookies?"

Soon, Kayla had a bowl filled with wet ingredients as Jasper measured the dry, using a recipe he'd located using his phone. As she scooped rounded tablespoons of dough onto the cookie sheet, she caught him watching her.

"Sorry my brothers made a big deal about inviting you to Thanksgiving. Two adults reduced to giggling preteens over—you know."

"It's no big deal." She forced a smile as she put the tray in the oven and set the timer.

"I would take you, but it would probably be uncomfortable since they all think—" He shrugged.

That you and I are sleeping together? Kayla almost finished his comment for him. She was tempted to remind him that he'd said it didn't matter what anyone thought.

"You're right," she said instead. "It would be awkward. Like slides under a microscope. Or primates at the zoo, throwing bananas."

She needed to stop agreeing with him, but she couldn't. This *un*-invitation bore no resemblance to her fantasy anyway. And being aware that Jasper had wanted to wait to invite someone special would only make her feel more like an interloper, while depriving him of the chance to make a statement one day with someone he loved.

"You do your family thing, and I will have a big date here. Just me and the remote. You and Bandit can even bring me a big doggie bag."

As if Jasper had missed the mental gymnastics routine she'd just performed, his gaze narrowed.

"But what will you do if you get a text from Presley? Or a call?"

Or a *visit*. He didn't say it, but they both had to be thinking it.

"I'll let you know when you get back. Or sooner, if it seems like it's important."

"But even if you did call, you would be too far away for me to get back quickly."

Kayla let out a frustrated breath. She couldn't help it. His eyes widened as if he didn't understand how unreasonable he was being. "What do you suggest I do?"

He shook his head, appearing equally irked. "I don't know."

"How about this? I'll stay at the barn until you return from dinner. I'll be close by in case something happens. I can check in on Dory. And I'll get a head start on our preparations for the storm."

"But it's a holiday."

For families. Jasper didn't get it, but people with a strong network never really understood what holidays were like for others like her. While for them, those days were cause for celebration, to her, they were scheduled reminders of everything she lacked.

"Other than it being a holiday, do you have any problem with the idea?"

Jasper considered it for several seconds and shook his head. "It's close, so I can come right away if you need me. You'll have your phone, too."

He paused and looked around. "Speaking of which, where is your phone? We used mine for the recipe."

She scanned the counter, then shot a glance to the table. Her hands automatically tapped her front jean pockets and then the back. All empty.

Jasper searched as well, scanning the tables in the living room and hurrying to the coat tree, where he checked her jacket.

"I can't remember when I had it last." She traced his steps into the living room and glanced down at the same tables, trying to recall when she'd last seen her phone or felt it in her pocket. "Maybe when we took Shadow to the pasture and returned the saddle?"

"I'll check the truck." He grabbed his coat and keys and headed out the front door.

While he was outside, she inspected the dresser in her room and the bathroom counter. Nothing. Her heart pounded in time with her steps, which moved faster with each failed search. She told herself it didn't matter that she'd had no access to her phone, but that not knowing creeped up on her again. Hands she couldn't see reached out with nothing to stop them. What if Presley had called her, determined that she was avoiding him when she didn't answer and decided to show up in person? Worse, if she'd been alone, she wouldn't even have had a way to call for help.

At the sound of the door opening and closing, she rushed into the hallway.

"Found it," he called out as he toed off his boots.

His voice sounded strange, but the wind had picked up since they'd been out earlier. Or maybe he was winded after running to the truck.

"Well, that's good," she said as she hurried over to him. "At least I didn't lose it."

But as she reached for the phone, his expression stopped her cold. "What is it?"

"You shouldn't spend tomorrow alone."

She might have argued, but he tapped the phone screen and turned it toward her. Though he didn't have her code and couldn't have opened her messages, her most recent text was centered on its background of clouds.

Have a wonderful Thanksgiving on the Gemini. It might be your last.

Chapter 14

Jasper rested his plate on the long, long, long Thanksgiving table in the lodge the next afternoon, forcing a smile that already made his jaws ache. Though Aubrey had outdone herself with the autumnal centerpieces, spaced along the orange lace runners that bisected the white tablecloths, there was no way he would tell her that. His twin wasn't his favorite person right now, after she'd tricked him into revealing too much.

That wasn't the only reason he couldn't get in a festive mood, even surrounded by most of his family, plus a bunch of guests, the room's walls practically vibrating with merriment and laughter. He didn't want to be there. On the other hand, he wasn't sure how to explain that he preferred to be in the barn with a ranch hand instead of celebrating with them. Well, technically two employees.

We'll be fine. Kayla's words from two hours earlier lingered in his ears, and he could still see her smirking at his insistence that she shouldn't be alone, even in the barn per their earlier agreement. In fact, had it been his choice, he wouldn't have left her behind. She would have been his unhappy plus-one for dinner, no matter what his siblings had to say about it. Kayla's compromise had been to convince her fellow ranch hand Vince to work with her. That didn't sit right with him, either.

He should have been the one with her. Not Vince, who only knew abridged details about the stalker. Jasper should have been the one working near her, keeping a watchful eye on her, prepared to take on Jed Presley right in the barn, if necessary, to keep her safe. He patted one pocket of his black trousers to ensure that his phone was still there and then tapped the other pocket for his keys. If Kayla or Vince called him for help, he would be ready to rush out of the building. If he had to skip picking up his coat in the cloakroom, he would do that, too.

"You're eating light this year." His mother's laughter-filled voice came from behind him.

"Hi, Mom." He turned to greet her with a hug and kiss.

Isadora Colton grinned at him as she pulled back, resting her hands on his forearms. She looked happy and healthy, her blond highlights fresh, her makeup carefully applied and her black-and-white outfit fashionable as always. Even if their mother still appeared younger than seventy-two, none of her children would take her health for granted anymore.

Oblivious to his concern, Isa pointed to Jasper's plate, its porcelain surface barely covered with turkey, cranberry sauce and his favorite candied yams, instead of piled high like most holidays. Leave it to a mom to pick up on signs that something was up with her kids.

"I'm just getting started. Plenty of time for round two." If his stomach would calm enough for him to eat the food he already had.

"At least I have a plate." He pointed to her empty hands. "Why are you so late? What took you and Chief Lawson so long to get here?"

As soon as the words were out of his mouth, he winced. He didn't want to know anything about what his mother and the guy who was probably her boyfriend had been doing to arrive at the party fashionably late. She'd even turned down offers from his siblings for rides to the dinner, saying that Lawson would pick her up since she was "right on his way."

Isa blushed like a teenager. "I'll have you know that *Theo* was right on time, but I couldn't find my keys, so I spent twenty minutes hunting for them."

"Again? We keep telling you to put them in the same place, so you don't lose them." He would have said "likely story" to her explanation, but this was his mother, and if there were a more personal reason for her delay, he didn't need to know it.

"Okay. I'll start doing that." She poked the deep red nail of her index finger at her son's chest. "And I keep telling you kids to stop calling him 'chief.' He's a family friend."

Friend, all right. He grinned at her, glad to see her happy. Twenty years was a long time to be alone.

"You and Aubrey have done an amazing job here." Isa gestured along the dinner table, where her sons and daughters, their spouses, partners and even a few children were taking their seats, and then to the food tables on the other side of the room. Turkeys and side dishes filled one and salads, breads and desserts lined the other. "We're so lucky you can host us at the Gemini. We have a packed house this year."

"There would have been more if Dom and Sami and Naomi and Philip could have made the trip," he said.

She shook her head. "Oh. No. We didn't want them on the roads if this storm hits. I'm happier knowing they're safe on the other side of the state."

He nodded as his mother's gaze brushed his for a second before she looked back to the table. No matter what Ben Colton had done, she'd lost her husband and the father of her children to an auto accident, and she would always worry about her children's safety when they traveled.

"In fact," Isa continued, "none of us better stay too late tonight in case the snow starts early. I'm surprised that you and Aubrey aren't already trying to sneak out of here to get your cattle and horses ready for the storm."

"Some of the staff are already getting started."

"Good thing."

She glanced up at the slate gray sky as if she expected it to start spitting snowflakes at any moment.

"Aubrey's disappointed that everyone couldn't be here today," he said to distract her. "That made me come up with an idea I want to discuss with you later, okay?"

He wondered if he should still plan the event for his twin, but he might feel differently after he was no longer angry with her.

"You have my number. And I haven't blocked yours

yet." She grinned and then gave him a sidelong glance. "What's going on with you and Aubrey, anyway? And, for that matter, what's this I hear about Kayla St. James moving into your place?"

The arrival of his mother's robust, silver-haired "family friend," his plate piled high with holiday fare, saved Jasper from having to explain that one for now. Even with twelve children, Isa seemed to have a sixth sense when they were having problems. She could be persistent in getting answers to her questions as well.

"Do I need to call for backup on a domestic disturbance?" Theo asked, grinning.

"No, Chief, everything's fine here." Jasper winked at his mother over his use of the man's title again as she stepped back, inviting the older man into the conversation.

Theo set his plate in the empty spot next to Jasper's, and the two men shook hands.

"Good to know," he said. "I've got baked macaroni and cheese *and* stuffing on that plate. I would hate to let any of this great food get cold while I'm busy handcuffing you both and waiting for a patrol car to pick you up."

The chief flashed the bright white smile Jasper guessed had won his mother over.

"Thanks for including me in your family event, by the way."

"And thank you for coming," Jasper told him. "The more the merrier."

"*More* is definitely the word with the Coltons," he agreed. He turned to Isa. "Why don't you get a plate? Those noodles over there are going fast."

Theo pulled out the chair next to Jasper's.

"I will, but don't get comfortable in that seat. Two sweet little blondes have saved places for us over there." She gestured to the opposite end, where Neve and Claire jumped up and down and pointed to spots near Ezra and their mother, Theresa.

"Ezra and Theresa get extra points this year for bringing me bonus grandchildren. Caleb and Nadine, too."

At the food tables, Caleb and Nadine were already helping Portia, Romeo and Juliet fix their plates.

"Guess baby Iris finally has some competition for Grandma's attention." Jasper grinned across the table at his sister Rachel, who carried two full plates, placing one in front of her spot and a second in front of her partner, James, as he wrestled their daughter into her highchair.

"There's more competition on the way," said a voice coming from behind them.

Jasper turned to find one of the triplets, Oliver, standing there holding two filled plates and grinning.

"Soon, too." Oliver tilted his head to indicate his love, Hilary, who stood next to him in a bright red tunic and leggings, her hands resting on her very pregnant belly.

Hilary shook her head, her blond bob fluttering. "Don't mind him. He's just getting excited. I am, too. We get to meet our little Robin and Marian in February."

Isa crossed over to Hilary, and with the young woman's nod, she brushed her hand lovingly over her abdomen. "With Gideon and Sophia expecting in May, too, it will be a good year for us."

Oliver gestured to the end of the table nearest the wall of windows, where Gideon was pulling out a chair for his wife, who rested her hand on her slightly rounded tummy.

"Oh, look at that cute baby bump," Hilary said.

"I see that you brought your baby, too." Oliver pointed to Bandit as the pup rested in the room's far corner, near the stone fireplace.

The poor puppy appeared exhausted after greeting so many guests. For all Jasper's worry about Bandit displaying good holiday manners, the dog had been on its best behavior.

"He's a good boy," Jasper said. "And if any of you have been giving him treats, I don't want to know about it."

Isa shook her finger at Jasper and then at Oliver. "I don't want to hear about competition for Grandma's attention from you, either. I have plenty of love to go around for grandchildren and grand pups. Hearts expand. They don't divide. I had plenty of practice with that while raising you twelve."

Theo squeezed Isa's shoulder. "Looks to me like you've done a fine job."

Jasper and Oliver glanced at each other and shrugged. They couldn't argue with their mother on her point or disagree with Theo on his. Isa had loved them all well, even while having to do it as a single parent for two decades.

As Jasper watched his mom and Theo make their way over to the young twins, and Oliver and Hilary took the two empty seats next to his, a wave of sadness poured over him. He pulled out his chair and sat in it, staring down at the food, even less appetizing now that it was getting cold. He'd been the third wheel with Aubrey and Luke before. But he'd never felt as lonely as he did at that moment, surrounded by so many of the people he loved.

This void he felt wasn't just about him needing *someone* by his side like most of his siblings had. Or even about him desiring a child, though he'd never thought much about it before today. He wanted Kayla with an intensity that nearly drove him to his knees. Just the idea of this strong, intelligent woman, with a tender side he was only beginning to know, carrying a child—*his* child—flooded his heart with yearning.

He'd told himself that if he couldn't have her, at least keeping her safe would be enough for him. And after those calls he'd made about The Rock Solid, he appreciated knowing he could do something else for her. But none of that would be enough for him. He wanted to be with *her.* Just the thought of years and Thanksgivings and Christmases without her beside him made his future look as bleak as one of the alfalfa fields, nibbled bare by the cattle. That future he couldn't bear.

When nearly all the guests had filled their plates and found places along the table, Aubrey stood next to Luke and lifted her hands to ask for quiet.

"Welcome, everyone. Jasper and I want to thank you all for coming to the Gemini for our family Thanksgiving celebration." She gestured to her twin. Their gazes met briefly, and then she looked away. "Not sure the Coltons would fit anywhere else these days with all our new additions."

Chuckles erupted around the table. Aubrey waited for quiet again before speaking. "The forecast doesn't look promising, so if any of you need to leave early, we understand, but we're so glad you're here now. Mom has asked to say a few words, so here she is." She gestured to their mother.

Isa stood and stretched her arms and then drew them in a circular motion until they came to rest at her heart. "I'm so happy to see so many of you here, in one place. We are blessed.

"I know most of you have already started eating. Or have finished and are headed off for seconds." She stopped and scanned the faces along both sides of the table. "Ezra and Oliver, I'm talking to you two here."

No one missed that she would have said *three* if Dom had been present with his triplet brothers, but Isa earned the laugh she'd been going for.

"Or some of us haven't even started." She gestured to the empty spot in front of her where her plate should have been.

"Those two have already eaten all the food. The mystery of the disappearing mashed potatoes...solved," Gavin announced, his partner, Jacqui, shaking her head.

Isa lifted her arms into the air. "Anyway, I'd like to give thanks for our meal."

Their mother said a prayer while they all joined hands. Some connected by blood. Others linked by love and commitment. All were family.

"And between dinner and dessert, I'd like us to revive the family tradition of each person sharing something you're thankful for," she said.

"Not *family tradition*," Ezra called out.

"All of us?" Oliver said. "We'll be *thankful* when it's over."

More chuckles spread around the room, with the children laughing the loudest.

From her place directly across from Jasper, Morgan, stood just as their mother sat. His oldest sister looked different today with her long, dark hair down instead of pinned up the way she always wore it for work as an attorney. She also seemed more solemn than usual, but Jasper admitted he might be projecting his feelings on her. They were the only two unattached Coltons now, after all.

"Tradition is important," she began, automatically slipping into the secondary parent role that she and her twin, Caleb, had assumed following their dad's death. "So, if Mom wants us to say what we're thankful for, then we'd better come up with something."

"We're thankful for you, Morgan," Gideon, the family social worker and one of the most sensitive among all their siblings, announced.

Morgan made a face. "You can say that one if you like, Gideon, but please wait for dessert. Your wife also might be hoping that you're thankful for *her.*"

As she sat again, she smiled across the table at Jasper in a moment of unspoken connection. Only he didn't want to be a part of their ever-shrinking singles club anymore. He couldn't help but to wonder if his sister felt the same, as her fortieth birthday approached.

The most recent defector from the Colton singles club, Alexa, waved at Jasper as she and her new boyfriend, Dane, took seats right next to Morgan. The two sisters pressed their cheeks together.

Jasper finally got down to the business of eating, his dinner barely lukewarm. He'd managed to choke down the last bite without tasting any of it when someone tapped him on the shoulder. Aubrey stood there alone.

"Can we talk?" Her gaze slid to the side, where she

caught Oliver and Hilary watching her curiously. "In the kitchen?"

He was tempted to tell her no, to let her stew in her guilt a few more days before he forgave her, but there were too many witnesses. Anyway, it wasn't his style. He followed her out of the dining room and into the commercial kitchen, which had received many upgrades during the renovation.

They passed the oven, where the turkeys had baked earlier, and restaurant-grade stoves with cooking utensils and pans dangling from the racks above them. She stopped at a prep area near the walk-in freezer and turned to face him.

"I hate it when we're not talking."

"We're talking." If "put that pan over there" and "that was the last of the turkeys" counted, anyway. It had been the quietest event preparation they'd had since opening the Gemini to guests.

"You know what I mean." She tilted her chin down and looked at him from beneath her lashes. "It wasn't cool of me to trick you into telling me something you didn't want to."

"No. It wasn't." Though she pursed her lips in the way she always did to get him to smile when he didn't want to, he refused to fall for it this time.

"But you should have told me what was really going on," she said. "I'm your partner. More than that, I'm your *twin*."

"That doesn't give you the right to—" He stopped and narrowed his gaze at her. "Wait. Who told you?"

"No one told me anything. That's the problem. Not Caleb. Not Ezra. Especially not *you*."

When he gave her a confused look, she added, "Ezra

suggested that I ask you if I wanted to know 'what's really going on.'" She made air quotes for the last part.

His arms shot straight down at his sides, his fists closing, until he recalled that they'd agreed they no longer needed to keep the secret. She watched him unfold his fingers.

"Someone has been cyberstalking Kayla."

Aubrey opened her mouth as if to ask more questions but then closed it and waited.

"We moved her into my house—with the dog—because we thought she would be safer there."

Though it exhausted him to tell the story again, he laid it out for her in abbreviated fashion. Just the facts.

"But she's okay now, right?" she asked when he was finished. "Have you told Chief Lawson?"

Aubrey started to the kitchen exit as if to do it herself, but he rested a hand on her arm.

"Kayla's not ready to go to the police yet?"

"What is she waiting for? The guy to come through the door?"

He shuddered automatically as the memory of that night in the barn slammed inside his mind. It could easily have been Presley who'd arrived that night, and Jasper wouldn't have been there to help her.

"She wants some answers first."

"But what about right now? Is she alone in the barn?" Again, she shifted as if to go handle the situation herself.

"Vince is with her."

She stopped, blinking. "You told Vince and not *me*?"

"Just this morning. I couldn't leave her alone after that message last night, and she wouldn't agree—"

"To show up at your family's holiday dinner and

face the questions from nearly all of your siblings? Particularly me?"

"Something like that," he said with a shrug.

"She paced away from him, past the freezer, and then turned around and came back. "I can see why you went to Caleb. I can kind of understand why you wanted to keep Luke and me out of the loop, though I disagree with your lack of faith in us about keeping the secret."

She tilted her head as if considering her next words. "But why did she tell you in the first place instead of coming to us both? Or just me?"

"I really don't know." Though Kayla had admitted that she'd never suspected him, even she hadn't understood why.

"About yesterday," Aubrey began, staring down at her clasped hands, "I really am sorry. I shouldn't have pressured you into admitting something when you weren't ready to do it."

"It's okay." It wasn't, but this was his sister. His twin. He could forgive her for it, even if it had been a lousy thing to do.

"Is it?"

He didn't get a chance to answer as Caleb strode into the kitchen, little Portia following him, dark ponytail trailing after her in her hurry.

"Are you two finished kissing and making up in here?" Caleb said. "The ruffians are getting anxious out there."

"Anxious? Why?" Aubrey asked.

The six-year-old answered for him. "Grandma Isa said no dessert until we all say thank-you."

"Mom's pumpkin bars are calling me, and we can't

even start saying what we're thankful for until you get out there." Caleb steepled his hands together as if in prayer. "Plus, have you looked outside? Think the meteorologists are right this time. We're going to get that blizzard, so we'll have to cut this party short."

As Portia and her foster father started for the dining room, the child glanced back and gestured for them to follow. "Are you coming?"

Aubrey held up an index finger. "Just give us one more minute, okay?"

The little girl planted her hands on her hips but allowed Caleb to lead her from the room.

Jasper turned back to his sister. "What is it? We'd better get out there."

"I just want to make sure we're okay. I mean, we're going to have quite a mess on the ranch for the next few days, so I need to know—"

"We're fine. Forget about it." He made an *X* across his heart just as they did when they were little. He would even move forward with his surprise idea for Aubrey that just might benefit him as well. But that would mean getting his mother and the rest of his siblings on board right away to start planning.

Aubrey was watching him when he looked back to her again. "One more thing before we *forget about it*?"

Cautiously, he met his sister's gaze, wondering if he was the only one with something up his sleeve. "Yes?"

"About that thing you told me yesterday. The one you didn't want to tell me."

"What about it?"

"The question is, when are you going to tell *her*?"

Chapter 15

Kayla pulled her hat lower over her eyes two days later, leaning forward in the saddle to block the wind. She curled in tighter so her wild rag scarf better covered her throat. Though the last daylight remained, the ice crystals pelting her face and the punishing wind made it both difficult to control her mount and to see more than one hundred feet in front of her.

Mother Nature had pulled off a post-Thanksgiving party that kept on giving, and the worst of it was expected that night. Even with the preparations they'd started on the holiday, the whole Gemini crew had to play catch-up from the moment that Jasper, Aubrey and Luke rushed to work following their Thanksgiving dinner. They'd barely stopped since, other than to take turns grabbing a bit of shut-eye, and though Jasper had brought a doggie bag back to the house for her, she hadn't taken the time yet for her first bite of leftover turkey.

It was a good thing she hadn't had the chance to ask Jasper how the holiday event had gone. And an even better one that she'd resisted her temptation to accept his obligatory invitation. The real celebration would only have paled compared to her daydream about it, anyway. Even now, her fingers warmed as she pictured them entwined with his, and her lips tingled as she anticipated a stolen kiss.

Oh, that was just the ice. She blinked the tiny shards of ice from her lashes and refocused on what little she could see of the path before her as that tingle transformed to a burn. At least Jasper and Aubrey had finally relented when she'd campaigned to ride alone as they spread out to check for stray cattle now that the rest of the herd was safe in the lower pasture.

She'd agreed to share her location with them on her cell phone, even if service was always hit-or-miss this far from the nearest cell tower. Probably more *miss* during the storm. The only thing worse than one overprotective Colton was a pair of them. Still, she'd told them they could cover far more land quickly if they scattered rather than requiring someone to babysit her. They couldn't argue with that.

When Reina jerked against the reins after a particularly strong gust, Kayla startled as well. Then she patted the horse's neck and leaned as far forward as she could.

"It's okay, girl. It's going to be fine."

The mare didn't seem to relax as it slowed briefly to a trot, but she could hardly blame the animal. Kayla wouldn't have been able to calm to soothing words, either, if someone shouted them in her ear.

She'd hated being so jumpy while working in the barn over the past few days, but it made even less sense now. Just like she'd told Jasper, no stalker would be stupid enough to attack during a blizzard. The land could be brutal in weather like this, separating the weak from the strong, with low visibility and winds expected to top thirty-five miles per hour. Escape routes that might have seemed clearer earlier could easily vanish beneath blowing and drifting snow.

After Kayla had completed a swipe along a bank of trees near the Gemini's western perimeter, movement near the pines caught her eye. She brushed her hand over the scabbard, where she'd tucked her Remington before leaving the barn. Now the smooth leather beneath her glove reassured her with its presence.

Since daylight was fading fast, and Jasper would worry if she didn't make it back soon, she pulled out her phone and sent him a voice-to-text message.

"Checking out something. Send."

Then, stowing her phone back in her pocket, she turned the horse and headed closer to the trees. Though it was probably a coyote, or even a wolf as the endangered species had been reintroduced to the area, she couldn't risk the life of one of the yearlings by not taking a look.

But just as she dismounted and reached for her rifle, more movement off to her left caught her attention. A man with a grizzly gray beard, gray coat and black stocking cap stepped out from behind a shield of trees. He pointed a handgun right at her.

"You won't be needing that rifle," he said as he continued to approach.

Kayla froze, as much from the sound of that voice as from the pistol's muzzle. Her heart thudded in her chest. Her lungs burned with the need to scream, but she couldn't afford to let it out. If she had any hope of walking away from this, she needed to keep her wits about her and shore up her unsteady legs.

"Move away from the horse," he called out.

She looked about wildly, trying to make sense of the situation. How had the man even gotten there? No horse. No vehicle. It was as if he'd dropped out of the sky. Just him and his gun.

"Who are you?" she asked to stall him, though she would have recognized his rasp anywhere. The same voice, probably the gruff work of decades spent smoking menthols, had been an unwelcome guest in her dreams more than once lately. "What do you want?"

As he stomped forward in the snow, he racked the Colt's slide. Stopping no more than ten feet from her, he planted his legs wide. "I'll answer the first question. Right now, I'm the guy who wants you to move away from that horse."

This time, she did as she was told, stepping several feet away from the mare. Reina watched her warily and shifted, picking up on the tension. At least the horse hadn't run off yet, taking with it her only chance to get to the rifle. Why hadn't she taken the time to holster her pistol as well?

"That's better, sweetheart." He grinned, revealing nicotine-stained teeth and a few gaps where others were missing. "Now we can have us a right civil chat, as long as you keep your hands where I can see them."

She doubted that was true, given that he still pointed a gun at her. How he was conducting a conversation at all, in a storm and dressed in jeans and running shoes, she wasn't sure. He had a hat and gloves on, but no scarf, and his coat didn't look particularly warm, either. Her attacker had underestimated his environment, so maybe he'd made other mistakes she could use to escape.

"Right. We haven't been properly introduced. I'm Jed Presley." He reached out the hand with the gun and, grinning, pulled it back. "We don't have to shake. I take it your daddy didn't tell you about me. That's too bad. He told me a lot about you. Cellmates get pretty close. Sometimes we share secrets. Your papa wasn't so great at keeping his."

Kayla couldn't help it. She shivered as revulsion tightened her throat. This slimy man probably had spent more time with her father than she had and knew things about him she didn't. She suspected she'd been better off not knowing.

"He kept photos of you on the wall. Pretty little girl." He scanned her body from hat to boots as though he could see right through her winter layers. "Turned into a right fine-looking woman, too. If I had the time…"

Kayla clenched her teeth, only her survival instinct preventing her from beating the crap out of him, gun or no gun.

"Why are you here?" she asked when she could finally loosen her jaw. She wouldn't ask him what he wanted again since it might be more than he'd demanded in the texts.

"We've already discussed this. I need you to tell me where it is. No. Scratch that." Still holding the gun with one hand, he slashed the empty one through the air. "I need you to *show* me. Now would be good."

"Show you what?"

"Good God, woman. *The money!* Where the hell is the money?"

She shook her head, holding out her hands until he jerked the pistol as though she were going for a weapon. Slowly, she pulled her elbows close to her sides again.

"Like I told you, I don't have anything. Money or anything else. Do you think I would live in the bunkhouse on someone else's ranch if I had access to *any* outside funds?"

Shivering, Jed pulled his hat over his ears with one hand. "Looks to me like you've moved right up to the boss's house these days."

She swallowed, bile bitter on her tongue. Of course, he'd been watching her. His last message had even mentioned Thanksgiving on the Gemini. Just what else had he seen? And if Jed had seen her and Jasper together, was he in danger, too?

"That's not—" She shook her head. "I don't need to explain myself to you."

"Good girl. You're more like your dad than I thought. He always had an angle."

"You don't know anything about—" Kayla almost said her dad. Presley's presence suggested that she had her argument backward. *She* didn't know anything about Mike St. James.

"I don't have time to talk all day, so knock off the pretending. He might have told anyone who'd listen that he was a victim, imprisoned by some corrupt judge, but good ol' Mike was as guilty as I was."

"You're wrong. And there is *no* money."

"Of course there is. Ever wonder about that fight

where your old man got hurt on the inside? Ever wonder *why*?"

He grinned over her shock. "I wasn't the only one who knew about the cash he stole, and those nice guys, who wanted what he'd taken from them back, had friends on the inside. As I said, your daddy talked too much."

"You're making all of this up."

"Stop playing innocent." He waved the gun at her. "You don't want me to get impatient."

"I'm not. I just don't know what you're talking about."

"Don't pretend you don't know about the money. That it wasn't enough for him to take kickbacks from those nice cocaine traffickers who needed their cash washed and used his new horse business to do it. Your daddy skimmed from them, too, to the tune of fifty thousand big ones. Thought it took basketball-sized balls to steal from guys with their kind of fire power."

"You're lying. About all of it." She spat the words but crossed her arms, pressing tightly to her rib cage, as if that could keep her insides from exploding into a million pieces.

"No, *Cup-Kay. He* was."

Kayla's stomach clenched, and a shiver of dread shook its way out of her. She'd heard him right on her cell, after all. And maybe she wouldn't have been facing Presley alone if she'd only told Jasper about her suspicion sooner. "He's the only one who called me that."

"I told you I knew him. And *he* said he told you all about the money. It was supposed to be hidden in the house. But I've been all over it and—"

"You went through the house? *Our* house?" Her

breath came in short gasps. The snow-covered field shifted in and out of focus. She was going to be sick.

"The bank's house. But that doesn't matter. I need that money to make a fresh start, and you're going to take me there. Now."

He closed the distance between them so quickly that she had no time to react. He grabbed her arm and started dragging her toward the fence row. Toward what, she didn't know.

"I can't leave Reina." She gestured to the gentle horse that had moved a few feet away to forage the cut alfalfa beneath the snow.

"Then she'll just have to leave *you*."

Kayla let out a mournful cry as he raised the gun as if to shoot the horse. He fired into the air instead. The terrified animal galloped across the open field.

His laughter rang out. "You thought that I could shoot—"

Presley didn't get the chance to finish what he'd started to say as Kayla took advantage of the distraction, swinging around to face him and thrusting a knee hard into his groin. He crumpled to the ground, his pistol flying from his hand and landing somewhere nearby. Where, she couldn't tell.

"You bitch," he called out, writhing on the ground. "I'll get you for this."

Kayla didn't look back as she rushed toward the fence row with a gravel road beyond it. She didn't stop when she reached it, either, but gripped the nearest vertical post, scrambled up the tightly stretched wires that probably cut through the rubber of her boots and threw herself over the top. Pain shot up through her knees when she landed on the ground, and her hands burned inside her gloves. But she got up again and kept running, now with the crunch of gravel beneath her feet.

The wind rushed at her face, the snow either having just picked up or gone unnoticed while she faced down the muzzle of Presley's handgun. Now her hat was missing. Her lungs ached with the effort of drawing in the heavy storm-weighted air. Her heart tried to battle its way out of her chest.

She couldn't think about the truth that trucks rarely traveled this road. That cars never did. Or whether Presley had followed her. Especially if he'd found the gun. If he caught up with her now, he would kill her, not caring whether she might be taking the location of her dad's loot to her grave.

Kayla kept running toward the ranch's southwest entrance, hoping it was closer than she thought. She wouldn't stop. She *couldn't* stop.

And then she heard him. At least she heard something. Lights followed the sound, or the other way around. Either way, a pair of headlights crested the hill that she approached and raced toward her at too high a speed for the conditions. It couldn't be Presley, right? Sure, she was disoriented, but hadn't he come from the wrong direction? Just because she hadn't seen him with a vehicle didn't mean he hadn't hidden one.

Taking no chances, she ducked off the road and worked her way to the fence. She refused to hear the voice inside suggesting he could drive off the gravel and pin her between the car and the sharp wires of the fence.

Only when the vehicle stopped in the center of the road did she realize it wasn't a car at all. It was a truck.

One she would have recognized immediately, even if the driver hadn't thrown open the door and flooded the cab with light. Jasper had come for her. Whether because he'd read something more in her message than she'd written or because he couldn't help being his overprotective self, she didn't care. He was there. Nothing else mattered.

Jasper rushed past the hood of the truck he'd left running, its headlights lighting the area in twin sprays. His heart pounded so hard it surely would explode. The gravel shifted beneath his boots, and he had to dodge the ice that had formed, but he couldn't stop, couldn't breathe, until he reached her, touched her, made sure she was safe. She'd met him halfway, pushing away from the fence and coming toward him, seeming almost relieved when his gloved hands gripped her upper arms.

"You're okay." His words came in a rush.

But she didn't appear okay. She looked shell-shocked. Her hat was gone, her hair wild, having escaped its ponytail.

She stepped back, just far enough to bend at the waist and gulp air in a way that would have announced that she'd been running, even if he hadn't seen her racing frantically. But he *had* seen her coming out of the dark in a slant of falling snow. And it had scared the hell out of him.

"Presley's…here," she managed, still gasping for breath.

"I know. Caleb called to tell me he saw an unfamiliar vehicle when he left the ranch." Thank God for that call, just before her text. He never would have forgiven himself if he'd missed the urgency in her message.

She shot a look back into the darkness from which she'd appeared.

"Where is he now? Is he still out there?"

"I don't know. But he—"

"Isn't going to get the chance to come after you again. Let's finish this now."

He nudged her toward the truck, opened the passenger door and closed it once she was inside. Then he ran around to climb behind the wheel. Following her gaze to his phone, still open to her shared location that had helped him find her quickly, he closed the app and tucked it in his coat pocket.

"Where did you see him last?" He started out at a less risky pace than he'd used to reach Kayla but still too fast, given the road conditions and the fog covering half the windshield.

"Presley has a gun. I mean, he *had* one. Until I sort of knocked it out of his hand after he fired—"

"He *shot* at you?" His stomach felt like a rock, and his throat gripped as tightly as his hands on the steering wheel. After all his plans to protect her, he'd failed her when she needed him most.

"Not at me. In the air. To scare Reina."

"When I saw Reina running up the fence line, still saddled, I thought—" He stopped himself, not even wanting to put words to the tragedy he'd imagined.

"We have to find her."

It was just like Kayla to think only of the horse's safety when Presley had threatened her life. Someone had to think of *her* first.

"Already called Hank and Charlie to round her up."

"He wouldn't let me get to my gun." She paused as if reliving those dark moments. "It's still with Reina."

She jerked her head to look behind her. In his rear-view mirror, he could see what had drawn her attention: the gun rack that was usually empty. He'd grabbed a box of shells and secured his .22 rifle there before driving off to reach her.

"It's about here." She pointed off to a long bank of trees northeast of the road.

He parked in the center of the road, leaving the engine running, and turned to unlatch his rifle.

When she reached for the door handle, he touched her coat sleeve. "I'll do this."

With his gun in his lap, he pulled a box of shells and a flashlight from the glove box. After loading the rifle, he tucked the light and the box in his pocket.

"I can't let you go after him alone," she said.

"You already told me he has a weapon. You don't."

She kept shaking her head. "But you don't know what he said."

"You'll tell me all of that later. Right now, we have to stop him. He'll keep coming back until you give him what he wants. Or he'll hurt you for not giving it to him."

As he pushed open the door, he glanced back at Kayla, her hand again on the handle. "Please, let me do this for you."

She seemed to consider what he'd said, then pulled away from the door and gripped her hands together.

"Okay. But promise you'll be careful."

For a flash of a second, he considered telling her

how he felt, just in case he didn't make it back. But there was no time. And keeping her safe mattered more than anything else.

"Promise me something, too." He pointed to the keys still in the ignition. "If he comes toward the truck, don't wait for me. Just drive."

He hopped down before she could argue, closed the door and trudged to the fence. Looping the gun sling over his shoulder, he scaled the wires and jumped. With a glance to ensure she hadn't followed, he started across the field, near darkness enveloping him as soon as he lost the benefit of the truck's headlights.

Using his flashlight, he crossed the field to the line of trees, the accumulating snow making progress a painstaking slog. As the brush became thicker, he slowed and listened, but the wind rustling the trees made it impossible to hear the other man's movements, even if he'd been only yards away.

"I know you're out here, Presley," he called out, anyway, his own voice swallowed in the vacuum. "You're not getting away."

Only he suspected that the ex-con already had. He wasn't sure how Presley had managed to trespass on the ranch and reach Kayla, but he appeared to have escaped the same way into the blizzard.

Jasper continued all the way down the bank of trees, dipping inside and scanning the wooded area with the inefficient beam of his flashlight. Finally, he turned back and crossed the field to the fence. When he hopped down, he tripped over something on the ground. From beneath new snow, he pulled out Kayla's smashed hat.

Once they were both back in the truck, Kayla cradled her hat in her lap and seemed to withdraw into herself. She'd insisted on returning to the barn to ensure that her fellow ranch hands had located Reina and had used a cooling sheet to protect the mare from a chill.

"Are you going to tell me what happened with Presley?" he asked when he couldn't take the silence any longer.

"I will."

She didn't say more, but he didn't push, hoping she would tell him when she was ready.

But as they drove past the bunkhouse, she straightened in her seat.

"Can we stop here?"

Dread filled him, but he parked near the building, beneath the bright safety lights. "After that run-in with Presley, you still want to stay here?"

When again she didn't answer, he watched her, ready to argue. He could breathe again after she shook her head.

"Need more clothes?"

She held up her index finger and opened the door. "Be right back."

He wondered if she'd lied again, choosing an easy way to walk out while avoiding an argument, but she'd left her hat on the seat. So he waited.

She didn't take long. As promised, she climbed back in the truck minutes later. In her lap, she settled a nondescript shoebox.

"Shoes? Now you made me stop for *shoes*?"

Only she didn't laugh. Or smile. She stared at the box without opening it. He didn't have to read her expression to know that it contained no shoes. And to understand that she wished she could walk away from whatever *was* inside as fast as her boots could carry her.

Chapter 16

Kayla leaned over the square coffee table, pushing her plate as far away as she could without knocking it or anything else on the floor. The tabletop had become a maze of plastic bags and clear containers, filled with left-over turkey and all the best sides, so she had to be careful. She dropped back onto the love seat, exhausted from more than just too much mashed potatoes and dressing.

It seemed as if a lifetime had passed since Jasper had offered her that pity invitation to his family Thanksgiving dinner two days before. A storm like the blizzard outside had ravaged her reality, tearing away the adornment of lies and leaving behind a foundation riddled with holes as real as those Presley had threatened with his gun. At the memory of the ex-con's sinister smile and the click of his pistol's slide, she shivered and twisted her damp braid for comfort.

Jasper pretended not to notice, but Kayla didn't buy it. Nor did she believe that he'd recovered from earlier, though, like her, he'd showered and traded his soaked clothes for cozy sweats. Though she'd nervously eaten her way through more calories than she usually consumed in a week during their late-night picnic, he'd only pushed candied yams around on his plate.

"Look at poor Bandit." She pointed to the pup, asleep by the woodstove after picking up on their stress and flitting between them when they'd returned to the house. "He's exhausted."

"Can you blame him?" He set his plate on the table, his turkey drying out, untouched. "It's been a long couple of days."

Kayla braced herself for Jasper to insist that she tell him what the shoebox contained, or at least give her the I-told-you-so lecture. He'd been right when he'd asked her to avoid working alone. But how could she have predicted that Presley would attack her in the middle of a blizzard?

"Sure you had enough to eat?" Jasper asked, instead, when he caught her watching him. He gestured to the dishes that she'd done a fair job of decimating.

"You were supposed to bring a doggie bag, not a doggie *cooler*. Just how many of me did you plan to feed?"

Like it had all night, their usual banter fell flat. But everything seemed off in the wake of Presley's words. Wrong. How could anything be right when she suspected that this smarmy stranger, who'd held her at gunpoint, had been more honest with her than either of her parents?

Jasper pushed a hand back through his damp hair

"I was so scared. If Caleb hadn't called…if you hadn't texted…"

At his words, those terrifying minutes flashed in her thoughts, panic gripping just as it had then. But as she recalled those approaching headlights, the outline of the man opening the truck door, calm flooded her system again.

"But he did call. And I did text." She smiled though his expression suggested he was still playing a dangerous game of what if. "Thank you again. For everything."

He nodded but didn't look at her. "I can't believe he got away. If the snow clears in the morning, I'll go back out there and see if he left any tracks. Or clues."

"Or the gun. And, by the way, we're both going."

Jasper opened his mouth to argue, but she crossed her arms.

"Fine," he said finally.

"I'll have my gun this time."

"We're also taking this to the police. We're not risking your life again."

This time his crossed arms and narrowed gaze dared her to argue. All her excuses for dragging her feet on reporting the stalker no longer made sense, anyway. Maybe they never had.

"All right."

Kayla's gaze slid to the shoebox on the end table. All through dinner, it had taunted her, waiting. As she caught Jasper staring at it, too, gooseflesh lifted on her arms. Answers to questions she'd avoided asking for years were trapped inside that cardboard prism, and the thought of letting them out blanketed her with foreboding.

"Want to tell me about the shoes?" Jasper asked.

Want to? She could have lived a lifetime without knowing some of this. Or being forced to believe it. For something to do with her anxious hands, she zipped the plastic bags closed and piled the containers inside the cooler. Then she stacked the plates. She would need the table space for the unpleasant task ahead, anyway.

"They're not shoes," she said finally. "They're letters."

"I figured something like that. Letters about what?"

"It's not the *what* that matters. It's the *who*. They're from my father."

Jasper stared at the box again but didn't reach for it. She couldn't bring herself to do that, either. Not when dread had already turned her few happy memories into a single lit bulb at the end of a long corridor. The distance between her and that light continued to stretch and distort.

"You never told me what Presley said about your dad."

Kayla's gaze shifted from the box to Jasper. "You're not going to beg to see the letters first?"

"It's up to you whether you tell me or show me anything. You don't have to talk at all if you don't want to."

A knot settled in her throat. Just like that other time when Jasper hadn't asked for more details about her father's conviction, he was simply there for her, just supporting her. Even after she'd brought danger to his ranch, he still asked for no more than she could give.

"I'm not like the other guy, you know," he said after a long pause.

"What guy?"

"The jerk you didn't tell me about. The one who wanted details about your dad."

"Right. *Bill*." She dampened her lips. "Not much to tell. He thought it would be cool to date a convict's daughter. Back then I didn't have any exciting information for him, so I guess he missed out."

"I was right. He was a jerk." His lips lifted. "And you're not kidding that he missed out."

Their gazes met, so warm that she had to look away from the heat.

"Has anyone ever told you that you're a really *nice* guy?"

He grabbed his chest and fake-collapsed on the couch. "You really know how to hurt a guy. I've heard those words before. Right before I got dumped."

Still chuckling, he carried the plates and the cooler into the kitchen.

"Then, whoever did that to you, she missed out, too."

Kayla might not have noticed the quick straightening of his back if she hadn't been watching closely. Her words had surprised her, too, but she found she didn't regret them. They were another truth in a day of dispelling lies. She liked knowing that at least some revelations didn't hurt so much.

Jasper took his time putting away the leftovers in the refrigerator. He seemed to be giving her the chance to decide if she was ready to let him in. To trust him with a story that she didn't fully know herself yet. That familiar tightness in her chest still shouted *no*. The risk was too great. But a gaping hole had formed inside her heart since hearing the news about her father. Though she didn't expect Jasper to fill it—no one could—she took comfort in knowing that he would at least listen while she tried to repair it herself.

When he returned to his seat, she blurted words that were almost too painful to speak at all, let alone to take her time saying. "Jed Presley was looking for the money that my father stole from his drug trafficking partners."

Jasper tilted his head. "Wait. I thought he was convicted of money laundering."

"Apparently, my father was an overachiever where his crimes were concerned."

He glanced at her and then away. It was the first time she'd confessed to believing her father was guilty. She couldn't even call him "my dad" anymore. The title felt too personal for someone she didn't know at all.

"If what Presley said is true, and I suspect it is, he pocketed a lot of money from his shady partners. Fifty thousand dollars, to be exact."

"Do you think he was involved in the other…?"

"You mean the drugs? Presley didn't say so." She shook her head. "But it wouldn't surprise me if he were. Nothing shocks me now."

"Since your dad cheated his partners, if he'd ever been released—" Jasper stopped himself, his eyes widening.

"Maybe." She hadn't thought about that before. Presley wasn't even the only criminal who could have come for that money. If her father had been released, his life would have been at risk, and he would have put her and her mother in danger at the same time.

He still had, even in death.

"Presley also called me 'Cup-Kay.'"

Jasper tilted his head to the side. "How did he…?"

"He was my father's cellmate." She drew her shoulders to her ears and lowered them. "Presley also used that nickname the first time he called me."

"Why didn't you tell me that?"

"I wasn't certain that was what he'd said."

He nodded, accepting her explanation, though he couldn't quite cover his hurt. Even after she'd promised, she'd held something back from him, and the regret settling heavily in her gut couldn't change that.

"Did Presley tell you about the letters?"

"No. He just made me realize I had to see what's in them."

Kayla glanced at the box. Only this time, she grabbed it, set it on the coffee table in front of her and pulled off the lid. They were still there in the almost empty box. Six envelopes, organized by postmark date, the same six-digit inmate number in the return address. A stamp in black ink on the front of each marked them as from the Delta Correctional Center.

Jasper leaned forward and peered into the box. "They still look sealed."

"I haven't opened them. I didn't even know about them until after my mother died. I found the box in her closet when I was cleaning out her things."

She waited for him to point out that her mother died five years ago. He didn't.

"Do you think she knew about the money?"

Kayla crossed her arms and allowed her head to droop forward. "I don't know. Maybe."

"Could it be that she didn't *want* to know the truth about him? Or you to know? Maybe she was a victim, too. Obviously, she didn't open the letters, either."

Kayla lifted her shoulder and lowered it. She could relate to that wish for oblivion.

"Is that why you didn't read them? Did you not want to know?"

"It felt like a betrayal. Of her memory. And his." She rested her hands on the edge of the table on either side of the box. "I'd already discovered enough about the difficult situation the ranch was in. It was too easy to put the letters away and pretend they didn't exist."

"But you kept them. And though you brought almost nothing from your ranch, you kept that box."

"I don't even know why."

"Are you sure that's true?" Jasper shook his head, making it clear that he disagreed. "I think you always believed that someday you would be ready to know the whole truth."

Had she really believed that, or had it just been another way to cling to her father's memory while shielding herself from the unsavory parts? Whatever her reason then, the situation had changed. *She* had changed.

She reached inside the box and took out the first letter. It was the oldest, postmarked a week before her fourteenth birthday and more than two years before her father's death. Ignoring the disconcerting quiver in her belly, she opened it, unfolded the lined paper and read.

My dearest Cup-Kay,
Happy Sweet Sixteen! I told your mother to wait until today to give you my letters. I can't wait to be home with you so we can go on a birthday treasure hunt outside, just like we did when you were little...

A sharp sound escaped her, and her hands opened, the paper fluttering to the floor. She covered her mouth with her hand, her breath fast and heated against her skin. Unable to bring herself to pick it up, she stared down at the familiar block-print handwriting. The first few lines already revealed so much. The ten or so others would only be more damning. There was a difference between suspecting and having proof. Even if it probably wouldn't have stood up in a court of law, she knew she'd found the truth.

"What is it? What does it say?"

When she didn't answer, Jasper crouched down and picked it up. He extended it to her without reading it. She waved it off. "I don't need to see more."

"Is it all right if I look?"

"Okay."

Holding the letter in both hands, Jasper read it.

"I don't understand," he said, as he rested it on the table. "I get that your mother knew about the letters before she received them. And he used the nickname from your snow globe. But what else does it show?"

She planted her elbows on her knees and rested her chin in the cradle formed between her hands.

"You know how all inmate mail from outside is opened and screened? And how inmates' mail can't be sealed until it's been examined?"

"I guess I generally knew that."

"So, that—" she paused and pointed to the letter "—is a game filled with clues."

Jasper picked it up and looked at it again. "You mean the number sixteen? He wrote that letter two years before that birthday."

"I don't know if that number means anything. He

might have just thought it was a good age for Mom to give me the letters."

"But like you said, you never found them until after she died. Maybe she planned to shield you from them. She could have decided to destroy them once and for all, but—"

"She was too weak?"

"No. Maybe *she* wasn't ready. Or it could have been right after your dad died, and she didn't want to upset you on your birthday by—"

She shook her head until he paused. "I was born in January. He died the September *after* I turned sixteen."

He lifted his hands. "Okay, I give up. What clues do you see?"

"The birthday is one. An *outdoor* treasure hunt? In January?"

"Makes sense. What's the other part?"

"The hunt itself." She pointed to those words. "My memories of when my dad lived with us are murky, but I'm pretty sure we never went on a treasure hunt together. Not once. He brought it up a few times when Mom and I visited him at the prison. He always used the same words to describe it. 'Just like when you were little.'"

"He was making sure it would stand out for you when you received the letters." Jasper poked a finger against the paper. "Only he didn't plan on dying while still on the inside."

"And he didn't expect Presley to come after me for the money."

"Sounds to me like he was only thinking about himself." Jasper pointed to the remaining letters, sealed with more potential to hurt her. "Are you going to look for more clues?"

Kayla returned to the box and opened the next letter and the next. She read each one aloud, absorbing the words that offered fresh blows to her heart and then attempting to decipher them. She'd expected more hints for a location, but most were happy messages, offering few clues, as if her father had hoped the treasure hunt would make her excited about the money.

"'Remember the horses in your snow globe?'" she read. "'We'll buy more with the money you've saved. Then when I come home, we'll ride and ride and *ride*.'"

Her voice broke on the last word, her throat thick with betrayal that felt like another death. Her dad had finally mentioned the money. When she glanced at Jasper, his eyes were shiny, too. He understood all too well what loss felt like when it mingled with shame.

"Do you want me to read the last letter for you?" he asked.

She shook her head, but her hands trembled as she slid her thumb under the flap. This was to be her last message, ever, from her father. Though she longed for an apology for the destruction his greed had caused their family, the best she could hope for was more hints on the cash's location. If he didn't provide that answer, she would have nothing to bargain with if Presley attacked her again.

"'We'll have so much work to do to get the barn ready to house the rest of the Thoroughbreds. First, we'll need to dig a new well, so—'" She stopped reading, her thoughts racing and tiny memories falling into place. "That's something."

"What do you mean?" Jasper held out his hand, and she gave him the letter. He read it and looked back to her. "What do you see?"

"Everything on The Rock Solid was old. The house. The barn. The tractors. There was one new thing on the whole ranch. The well. The old well had dried up, so my father had to have a new one drilled."

"He wouldn't have hid money in the well, would he?"

"That would be dumb, but it could be a hint." She closed her eyes, trying to recall more, and then opened them again. "The barn could be a hint, too. He talked about the money I'd saved, too. Maybe my piggy bank? I don't know what happened to that."

"Your dad never counted on the ranch ending up in foreclosure. Wherever he put the money, it could have gotten wet. Even moldy."

"That would serve him right."

She'd meant it as a joke, but her own words bounced back, their humor gone. Her father wasn't there to deal with the consequences of all his scheming. No, that would fall to her. The embarrassment and the shame, those would all be hers.

"He didn't care about us. Money." She spat the word. "That was all he thought about."

"Your dad cared about you. He sent you the snow globe and—"

"And he probably bought that with stolen money, too."

"Maybe he made some mistakes, but he—"

She shook her head until he stopped. "I know you're trying to help, but don't defend him. You didn't even know him. And it's very clear now, neither did I."

With Jasper on the sofa and Kayla on the love seat, their knees nearly touching at the corner of the coffee table, he reached out and took her hand.

"This doesn't change anything."

She jerked her arm back, heat rising behind her eyes. "Don't you understand? It changes *everything*."

Her words poured in a torrent that wouldn't stop. Tears had started as well, hot twin streams blazing trails down her cheeks for others to follow.

"Before, he was a…victim. An innocent man, unfairly judged by your father." She gulped a breath and used a sleeve to swipe at her tears. "Now he's just a criminal. And I'm no longer the daughter of a wrongly convicted man. My righteous indignation was a joke. *I* was a joke, too."

"You're not."

"Maybe not, but I'm the daughter of a selfish, cruel man who would do anything and hurt anyone just to get a little free cash."

"What your father did doesn't define you. That's all on him. But that said, people make mistakes. Even big ones. That doesn't mean your dad didn't love—"

"No! I said don't defend him. And don't defend *me*. Not when I blamed your dad. I blamed—I don't know—even you."

Burying her face in her hands, she let the sobs come, sounds of loneliness and betrayal ripped from her soul. She wasn't sure when Jasper stood up and moved closer, but suddenly he was sitting next to her, his hand on her shoulder.

"Don't you feel sorry for me. I don't want your pity." Kayla tightened her shoulders when he pulled her close, her arms pressed to her sides. She couldn't let go, couldn't let herself fall into the safety of his arms. If she did, she might lose herself, might never get the chance to draw it all back in. Might never reclaim control.

Jasper held on, not so tightly that she couldn't pull away if she chose to, but with strength and structure to comfort her if she could let him. And she wanted to let him.

After a long while, he pulled back, his hands still gently closed over her arms. He stared into her eyes.

"We spoke before about how our situations were different." His shoulder shifted. "Maybe not as different as we thought, but still. You said something to me that I needed to hear, and now you need to hear it, too. I don't need to have met him to know this. You're nothing like your father."

With that, he brushed his lips over her forehead. It was the sweet, consoling kind of kiss that she, as a six-year-old, might have given ten-year-old Jasper at his father's funeral or he might have offered her when her dad died ten years later. A recognition of unimaginable loss.

He stared into her eyes, his own reflecting back at hers as pools of compassion, open and vulnerable and a little fearful. Then he dipped his head and pressed his lips to hers in the gentlest, most perfect kiss she'd ever known. He smiled against her lips, and with her eyes still open, she grinned back, sliding her arms up over his shoulders and around his neck. She knew in her heart that this would change everything, too.

Chapter 17

Jasper hadn't intended to kiss her. At least he hadn't planned beyond that initial brush of his lips on the soft skin of Kayla's forehead. It was to be just an offer of compassion and solace on one of the worst days of her life. He'd even planned to keep that promise to himself that he would never kiss her again, not after the last time, when he'd longed for everything she could give, and she'd wanted nothing he offered. A man could take only so much rejection.

But as he'd sat next to her, so close that the heat from her body already melded with his, and she'd stared back at him with rare vulnerability softening her features and what he hoped was trust easing her spine, he lost the battle with his better angels.

He could no more have resisted kissing her, just once more, than he could have shoved her out the front door into the blizzard. So he sank into the plushness of her lips and slowly allowed himself to drown in her sweet taste and texture and essence. For just this moment, he dared to believe that the woman he loved could truly be his.

Then she slanted her mouth over his, and he was convinced that tonight *possible* had dumped *impossible* on its head. He tried to remember that this was only a kiss, but the way she leaned into him and took his mouth had him questioning his own supposition. And feeling so grateful to be wrong.

He kissed her gently, thoroughly, beginning the sweet, slow seduction he'd replayed hundreds of times in his best daydreams, but she had plans of her own. She shifted to straddle him and then settled herself *right there.* His eyes flew open at that first point of intimate contact, the sensation intensifying once he realized only the soft cotton of their sweatpants separated them.

She drew on his bottom lip and captured his mouth in another searing kiss. When it ended, though he hadn't yet had the chance to see her amazing body or to touch and taste all she offered, he could think of nothing beyond the need to bring them together, making her his own and letting her claim him as hers.

Jasper dragged his mouth to her cheek to gasp for breath and reclaim his senses before, with the tiniest shift of clothing, he would do exactly as his body demanded.

"Uh, Kayla."

She dipped her chin to her chest, her braid brushing her cheek, and leaned her forehead against his.

"Please don't tell me that you want to stop again," she pleaded.

"What? Again?" He leaned his head back so he could look in her eyes. "You thought before that I didn't—or now that I wouldn't— Oh, hell, no."

"That's good to hear."

She traced her tongue over his lip. He pulled his head back slightly.

"Don't doubt for a minute that I want you. That I've wanted you probably from the day you arrived on the Gemini." He cleared his throat. "I mean, can't you tell?"

"Oh, I can tell."

Leaning to the side, she kissed her way down his neck. "So, you were saying?"

"What?" He blinked several times, trying to remember. "I just needed to say that you might want to think about this. Before it goes any further."

She covered the other side of his neck in wet, open-mouth kisses and returned to his lips. He couldn't resist going in for another taste.

"You've had quite a shock today," he said when the kiss broke off again. "I don't want you to do anything you'll regret later because you're feeling vulnerable. Unless you're sure?"

"Oh, I'm sure." She glided her fingers over the notch at the base of his neck.

"I mean, we can just talk all night, too. If you'd rather."

"I'm sure." She leaned back and spread her hands over his chest.

"I just want you to know that you can back out now. Or even…uh…later if you need to."

"So, Jasper?"

"Yeah."

"How many more ways do I need to say yes?"

"I guess that would be enough." He chuckled, more

nervous than he cared to admit. "One more thing. It's… um…been a while, so I'll do my best to take it slow but—"

"We'll see about that."

She scrambled off his lap, grinning when he automatically covered himself with his arms.

"How about we reconvene this party in five minutes in my room? Do you have condoms?"

He nodded. "Upstairs. I could dust them off."

"You do that."

When he stood, she slid her arms around his neck and kissed him so long and hard that he was certain he would make a short night of it. Then she pulled away and started toward the bedroom. Outside the door, she turned back.

"And Jasper, could you do me a favor?"

"Anything," he said, meaning it.

"Could you wear the cow pajama bottoms?" Her smile was so wicked that he felt it all the way to his toes.

"Will do. But what about him?" He pointed to the pup that had awakened from all the movement and stood with tail wagging.

"I'll let him outside. You can give him a snack when he comes back in. Then he can have some quiet time," she paused, shaking her head at Bandit. "Because for this, he's not invited."

As promised, Jasper arrived at Kayla's closed door several minutes later, having completed the list of tasks she'd given him at record speed. He glanced down and patted his pocket for the small box of condoms that, indeed, had a little dust on it.

Suddenly, those ridiculous pajama pants that he'd

paired with a wide-neck, black T-shirt didn't seem like such a great idea after all. She'd probably been joking when she'd asked him to wear them. How was he supposed to be sexy with a bunch of Charolais cows all over his butt? And he really wanted to be sexy for Kayla right now, even if his mouth was dry, and moths like he hadn't seen since September were performing acrobatic stunts in his gut.

"It's like riding a bike, isn't it?"

His whisper must have been louder than he'd thought as Bandit's ears popped up, though the dog had been across the room. He probably wouldn't have to worry about climbing on a bicycle seat and peddling tonight, anyway. With a few minutes to reconsider, Kayla had probably changed her mind about this whole thing. Could he blame her? He shook his head, though just the thought of *not* touching her made his whole body ache.

Still, he pushed his shoulders back and stepped closer to her door. He'd never wanted any woman the way he wanted Kayla, and if there was a chance that she might still choose to be with him, he would take it. He reached for the door handle and tested it. Locked. He lowered his head.

"Jasper, are you out there?"

He lifted his head, blinking. "Yeah, I just—uh, the door's locked."

For several seconds, she said nothing. He'd wanted an answer. This wasn't the one he'd hoped for, but he would accept it. He turned and took a step toward the stairs.

"Use the key," she called out.

He let his head fall back. That phrase was one of the best he'd heard all day. *I'm sure* was the other. He reached for the key that, as with all the other bedrooms and bathrooms in his house, rested just above the door-frame. He unlocked the door, then scooted through the opening while edging his canine friend out of it.

"Sorry, buddy."

Once inside, he closed the door and pressed his back against it.

Kayla sat on top of the comforter in the center of the bed, the lamp from the nightstand outlining her delicate features in soft light. Still dressed in that lavender sweatsuit from earlier, her hair tied in that same braid, she stared down at her hands in her lap.

"You might want to lock the door. Bandit kept opening it," she said before finally looking up. Even then, she didn't quite meet his gaze.

"Right." How he'd forgotten about his escape-artist pup, he wasn't sure. He shifted from one bare foot to the other, her unease becoming his, but finally he turned to twist the lock inside the door handle. "By now, he probably thinks this *is* his room."

"Not right now it isn't."

Kayla stared at her lap again. It didn't make sense. She'd said the right things, but her actions weren't matching her words. Was she as nervous as he was? Or could it have been something more than that? Her hand shifted, making it easier for him to see that she held her phone.

His pulse immediately raced. "What is it? Was it Presley? Did he threaten you again?"

A moment ago, he would have had to work up the courage to cross the room to her, but now Jasper found himself next to her bed, ready to help her if she needed him.

She looked up from the phone and shook her head.

"That's just it. There's nothing. Not after we returned to the barn. Not since we've been back here. After... earlier... I would have expected a tirade of texts from all the numbers."

When she handed him the phone, she hugged her knees to her chest and watched him scroll through the messages from the cyber stalker. The last one had been from the night before Thanksgiving. The thought that Presley could have made good on that threat today caused Jasper's hands to sweat. He passed her cell back to her, and she set it aside.

"Let me get this straight. You're worried because he *hasn't* texted or called?"

"I guess that sounds ridiculous." She pointed to the window. "But he's still out there somewhere."

Since he shivered over that truth, he appreciated that she was still staring at the closed blinds.

"You're right. But if he has any sense at all, he won't try again during the storm. Even if he were dumb enough to try, we have the motion-activated lights to warn us, and Bandit will let us know if anyone is here."

Jasper paused, considering it again, and then shook his head. "He won't come out tonight. He's probably hunkered down like we are and waiting for the storm to pass. We can relax for now."

He looked down at his feet. If he'd located Presley like he should have earlier, he would have been able to promise that she was safe. Now he could only offer her a reprieve rather than a guarantee.

"Is that what you call this?" She gestured to the mattress. "'Hunkering down?'"

"I'd call it a very pleasant near miss." He gestured to his pajamas. "Is it the pants?"

She didn't even smile at his joke. "No, it's—I don't know."

Her gaze flitted to the snow globe on the dresser, showing that even when she searched for a distraction, her father—and now his betrayal—was never far from her mind.

Though Kayla returned her attention to Jasper, she appeared even more troubled than before. He considered trying to come up with more clever words, relying on the humor they'd both used to cover their discomfort, but tonight was too important, whether or not they ultimately made love.

"I know you're scared. I'm scared, too. But the decision is yours." He smiled down at her. "I'm already all in."

Jasper extended a hand, realizing he'd asked a lot of her. There was a difference between climbing into his lap in an emotionally charged moment and making a clear-headed choice to trust him with her body, even if with nothing more. She stared at his hand without moving. He waited several heartbeats and then swallowed, accepting the rejection reflected in her inaction.

But just as he started to pull away, she rested her hand on his. A sense of weightlessness filled him as he closed his fingers and drew her, first to her feet and then into his arms. The emotion clogging his chest made it tough to breathe. For a long time, he just held her, feeling each breath she drew against his chest, recognizing the gift as she relaxed against him.

With utmost care, he leaned in and pressed his lips to hers. He didn't hurry or ask for more than she was ready to give, gently tasting the now familiar and reveling in new discoveries. When she slid her arms around his neck and touched the corner of his mouth with her tongue, warmth spread in his chest. She opened for him, and he deepened the kiss, the moment less frantic than earlier but far more intense. As she reached behind her, drawing her braid to the side, he stilled her hand.

"May I? I've been dreaming about this for months."

"Okay," she whispered against his mouth.

He took his time, sliding his fingers through the damp silk, unraveling the strands and allowing her hair to fall down her back. Then he sank his hands in the mass while tracing a line of kisses along her jaw and past her chin to her collarbone.

"This is exactly what everyone thought we were doing," she said. "They probably had a pool going on when it would happen."

Recognizing her attempt to distract, he continued adoring her neck, especially that sensitive spot at the base of her throat.

"Who do you think started the pool?"

When she frowned at him, he shrugged. "Had to increase my odds."

His lips returning to hers, Jasper slowly walked her backward until her legs touched the edge of the mattress. She did the rest herself, first sitting and then scooting back and lying across the covers, but she didn't look at him. He stretched out on his side, next to her.

He brushed her hair back and tucked it behind her ear. "You're so beautiful."

She shifted, as if she rarely heard those words, when someone should have been telling her that every day. He knew who would volunteer for that job.

"Everyone probably thinks I took advantage—"

"Of me? That couldn't be further from the truth.

Besides, I don't care what any of them think. And neither should you."

She flipped onto her side and stared at him. "You're the owner. I'm just the help."

"That's not close to being true," he said, though in the most basic sense, he remained her employer. As tonight's revelation that her father was guilty had removed one of the obstacles for them to be together, she had recycled the other one, lesser in his eyes, but still significant to her.

His chest tightened, his throat closing. Just like before, she was pulling back, rebuilding the wall that she'd used to shield herself from hurt.

"Stay with me, Kayla. Please."

Though she couldn't have known that he'd meant those words on so many more levels than this one bed or this one night, she looked up at him, uncertain. She had no idea how amazing she was or how deeply she'd embedded herself in his heart, even if he wasn't ready to share those words.

"I need you." His voice sounded raw, but he had to let her know. "And I think you need me."

The silence was so profound that he could almost hear his heart pounding as he waited for her to decide. Then she leaned forward and kissed him. It felt like a gift. This moment of trust went beyond two bodies seeking comfort and relief, and he had to believe that she recognized it, too.

Jasper touched his lips to hers, then backed a breath away and repeated that movement, an approach with anticipation and a retreat with regret, again and again and again. Until, on the last advance, her arms slid around his shoulders, her fingers linking behind his neck. As she held him near, she pressed her whole body down the length of his. Lips to lips. Breasts to chest. One rider's muscular thighs tight against those of the other. She fit perfectly to him, as if they'd both been built for the sheer purpose of coming together like this. Their hands moved and found each other as well, their fingers smoothly entwining like muscle memory from a couple who'd spent a lifetime making love.

When she pulled back, every inch of him yearned for her touch and her warmth. Some parts more than others. But he reminded himself he'd said he would take this slow. That would be more difficult than he'd thought.

Releasing her hand, Jasper slid the backs of his fingertips up her side until they passed the curve of her breast. Then he covered its fullness with his palm.

"Incredible," he breathed.

Her arm snaked beneath him, and her free hand slid under the hem of his T-shirt and slowly edged it up. To make her task easier, Jasper draped his legs over the side of the bed, reached up and pulled the shirt off with one hand.

"You weren't kidding," she said as her gaze traced his form. "Incredible."

"Fair is fair." He reached for the hem of her sweatshirt and guided it over her head but was surprised to find a black lace bra beneath.

"I changed a little while you were upstairs," she admitted with a sexy smile.

She even assisted him as he helped her out of her sweatpants, revealing the second half of that black lace set. Then she reached for the waistband of his pajama pants.

"As much as I hate to see these go…" She pushed one side over his hip, her eyes widening as she revealed the bare skin beneath since he'd skipped the underwear.

"They've already worked their magic," he agreed as he removed the pajamas.

He couldn't help her out of her lacy things quickly enough, but soon they'd pulled the covers back, and that exquisite beauty lay fully naked, just inches from him. They touched only with their gazes, following contours in slow, steady appreciation, their breaths and the heat from their bodies mingling with anticipation.

They reached for each other at the same time. Jasper worked slowly, loving all of her with fingertips first and then with his lips. Kayla explored with that same enthusiasm, touching and tasting all that he had to offer. Until he couldn't bear but to volunteer more.

After rolling on a condom, he braced himself above her, waiting for that final yes.

She dampened her lips, already swollen from his many kisses. "I haven't done this in a while, either. A long, long while."

"We can figure it out together." His arms began to shake with the exertion of holding himself up, but still he waited.

"Yes," she breathed. "Yes, we can."

Jasper brought them together, slowly waiting for her body to adjust before going further. Finally, she lifted her hips to fully seat him.

"You don't know how long I've wanted this. Wanted *you*." He closed his eyes, his throat filling with emotion over the enormity of the moment.

He was in love with Kayla St. James. No going back now. No recovery for his heart if she stomped all over it.

"Good thing that wait is over," she said with a laugh.

She lifted up again, and they moved together, equal partners in the chase. Their lips found each other again as they swayed, tasting and sharing, swallowing each other's sighs. She called out in her release, which sent him over the edge as well. Cuddled together, they fell asleep in each other's arms, the room still flooded with light.

Jasper awoke to the sounds of scratching and a whimper outside the bedroom door. He slid on his pajama pants and pulled it open. The puppy made happy circles around his legs. As he returned to the bed, with Bandit curled up at the foot, he left the light on a little longer so he could watch Kayla sleep.

His chest squeezed with the hard truth that even with all the things they'd said, all the feelings swelling in his heart, they'd made no promises. He hadn't even told her about his surprise yet. But after tonight, after getting as close to her as two humans ever could be, Jasper worried he wouldn't survive if he ever had to let her go.

Chapter 18

Kayla awoke with a start and lifted her head, looking back and forth and trying to make sense of the darkened room. In her dream, the lamp next to her bed had been switched on, framing Jasper's face in soft yellow light. She blinked several times, trying to clear her thoughts. Had it really happened, or had she just dreamed it, complete with all the tastes and sensations?

Her hand automatically reached for the pillow next to hers. No one was there. Maybe she'd fantasized all of it, even if she could describe the event and Jasper's form in such precise detail that her cheeks burned to recall it. That her pulse picked up and her body steamed up in places it had no business warming, made it even more confusing. To settle the matter, she reached beneath her covers and touched…bare skin.

She gasped as more memories bombarded her, both

sweet and alluring. Jasper's precious words and his strong arms. His skilled, if allegedly out of practice, hands. She lifted her fingers to her mouth, her lips sensitive and slightly chapped. Her most feminine places were tender as well. Yanking the comforter with her, she sat up in bed, tucking the blanket under her armpits. She brushed her hand over the pillow on the other side of the bed again. This time, her fingers sank into the depression left by his head.

But where was he now?

After all those comforting words, his sincerity more enticing to her than any roses-and-chocolate seduction, could he have made love to her and then just switched off the lamp and slipped away to sleep in his own room? Had it only been sex for him, when to her it had been so much more?

Her breath caught as the truth presented itself for the first time, daring her to challenge it. If she wasn't in love with Jasper Colton, she was something darn close to it. She'd put up a valiant fight, trying to avoid letting herself rely on him. But he was just too good at being there for her. She'd refused to let him past the walls she'd built for self-preservation. He'd only kept knocking on the door and waiting.

He'd wanted her to trust him, without recognizing what a monumental request that was. Then last night he'd said he needed her, and every sound reason she could think of for not being with him slid away as quickly as their clothes. Didn't he realize that making love with him was that ultimate act of trust? If he did, he wouldn't have left her there. To wake up in the dark. Alone.

At a knock, she started again. A thick stripe of light

seeped in from the hall as Jasper cracked open the door. She automatically tucked the blankets tighter under her arms and drew her knees toward her chest. She had to look ridiculous using the blankets to cover herself when he'd already seen and sampled everything she tried to hide.

"Oh, good. You're awake." He pushed the door fully open and switched on the lamp from the wall plate as the puppy scooted past him into the room. Dressed in the same clothes he'd shed in her presence earlier, Jasper stood in the doorway, shifting from one foot to the other.

"Bandit says good morning, too," he said.

"I see that."

She didn't miss the food tray in Jasper's arms or the truth that while she'd been jumping to conclusions about his reasons for leaving her after their night of intimacy, he'd been making *her* breakfast. The smells of coffee and bacon that wafted her way made her slightly nauseous rather than triggering her appetite. Why was it always so easy for her to believe the worst about people? Especially Jasper, who'd never done anything to make her question him.

"Thanks…for this," she managed.

"I had some paperwork to do." He paused and cleared his throat. "Uh, I wanted to let you sleep for as long as you could."

He gestured to the dog. "I had to give him bacon just to keep him from opening the door again. Anyway, I figured you'd need something to eat before we go."

"You're not going to make me come over and get it, are you?"

"Of course not." A tiny smile played on his lips when he slid a glance her way. "Sorry."

He stepped around the end of the bed and bent to hand her a filled coffee mug. It was then that she noticed two small plates with breakfast sandwiches and fruit on the tray, plus another filled mug. Not just *her* breakfast. He'd made breakfast in bed for two. She'd thought he was stepping away from her, but even with their morning-after nervousness, he intended to stay.

After returning to the opposite side of the bed, he settled the tray near the foot of it.

"You guard the food, and I'll find your things."

At least he didn't say *clothes* and didn't watch her while he went to work on his promise. He gathered her sweatshirt on one side of the bed and her pants, partially inside-out, on the other, her bra just off the end. Kayla's face heated as he hunted for her panties, finally finding them on the table next to the lamp.

He set all her clothes on her side of the bed, almost on top of her toes. Then he whistled.

"Come on, boy. Let's give the lady some privacy."

Bandit followed him from the room, and Jasper closed the door behind them. Though Kayla quickly dressed again, the sexy underwear felt silly, especially after she caught sight of herself in the bureau mirror, looking like Medusa in training. She hurried into the bathroom and combed her hair and brushed her teeth before he knocked again.

"Okay to come in?"

"It's fine."

She'd straightened the comforter and sat in the middle of the bed, so it felt like déjà vu from the night before. But this time, he stepped inside right away and sat on the edge of the bed.

"I didn't want to rush you, but the food's getting cold, and we need to get going." He grabbed his plate and took a bite of his sandwich.

"Are we headed to the horses first or the cattle in the lower pasture?" She lifted her plate and popped a grape in her mouth.

"Neither. Aubrey and the guys will take care of them all this morning." He took a sip of coffee and rested the mug back on the tray. "I thought you'd want to go to The Rock Solid."

At her confused look, he pointed to the window. "Have you looked outside? The snow stopped."

She set down the food on the plate and rushed to open the blinds so she could see for herself. Snow blanketed the ground, leaving barely any marks to show the outline of his driveway, but as Jasper said, the snow had stopped. The wind had died down as well.

"I have some ideas from my father's letters, but if I go, I'm still not sure I'll be able to figure out where he hid the money."

"You mean if *we* go," he said. "And it's worth a shot, right?"

She couldn't help smiling at Jasper as she returned to sit on the edge of the bed. He'd never once questioned whether he would be the one taking her to The Rock Solid and even made arrangements with Aubrey. She didn't mind the extra security of knowing he would be there, either. Still, there was one area on which they didn't agree.

"With Presley still running free, you probably think I should go to the police first."

"Would you go if I asked you to?"

She tilted her head back and forth. "The police weren't exactly nice about me wanting to stay in my home when the bank foreclosed. Do you think they'll be happy knowing I'm about to break in?"

"I'm thinking no."

"But I'd still like to get the chance to figure out what my father did with the money before the police descend on the property."

"Still haven't heard from Presley?" He reached for her phone, still plugged in on the bedside table, disconnected it and handed it to her without looking at the screen.

"I didn't hear it vibrate or anything before, I mean, I—" He stopped, giving her a sheepish grin. "You know what I mean. Nothing woke Bandit up, either."

She glanced at the dog at the foot of the bed. "He slept in here?"

"You seemed pretty tired. Guess he didn't wake you."

His smile made something flutter in her belly, so she turned away, planted her bare feet on the floor and focused on checking her messages. The last thing she needed right now was to think about Jasper, Bandit and her all snuggling together like a little family. She scrolled through the messages and clicked out of her inbox.

"Still nothing. All I can think of is that Presley grew tired of his old game and is starting a new one."

"Whatever he's trying, the police should be involved in finding him this time," he said.

He met her gaze when she looked back at him and then lifted his chin. Apparently, Jasper could be stubborn, too. She had to admit that he was right. Now that she had the answer to her question about what Presley wanted from her, it didn't make sense for her to put Jasper or herself at risk to stop him. The Blue Larkspur Police Department could have that job, and she would give it to them right after they checked out her father's clues to locate the money.

Having eaten as much as her sensitive stomach could handle, she took another swallow of coffee and set the mug back on the tray. "I'll just shower. I can be ready in twenty."

Neither mentioned why she would want to bathe again when they were headed to possibly dirty work digging through her abandoned former home.

"I'll do that, too," he said.

She prayed he wouldn't suggest that they shower together to conserve water or some other ridiculous excuse since she would have a difficult time picking holes in his logic. For right now, she needed to wash his scent off her skin and reclaim a little of her equilibrium.

She pointed to the tray. "So, if you have this, I'll go do that."

"Kayla," Jasper called after her as she started for the bathroom.

She stopped and turned back to him.

"We need to talk about what happened between us last night. What it means."

"I know." She cleared her throat. "We will. Later."

Much later if it was up to her. How could she tell him what it meant to her when she wasn't sure about that herself yet?

"Just want you to know, when you're ready to talk about it," he said, "I'll be ready, too."

* * *

Kayla's boots crunched over the broken dishes and splintered wood that stretched across her mother's old kitchen. A toaster lay mangled, having been thrown against the wall. Even the old hardwood floor that she'd one day planned to resurface had become a checkerboard of missing pieces, loose planks pulled off the floor in search of treasure beneath.

It was all she could do not to sit on the floor and sob. Someone had taken the home of her childhood from her, not once but twice, and the journey through each room offered another small, painful death to her memories.

At the sound of more crunching porcelain, she turned back to find Jasper and Bandit standing in the doorway, the dog's leash wrapped several times around Jasper's hand.

"We've got to keep him out of here." She pointed to what was left of her mother's everyday dishes. "He'll get a splinter in his paw."

"He also might notice something that we're missing."

She couldn't argue with that. They'd brought Bandit along for just that reason.

"There's nothing else you can think of for us to look at in your old bedroom?"

She shook her head. "That secondary entrance to the attic from my closet was the only other one I could think of. You didn't see anything, either, did you?"

"You know what you're looking for. I don't."

"Unfortunately, I don't know any better than you do." As she looked around the house, at spaces that should have reminded her of her father, she couldn't picture him in any of them. The life she'd known on The Rock Solid had barely involved him at all.

"We've already looked all the places Presley tried. Where didn't he look?"

Kayla recalled the specifics from the letters, trying to think like her father would have. But that was impossible. They were strangers.

"We still need to check out the barn and the new well," she said. "He definitely mentioned those."

"Let's try those then. It can't be any colder out there than it is in here." Jasper gestured to the door and then carried Bandit across the kitchen floor as he had when they'd entered.

It was colder, after all, the residual wind from the storm refusing to give up its final gusts. With the dog racing ahead, they stomped across the snow, through tangles of tall dead vegetation, to what used to be the barn. Its three remaining walls made it look more like a lean-to, the still-gray sky visible through the slanted roof. Jasper walked around, kicking the dirt and testing the strength of the wood, which split under a little pressure.

"Do you think he would have buried it under the barn?"

"Somehow I don't think so."

Kayla closed her eyes, trying to remember those last days with her father still in their home. It seemed so far away now, hopeless like trying to mine some other person's recollections. Her chest ached over the void on behalf of the child she barely recognized as herself.

"The last memory I have of my father here was on a snowy day like today. But then I'm relying on the memories of a six-year-old. My mind might have edited them, anyway, to make them a little less sad."

"Don't discount anything you're remembering. What happened that day? Even little things might spark another memory."

She stared out into the drifting snow, letting her mind peel back the years.

"He told me he was too busy to build a snowman with me. That wasn't anything new. He was always working. But Mom wasn't feeling well that day, and I couldn't build one by myself, so he said yes. I was so happy."

Her pitiful temptation to smile only made her angrier at her father. Even on this rare happy moment in her childhood, he would have preferred to brush her aside, choosing his money over her. She scanned the property, still longing for a time that had never been.

"I'm sure we built that snowman quickly, but it stood nearly as tall as I did. Then he told me to go play."

She stopped, blinking and trying to grasp those final details that remained on the fuzzy edges of her memory. A shiver fluttered up her spine as the blurry lines cleared.

Jasper returned to stand in front of her, his brows pinched together.

"What is it? What do you remember?"

"He was carrying a shovel. A pointed *digging* shovel. Not one for the snow."

"Now if we could just figure out where…"

"That's just it. He told me to stay away from both the wells because I would get all muddy."

"Not just the new one?"

She shook her head. "I can see that there would be

mud around the spot where a new well had just been dug, but the old one?"

They traded one more look and then tromped to the truck, only the snow slowing them down. Recognizing a new game, the puppy chased after them but beat them to the pickup. Jasper pulled two garden shovels from the truck bed and then lifted out a pick.

"Okay, where's the old well?" he asked.

She shot a glance back at the open field. "I only ever had to deal with the new one, but if I can find that, I think I'll be able to figure out where the other one is. It's about an acre farther from the house in kind of the same line."

Kayla directed him through the brambles and overgrown vegetation, constantly looking back to determine her location, just as she'd always done while working on the ranch. But the farther they moved from the house, the deeper the snow became.

"Are you sure you know where it is?" Jasper asked when the snow reached the top of his boots.

"I think so. It's somewhere close to here." She glanced to the house and back again, trying to judge the distance. "The well head is only about two feet tall."

They both moved in widening circles, trying to increase the distance from the house at the same rate.

"You could easily have the distances off." Jasper pointed to the row of trees ahead. "Do you have any other markers— Ouch!"

She glanced over at him. "What is it?"

"Found it." He closed his eyes, pressing his top teeth into his bottom lip.

"Sorry."

He bent his knee and gripped his boot, somehow

managing not to fall over. "Okay, we've found this one. Where's the other one?"

She pointed to the trees. "Keep going that way."

Jasper stomped on, favoring one foot. "We couldn't have picked worse weather to do this."

"Sure about that? We just had a blizzard."

It came as a surprise that the old well was easier to find since the trees nearby had blocked some of the snow. First, Kayla cleared a full circle around the pipe-shaped well, hoping to find subtle differences in the land. It hadn't been touched with anything beyond a tractor's lawnmower blade in more than twenty years, after all, and probably nothing in the past two.

Finally, she made her best guess and jammed the tip of her shovel against the frozen ground, and the bounce back strained her arm. She gestured to him.

"Why don't you try?"

Even with both taking turns with the pick, their progress remained slow. When it was Kayla's turn again, Jasper stretched his neck back and forth.

"If this isn't the right side, we're going to be too tired to start on the other one."

"Speak for yourself." She swung the tool again. "I'm pretty motivated to find this thing before someone else does."

With the dirt on the surface fairly broken up, they both went to work with their shovels. Kayla's shoulders ached, her hands burned beneath the work gloves and she was sweating, but she wouldn't stop. Couldn't let her father win. Her body surrendered in slow steps, the shovel becoming too heavy, her eyes welling with tears that went beyond the exhaustion that she felt in every joint and muscle and bone.

And then her shovel hit something with a thud. Her breath caught in her throat. She and Jasper stared at each other and then dropped on their knees in the snow and dug with their gloved hands.

"I might have just hit the side of the well," she said, digging harder.

"You might not have."

Her fingers came into contact with something that definitely wasn't the side of the well. As Jasper pulled back, Kayla wiped off the top of it with her gloves. She'd uncovered a forest-green container.

"It's a box of some sort. Waterproof, maybe?"

"Let's hope it was."

Jasper handed Kayla her shovel again, and they both dug around the outside the container, which looked more like a case to store ammunition. He leaned in and shook the case loose before straightening.

"You do it. This is all yours."

Kayla's chest squeezed beneath her coat. Jasper seemed to understand how important this was to her. After years of trying to right his dad's wrongs, he could relate to her need to do the same. A rush of gratitude filled her over the sacrifice Jasper had made for her, then and now. She bent down and lifted the hard-plastic container, the size of two Western-boot boxes stacked on top of each other, and then set it on the snow.

"You think this is it?" For some reason, her hand shook as she stared down at it. Until now, all of her "proof" of her dad's crimes had come in hearsay and in clues in the notes. Now she would have the kind that no court would deny.

"Only one way to find out. Can you open it?"

She ran her gloved fingers along the top and turned

the box. There was an intricate latch on the other side.
And a lock. She tried it, anyway. It wouldn't budge.

"He locked it?" She stared at it incredulously.

"He probably didn't want anyone else to be able to
open it in the unlikely event that they would find it before he was released." He leaned close to examine the
lock. "Guess he'd never heard of power tools."

"Or picks," she said.

But just as she stood and reached for the one they'd
been using, Bandit growled.

The dog that had been milling back and forth around
them as they dug now stood about fifteen feet away,
staring at something behind the trees. The pup that
rarely barked wouldn't stop, floppy ears lifted, its
stance one of attack.

The chill she'd felt moments before was nothing
compared to the rumble of terror that spread through
her now.

"He's back." Kayla glanced from side to side and
then signaled to Jasper before reaching for the .22 pistol
she'd thought to holster that morning. No way would
she let Presley get away this time.

Jasper must have missed her signal, or ignored it,
as he creeped over to the dog, the leash in his hand.
Bandit continued to growl, canines bared.

A shotgun blast seemed to shake the ground and all
the trees. It thundered in her ears and in her gut as if
she'd been struck.

"Run, Kayla!"

Jasper's words pounded in her ears as well, but
she shook her head. She refused to run from Presley,
wouldn't hide from the creep who'd terrorized her and
now wanted to do the same to Jasper. But her gaze

flicked to the pistol in her hand. She'd already heard the sound of a semiautomatic shotgun being fired. To take him on with this would be like taking a butter knife to a mortar fight. Not only couldn't she stop Presley with this weapon, but she also couldn't protect Jasper, who was unarmed, or the pup that might die trying to protect them.

So she ran, struggling through the snow toward the house. After rethinking, she veered to the truck. When she glanced back, her heart froze. Jasper wasn't behind her. Had he gone back for Bandit? Or worse, had he decided to take Presley on by himself? Panic swelling in her throat, she slowed and then turned. It might be a suicidal choice, but if he planned to stand and fight, she would battle right there beside him.

"What are you doing?" Jasper called as he ran up beside her. "Get in the truck!"

Kayla sped up again, her hands hitting the side of the pickup bed just as Bandit reached her. Jasper was only a few steps behind. He hit the lock, and they both rushed for the doors, the dog leaping between them. Turning the truck around, he raced out of the driveway.

"You're not going back?" She gestured to the rifle, still attached to the gun rack.

"Not a chance," he said.

He barely stopped to make the turn at the end of the driveway, the pickup fishtailing as he pulled onto the road.

"If it were just me, maybe," he continued without looking away from the pavement. "But I'm not going to put you or Bandit at risk just because this guy deserves—"

Jasper stopped himself, but Kayla didn't need him

to clarify what he believed Jed Presley deserved. His hands gripped the steering wheel so tightly that his knuckles flashed white.

"I was afraid you weren't going to be able to convince Bandit to come with you, or that you would go after Presley, and you would—"

This time she stopped. She couldn't bring herself to say it.

"I didn't think he would come, either."

Jasper didn't even address her fears for him. An unsettling certainty filled her that if she hadn't been with him, he would have gone back for Presley, and one of them wouldn't have made it out alive. She shivered with gratitude that he hadn't had the opportunity to make that choice.

"Presley had more fire power this time, too," Jasper said without looking over at her.

"What do you mean?" She squinted until realization dawned. "Before, he had a pistol. That was a shotgun."

They drove on in a tense silence. Only after they reached the main highway did Jasper guide the truck onto the shoulder of the road and stop. He pulled out his phone, searched for a number and dialed.

A loud male voice offered a greeting from the Blue Larkspur Police Department and asked how he could help.

"My name is Jasper Colton," he answered. "I'd like to speak with Chief Lawson."

Chapter 19

The sun had lowered in the sky by the time Jasper pulled his pickup back onto The Rock Solid with Kayla and Bandit again in the cab. As if giving their reports together at the police station hadn't been tough enough, he'd had to excuse himself to the restroom a few times to answer emails from the Realtor without making everyone believe he had a prostate problem.

Kayla's former home looked different this time, with several patrol cars lining the drive and crime-scene tape stretched around the house. He had no doubt they would find more tape near the wells in the back.

Wearing a long wool coat, a stocking cap and a frown, Chief Lawson met them outside the truck.

"I heard from Dispatch that you already filed your report," Theo said as soon as Jasper opened the door.

"Just getting back from there," Jasper said.

He let the pup out of the truck, and Kayla met the two men near the front bumper.

Jasper cleared his throat. "Like I said on the phone, we really are sorry for not reporting everything sooner."

"Yes, we really are—"

Theo raised his hand to cut off Kayla. "You should be. Both of you. You could have gotten yourselves killed."

Jasper was glad they hadn't started walking toward the well since his limbs trembled so hard that he would have fallen on his face in the snow. For the hundredth time in the past few hours, he'd berated himself for not insisting that they go to the police earlier. If Kayla had been killed, it would have been his fault. Especially after Presley's attack, he should have called the cops, no matter what she'd said. But he'd been too busy building a cocoon in which to keep her safe with him, and then loving her inside it, to do the right thing.

Still, as Theo stared them both down by turns, Jasper had to hold back a smile. The man's anger and his words seemed to come more from his mom's boyfriend than the police chief of a small city. Unfortunately, the guy was both. And he was right.

"Yeah, we know," Jasper said.

The older man crossed his arms and tapped a gloved index finger on his sleeve. "Your brothers, Caleb and Ezra, are on the hot seat for this one, too. Playing detective? What were you all thinking?

"And for that matter, you two were trespassers on this property." He paused to look back and forth between them. "You're lucky not to be charged yourselves."

Now he sounded more like a disappointed parent, but Jasper didn't dare point that out. Theo turned and trudged toward the wells at the back of the house, leaving Jasper and Kayla to trail after him.

"The only reason you're being allowed on this crime scene at all is so you can help Detective Beaulieu with his report," he said when they caught up with him. "He's the only one who's a paid police detective here."

"We get it," Jasper answered for them both. He expected a second lecture from the detective.

As they approached the wooded area beyond the old well, Kayla pointed in that direction. "The shot came from somewhere in there, and Bandit definitely saw something in the woods."

"We've had officers combing that area, the perimeter of this ranch and some of the areas you mentioned related to the confrontation with the suspect on the Gemini," Theo said. "We located an abandoned vehicle just off the Gemini property, but we're still following up on that. We would have been further in this investigation if…"

He didn't bother finishing what he'd started to say as Dane approached them. They all knew what he meant.

Theo gestured from Dane to Jasper and Kayla. "Detective Beaulieu, you already know Jasper, but I'd like you to meet Kayla St. James."

"Alexa's told me great things about your work with horses," Dane said as they shook hands.

At least the guy managed to keep a straight face. Since Colton news spread faster than anything in the media, Jasper could only imagine what other information he'd heard.

After Theo left them to check in with the forensic specialists inside the house, Dane led them back to the site of the old well. Like Jasper had predicted, another long stripe of crime-scene tape had been draped around the area, attached to nearby trees. The hole was the same as when they'd run from it, dark brown earth piled on top of the snow all around it. But the green box that just might have contained fifty grand was gone.

"Ever heard the one about the victims who dig up the money just in time for a suspect to scare them off the property?" Dane asked as he pointed to the hole.

Jasper frowned at the detective, already known in the Colton family for his corny jokes. "No. But I know the punch line. The creep gets away with the cash."

"Aw, you've heard that one."

"Is this a joke to you two?" Kayla's gaze narrowed at both of them.

Dane shook his head. "No, miss."

The conversation became serious after that as Jasper and Kayla gave the detectives all the specifics they could about the gunshot and the clues that led them to the site of the container. They'd already agreed to drop the letters from her father off at the police department the next day.

"Well, at least we don't have to worry about Presley anymore since he got what he was looking for," Kayla said when the detective stopped writing in his little notebook.

Jasper shook his head and found Dane doing the same.

"First, you're still facing a threat until Presley can be apprehended," Dane said. "And second, since you were unable to open the box, we can't be confident that it even contained the money you were searching for. Any others who might be interested in that money could still show up here or seek you out, guessing you might know of a second location."

She lowered her head. "It's never going to end, is it?"

"We'll do our best to locate the suspect," Dane assured her.

Kayla thanked him for his effort, but she was still brooding when they returned to the truck.

"I'm never going to get my life back." She stared out the passenger window at the darkening sky. "And now I've dragged you into this mess."

Though he felt her frustration, he couldn't help but to chuckle at the last part. "I never saw me kicking and screaming while you were dragging me. In fact, I'm pretty sure I volunteered for the job."

"You shouldn't have."

"I'm glad I did," he said as he pulled onto the two-lane highway that led back to the Gemini.

Usually, she would have said something about him not having the good sense to avoid stringing fence wire during a thunderstorm, but she was quiet, lost in her own thoughts.

He would let her think for now. There was plenty of time for them to talk once they got back to the house. But they did need to talk. He had to tell her how he felt about her. Or at least *begin* to tell her. Though his chest tightened at the prospect of it, she needed to know that their lovemaking wasn't a one-night thing for him. And that he hoped it would be the beginning of something more.

He'd told her they would talk when *she* was ready, but he realized he would have to be the one to broach the subject. He had to figure out how. With the disturbing revelations she'd faced the past few days, she might not be ready to bring it up herself for months. He couldn't bear the idea of waiting more hours and more days before she would return to his arms again.

Suddenly, he smiled at the road ahead of him with snow piled high on either side. He did happen to have a couple of conversation starters that just might work. Though he hadn't planned to tell her about them yet, when he hadn't settled the details for either surprise, he realized now that they might be perfect. One question and one revelation. Now he just had to pick the perfect time to let her in on the secrets.

Kayla couldn't shake the funk she felt once they returned to Jasper's house. She could barely muster a smile, despite his obvious attempts to cheer her up all through dinner, which consisted of the last of the holiday leftovers. The homemade whipped cream, which had lost its gentle peaks and become just a cold, sweetened soup in the bottom of the plastic storage container, said it all. Dreams she hadn't wanted to admit she possessed fell flat all around her, leaving her with an overwhelming sense of loss over what could have been.

No matter how much she wanted to be with Jasper and to stay with him in his perfect little house, she had to admit that it wasn't fair to him or to any of the staff on the Gemini. *Any others who might be interested in that money.* The detective's words replayed in her mind.

Even if the police caught Presley, there might be others who could still come to The Rock Solid searching for the cash her father bragged about in prison. Then they would come to the Gemini, looking for her. This meant she couldn't stay on Jasper's ranch, and even if she could afford to buy it back, she couldn't go home.

"You're killing me over here," Jasper said from the sink, where he was rinsing the plates before loading them into the dishwasher.

She carried over the last of the dishes and set them next to him. "What are you talking about?"

"I've told my best jokes all night, and I'm not even getting a pretend laugh out of you."

"Sorry. I'll try to pretend better."

"Good. Glad we have that settled." He turned around and pressed his back to the counter, his smile gone now. "I know today was tough for you. Especially the part about losing the money. I know how much you wanted to make that right."

"You heard Detective Beaulieu. We don't have proof that the money was in that case." She sighed and closed her eyes.

"*We* know it was."

"It doesn't matter. It's gone."

Jasper's phone vibrated in his pocket. He pulled it out and glanced at the screen, and then his gaze flicked her way. "Sorry. I have to take this."

Without giving any indication who was on the call, he touched the button to answer it and strode from the room and up the stairs.

"This is Jasper Colton," he said before closing his bedroom door.

An unsettling sensation covered her as she waited. Was this how Jasper had felt when he knew she'd lied that day about one of the texts? He wasn't telling her something. She couldn't resist checking her own phone while he was gone. She still hadn't received any more texts from Presley, but she didn't think that she would. He had what he'd wanted now. Hopefully, he would leave her alone.

When Jasper returned only a few minutes later, he was having difficulty keeping from grinning.

"Good news?"

"Possibly."

He tucked his phone in his pocket and gestured for her to follow him into the living room. On the sofa, he patted the cushion next to him for her to join him. An odd sense of foreboding made her insides quiver. She had to focus on breathing evenly. He turned to face her, and she shifted toward him as well.

Just last night she'd invited him into her body, and now she was nervous just sitting next to him.

"I thought we should talk about last night," he said.

She shook her head. "Didn't we agree—"

"I know what I said before, but I need to tell you this."

If he hadn't reached for her hand then, she might have argued. No matter what the right thing to do was, she couldn't pull away.

"Last night wasn't a onetime thing for me," he said. "I want more. I think that we can make this work."

She did pull back this time, her arms crossing in a tight self-hug. It was like having a dream in full color and not wanting to wake up to a life printed only in grayscale.

"Like I said before, you heard the detective. I won't be able to walk away from this. My dad's crimes will follow me. I can't continue to expose you, and everyone else on the Gemini, to whatever is coming next."

"And like *I* said before, I'm a volunteer." He shook his head, a small smile spreading on his lips. "You don't get it, do you? I'm in love with you. I didn't know if I was ready to tell you until just now, but there it is. And whatever happens with Presley, we can face it together."

Kayla couldn't help it. She leaned forward, wrapped her arms around his neck and kissed him in a way she hoped would reveal what was in her heart, even if she couldn't say it out loud yet. They were both breathless when he set her back slightly and pressed his forehead to hers.

"I just wanted to ask you a question."

He pushed his shoulders back and cleared his throat.

"Kayla St. James, would you do me the honor of being my date to the Colton Christmas party in two weeks?"

"What? I don't understand." Her heart was beating so hard that he had to hear it. Had she thought he'd planned to *propose* to her? What would she have said if he'd asked?

"It's kind of a surprise for Aubrey. She was upset that not everyone could make it for our Thanksgiving dinner, so I talked to Mom about reviving the Colton Christmas party. Just for family and close friends, though."

"You're sure about this? About inviting *me*?"

He nodded emphatically. "I know my brothers told you I've never taken a date to any family event. No one was ever important enough to me. Until now."

Jasper tilted his head and gave her a hopeful, boyish grin. "So, will you come?"

"Of course I will." She couldn't believe it. A few moments ago, she'd wondered whether she should stay away from Jasper for his own good, and now she'd just agreed to go public with their relationship. Was it a mistake? Maybe. But she longed to be with him, and he wanted to be with her. That was all that mattered.

"There's one other thing. I have a surprise for you, too."

He paused for too long, and that unsettling feeling inside her returned.

"You know that call from before and all those emails from earlier today?" He held his hands wide, grinning. "Well, I put an offer on The Rock Solid today. And I just heard it was accepted."

"What? Are you joking?" She leaped up from the sofa. "Is that what all of this has been about? You did it because you want my *land*?"

With every question, he kept shaking his head. "No. You've got it all wrong."

"Do I?" She crossed her arms to stop her hands from shaking. "It all makes sense now. Maybe you weren't the one sending those texts to me, but you wanted something from me, just like Presley did. You wanted my land. How could I have *trusted* you?"

The injured look in his eyes told her she'd hit her mark, but he deserved a taste of the hurt he'd given her.

"Please, let me explain," he said, anyway.

She couldn't. Not when whatever he said next would keep spitting in the face of her conviction that he'd always been honest with her.

She turned away and rushed into her bedroom. He trailed after her. When she didn't close the door, he followed but stopped in the doorway.

"Okay, I was wrong. I should have told you first, but you said you wanted to own the property again. I checked into it and found I could get it at a great price, so I—"

"Just bought it? Good way to ensure I could never have it."

"I'm buying it so you *can* have it."

Without letting herself look his way, she crossed to the closet and pulled out her duffel. She stalked back and dumped it on the bed. "When I told you I wanted to buy it back, somehow I never pictured having the chance to *rent* my own home from the magnanimous Jasper Colton."

"You're misunderstanding. We'll set up a land contract. You'll be buying it."

"From you," she spat. "You said your dad was like the puppet master, determining other people's fates. Well, what are *you*?"

In her peripheral vision, she saw him jerk back as if she'd slapped him. She wished it didn't matter to her that she'd hurt him, but it did. Still, she stepped back to the closet and started yanking clothes from hangers. At the bed, she folded shirts and pants haphazardly and stuffed them inside the bag.

"Why are you packing your stuff?" he asked from behind her. "Stay. Let's talk about it."

She shook her head as she moved to the dresser and added her underwear and socks to the rest of the items in the bag.

"I'm going to need you to drive me back to the bunkhouse. I'll figure out my next steps tomorrow. New job. New place to live."

"Don't go." After a long pause, he added, "I did it for *you*."

The anguish in his voice was nearly her undoing. But she needed to stay strong. Couldn't let him hurt her the way— No, she couldn't think about her father now. "You did it for yourself. If you don't realize that, you have bigger problems than just an ex-con taking a shot at us."

"Have you looked in the mirror?"

Kayla had wrapped the snow globe in the miniature quilt, but at his words, her hands jerked back. She bobbled it but managed not to drop it.

"You're talking about *my* problems when you pull away every time someone tries to get close to you," he said.

"You were upset when I didn't tell you about Presley maybe using the nickname, and you didn't tell me you were trying *buy my land*? That's one hell of an omission."

He shook his head. "It was supposed to be a surprise, but it doesn't matter. You were looking for an excuse to push me away. I'm just the bonehead who gave you one."

She carefully set the snow globe in the bag, tucked in the letters that they would need to take to the police and zipped it closed.

"I need you to drive me to the bunkhouse," she repeated.

"You'd never be able to trust me, anyway. And I won't allow myself to be with someone who can't."

She hoisted the bag on her shoulder and plowed past him to set it down by the front door. "Take me now, or I'll walk."

Whatever he'd been about to say fell away as his phone rang in his pocket again.

"Guess you have a real-estate transaction to negotiate," she said over his shoulder.

Jasper pulled the phone out of his pocket and stared down at the screen. "It's Chief Lawson."

He clicked to answer and immediately hit the speaker button. "Jasper Colton here."

"Jasper, is Miss St. James with you?"

He shot a glance her way before returning his focus to the phone in his hand. "She's here. You're on Speaker."

"I wanted to let you both know that a body was located tonight on the Gemini property," Theo said. "Positive identification is pending, but the body is believed to be that of Jedediah Presley."

Chapter 20

The room shifted in and out of focus as Jasper's gaze moved from the phone on the coffee table to Kayla. She sat on the love seat, a shell-shocked look that probably resembled his own on her face. Then he glanced once more to her bag, still resting by the front door. As awkward as it felt to sit here after the things they'd just said to each other—words they could never take back—they had no choice now. No matter what had happened between them, no matter that his heart was breaking, he had to put all that aside. He had to keep her safe.

She leaned closer to the phone, still on Speaker. "Are you sure it's Presley?"

Theo cleared his throat. "As I said—"

"Oh. Right." She shook her head as if to clear her thoughts. "Pending positive ID."

Jasper bent forward and asked his own question.

"Do you know how long Presley—I mean, *the body*—had been out there?"

"Time and cause of death are also pending prior to autopsy, and the freezing temperatures and accumulation of snow make time more difficult to pinpoint," Theo said. "Still, the county coroner believes the individual had been dead just under twenty-four hours, and tentative cause of death is exposure."

Kayla sat staring back at him, so Jasper spoke aloud the conclusion all three must have reached.

"This means that whoever shot at us on The Rock Solid, it likely wasn't Jed Presley."

"Correct," the chief said.

"And I have a good idea who it might be." Jasper looked to Kayla and then back to the phone. "Ronald Spence."

"Definitely a suspect, but we don't have much evidence yet," Theo said. "We'll move forward with the investigation, but I wanted to make you aware that Spence still might be in the area. You need to keep your eyes open."

"The alleged money we dug up is probably gone for good then, right?" Jasper asked.

Theo chuckled at that. "I guess you haven't heard that part of the story. Apparently, twenty years ago, the FBI was working a case to take down a group of drug traffickers. Special agents performed several key drug purchases, using bills with traceable serial numbers, and then part of that money was never recovered, possibly because an associate of the traffickers was skimming from the proceeds to the tune of fifty thousand dollars."

"You're kidding," Kayla called out.

"Not kidding," Theo continued. "Fast-forward twenty years. We believe that the cash never surfaced because it was buried on a ranch in Blue Larkspur, Colorado. If a suspect in a different series of crimes were to steal said money and try to spend it, then we would be able to track him."

"That's amazing," Jasper said. "You can't make this stuff up."

When Jasper ended the call, he turned back to Kayla, who still wore that shocked look, which he guessed was only partially because of the news they'd received.

"You've heard the stories about Spence, right? He's the guy that my siblings helped to free through The Truth Foundation, only to realize he was guilty after all."

She nodded. "I remember reading about him."

"Well, Morgan sent all of us a few photos of Spence." He grabbed his phone and looked up the old email. "Like the chief said, we need to be on the lookout for him. He's seeking vengeance against my family for trying to stop his crime ring, and he's dangerous."

He finally located it and handed the phone to her. "The first one is his arrest photo from years ago. The other one is more recent."

Kayla studied the photos for several seconds. When she looked up again, her eyes were wide. "I saw that man on the Gemini the other day. I thought he was one of the few straggler guests."

"You mean he's been right here under our noses all along?" He jumped up from the seat and started pacing. "How could I have missed it? He could have been here to kill one or all of my family members, especially on Thanksgiving, and I didn't even notice him."

"It's my fault." Kayla gripped her hands in front of her. "You've been preoccupied with my problems. My stalker. I'm sorry."

He waved off her apology as he continued to pace back and forth across the room. "We can't worry about that now. Besides, I would have done nothing differently. Nothing."

"But if he has the money now, then maybe he's gone."

He stopped, considered what she'd said and shook his head. "We can't count on that. He hates my family too much, and vengeance is a powerful thing. That also means it isn't safe for you to return to the bunkhouse."

"You're wrong about that." She stood and lifted her chin. "There's no reason that I can't go back there. Presley is likely dead. This Spence, if he's the one who fired the shot earlier, doesn't have a beef with me, so I would be safer away from a Colton than closer to one. And he already has the money."

As Kayla lined up her reasons, Jasper felt himself losing the argument. She was right. When it came to Spence, her proximity to him made her less safe instead of more so, even with Bandit there.

"We could just wait," he reasoned, trying not to plead. "I'll take you back there tomorrow morning."

"Jasper." She waited until he met her gaze to continue. "I *can't*. Please. I can't stay here."

Finally, he nodded. He crossed to the coat tree, put on his jacket and grabbed his keys. "I'll warm up the truck."

Kayla leaned her rifle case against her duffel. "I'll get the rest of my toiletries and be out in a minute."

When he glanced back at her once more, she mouthed "thank you." He nodded, his throat feeling thick, and headed out the door before she could see the moisture in his eyes.

A shotgun blast shattered the silence just as he stepped off the porch. He dove into the snow, certain that shell had nearly hit him.

"It's not fun being the target, is it, Colton?" a voice called to him out of the dark.

Jasper lifted up to a squatting position, wiping the snow from his face with his sleeve. He tried to locate the voice. It could have come from beside his storage shed or from behind the line of pine trees. He couldn't tell which.

"What do you want, Spence?"

"Well, you finally know my name. We're going to have to stop meeting like this. You and your pretty lady."

"I said, what do you want?" Jasper asked again through clenched teeth. He had to stop the guy before he reached the house. Had the chance to hurt Kayla.

"You'd be wise to be nice to me, Colton. I'm the one holding the gun."

Jasper could have sworn he heard a horse whinny. Spence was riding around the ranch? Had he taken one of the horses from the Gemini stock?

"Well?" Jasper sneaked a glance behind him, hoping Kayla hadn't followed him outside. The door was still closed.

"I want you Coltons to leave me alone," Spence said. "Me. My business associates. All of us."

"And if we don't?"

"You'll be as dead as your daddy. You and the rest of your family. Maybe your little girlfriend, too."

"I'll keep that in mind," Jasper said, despite the

shiver running through him. Spence would have to get through him to reach any of those he loved. Especially Kayla.

"Let's go."

At first, Jasper thought those words were directed at him, but out of the corner of his eye, he caught a flash of Spence on horseback. From off to his side, Kayla, who'd carefully cracked open the door, leaped out onto the porch, aimed her rifle and fired a shot as the man disappeared from sight.

A human howl of pain echoed after the sound of the blast.

"You hit him," Jasper said as he rushed after her into the house. "Thank you."

With a nod, she acknowledged that she'd protected him this time, and she stowed her rifle back in its case. Then she stepped behind him and locked the front door. A loud thud and a bark from inside the bedroom answered his question about how she'd managed to keep Bandit in the house. She slid the key from the top of the doorframe and unlocked it.

Kayla had protected them both.

She didn't ask Jasper to drive her to the bunkhouse again. Instead, she grabbed her bag, returned to her bedroom and closed the door behind her.

Daylight had just broken when Kayla carried her bag and her gun case outside. They'd barely gotten any sleep since they'd been forced to file another police report, this time about Ronald Spence's appearance on the Gemini. Now her eyes burned, and her stomach churned with the same nausea that had kept her up the rest of the night. No matter what she felt about Jasper's actions involving The Rock Solid, when he'd been in danger, her instinct to protect him had overtaken everything else. Then she'd lain awake in bed, battling her heart as it warred with her head. Neither had claimed victory. Neither had bowed in defeat.

Having just returned from feeding the horses, Jasper had left the truck running. But she found the cab empty, except for the dog, when she set her bag in the back and carefully opened the door to slide her gun case behind the seat.

"Over here," Jasper called out.

She jogged over to where he stood, near the line of pines. He pointed down at the snow.

"You think that's blood?"

She examined the deep red drops. "Looks like it to me."

"The police missed it last night, but they'll be back to resume the investigation soon. How badly do you think he's hurt?" Already, Jasper clicked on Detective Beaulieu's number in his contacts.

"Bad enough to yowl like a baby, anyway. I was only glad I didn't hit the horse."

"Me, too." He held the phone to his ear. "I still worry it was one of ours."

She shook her head. "I just couldn't tell."

He spoke into the phone. "Hey, Dane, are you on your way? I think we've found the blood stains you were looking for."

Jasper spoke two minutes longer, nodding at the speaker, who couldn't see him.

"You're right about that. See you soon," he said as he ended the call.

"What did he say?" Kayla asked as he returned the phone to his pocket.

"Oh, that. He said with as much time as the Blue Larkspur Police Department is spending on the ranch that they'll need their own cabin."

They rode in silence from his house to the bunkhouse, but when they stopped, Jasper turned to her.

"Could you do me a favor? If you're still planning to quit, could you wait until we find a replacement? It's going to be tough replacing such a fine horsewoman."

Her chest felt so tight that she had to concentrate to breathe. "I don't know, Jasper. I'm not sure if I can."

"Whatever happened between us, or didn't, I know you love the animals, and you wouldn't want them to suffer because of something I did."

She shifted closer to the passenger door. As with most of his observations about her, he was right.

"Just think about it, okay?"

"I will."

She grabbed her gun case from behind the seat and her bag from the back and headed inside, entering by the code lock on the door. At least the others had already gone to feed the cattle, so she didn't have to face them and her uncomfortable return at the same time.

After pulling open the door to her room, she paused before stepping inside. She wouldn't have believed that anything could be worse than that first day when she'd moved to the bunkhouse, having lost everything that mattered to her at the time, and yet this was. She missed the house at the higher elevation, the warmth from the woodstove and cuddling with that puppy. But more than any of that, she missed Jasper, the man who'd hurt her more than he would ever understand. The man for whom her heart still yearned.

She set her bag on the bed but didn't unpack it. Though she needed to get dressed and return to the barn to start her chores, she sat on the edge of the bed, covered her face and let herself cry just a few precious tears. Later, she would hide her feelings and get on with the job. She was good at hiding. A master. But for now, she allowed herself to experience it all. She'd never felt more alone.

The knock on Kayla's bedroom door two weeks later rumbled the room's thin walls. She sat up in bed, where she'd been reading words she wouldn't remember from a book that didn't interest her after the second-longest workweek of her life. Second only to the week before when her feelings were even rawer.

Just the effort of being so close to Jasper, feeling his gaze on her, and having to force herself not to look back, exhausted her. She wanted to look back. She would *always* want to look back. Tonight was worse. Not far up the road at the lodge, the Coltons were having their Christmas party. The event that Jasper had asked her to attend as his date. No matter how much he'd hurt her, part of her still ached to be there with him.

A second knock came, louder than the first, her walls repeating their vibration.

"No, Vince, I don't want to watch sports out there with you all," she called out. She'd had enough of their pitying glances at dinner, thank you very much.

"It's not Vince," a female voice answered.

"Aubrey?"

"Are you going to make me talk to you from the other side of the door?"

Kayla sat up on the bed and brushed back her hair. "It's unlocked."

Her boss opened the door and stuck her head inside. "So this is how you spend your Friday nights."

Aubrey stepped inside the tight space, dressed fancier than Kayla could ever remember seeing her, except in photos from Caleb and Nadine's wedding. She wore a long black skirt and a red silk blouse under a wool dress coat. She even sported a pair of heels.

"Wow. You look great."

"Well, you look…" She gave Kayla an appraising glance over the frames of her glasses. "*Not* great."

"That was the opposite of encouraging."

"Just being honest." As if forgetting her mission as soon as she was inside Kayla's little room, Aubrey flounced her hair, to which she'd added dozens of spiral curls. "I'm going to a surprise Christmas party tonight."

"You knew about it?"

"Of course I knew." She rolled her eyes. "My brother really thought he could keep a secret from me when there were ten other siblings just waiting to slip up. I've already promised three of them to pretend to be surprised when Luke and I show up for our dinner with just Jasper."

"It was really nice what your brother did for you."

Aubrey grinned. "That's Jasper. That's who he is. And like the party he planned for me, that thing at The Rock Solid, he did that for you."

Kayla shook her head and raised both hands to make

Aubrey stop. "Can we not do this? I've already decided that I'm going to leave the Gemini. I *have* to."

Aubrey nodded, offering a compassionate smile that reminded Kayla so much of the woman's twin. "Do what you have to do, but please, hear me out first."

Kayla leaned back against the wall since the bed had no headboard and waited. The sooner they got this over with, the sooner Aubrey would leave.

"My brother put the offer on the ranch not because he wanted the land, but because he wanted to make sure you wouldn't lose it to some other buyer. He was putting it in holding for you. Just like when he tried to make up for our dad sending yours to prison. No matter how that turned out, he did it for you."

"I don't know what to think."

"Stop thinking so hard and try trusting for once." Aubrey shook her head, her curls fluttering around her face. "Besides, if you can believe that Jasper Colton would do anything less than honorable, you not only don't know him at all, you also don't *deserve* him."

Kayla did know him. That was the thing. Believing he would have intentionally taken advantage of her to get to her land went against everything she knew about him. And everything she believed in her heart.

"I told you once if you hurt him, you would have to answer to me. Well, you hurt him."

She nodded, her heart aching over that fact. "He hurt me, too."

"He knows he did." Aubrey held her hands wide, as if she offered a simple solution. "So stop hurting each other."

If only it were that easy. She rolled her eyes, but she couldn't help grinning back at Aubrey's hopeful smile.

"Now I have to fly. Luke is waiting for me in the car. But I brought something for you."

She stepped outside the bedroom door and returned seconds later with something draped under a plastic dry-cleaning bag and another small shopping bag.

"These are from Alexa. You two are about the same size. I'm going to leave these here. I just wanted to make sure if you decided to go to a party tonight, even if you didn't bring anything with you to the ranch, that you'd still have something nice to wear."

She waved and was out the door before Kayla had time to argue.

For the longest time, Kayla just stared at the bags on the bottom of her bed. Jasper's twin hadn't told her anything she didn't already know about him. From the beginning, she'd gone against her instinct and trusted him enough to tell him about her stalker. She'd put her safety in his hands, just as he had his in hers.

They'd told each other on separate occasions that they weren't like their own fathers. Well, the truth was Jasper wasn't like *her* dad, either. Not at all.

Her gaze moved to the snow globe that she'd placed in its usual spot the day after returning to the bunkhouse. Even the glittery snow didn't help it to shine as brightly anymore. Like a statue of remembrance for promises broken.

Kayla scooted around the bed to pick up the globe. It was so heavy in her hands. So substantial for a relationship that had been little more than smoke and mirrors. She reached for the bottom and turned the knob, the tune playing another lie. Her father hadn't come home for Christmas, but he hadn't cared enough to do right by those living there, anyway.

Her arm jerked as she set the globe back on the dresser, its smooth glass slipping from her fingers. The globe hit the concrete floor, and water, glitter and hundreds of tiny shards of glass shot from her dresser to the bed. The base cracked as well, its bottom landing near the door .

She stared down at the mess, unable to breathe. But then she caught sight of something in the puddle. She reached down and picked up a tiny, laminated card and plastic-sealed key that appeared to have been stored in the base. For several seconds, she held the two pieces that her father had gone to so much trouble to send to her. She didn't have to ask what the key was for. The missing green storage container had been opened by now without the key, anyway. The message on the card was harder to take.

I did it all for you.

"That wasn't for me," she whispered. "None of it was for me. Even the globe. You did it all for yourself."

Her throat clogged, and heat built behind her eyes, but she shook the emotions away. She was done crying over her father. And she was finished letting a man who'd loved only himself destroy her happiness with someone who really loved *her.* Someone who'd made a grand gesture, just for her.

"What was that?" Vince called from outside her door.

"Come in and see."

Vince and Hank stepped inside and stared down at the mess.

"What are you still doing in here?" Hank asked.

"Aubrey told us outside that you might need a ride to a party, and then you're in here breaking things."

"It was an accident." She glanced at her watch. "That's going to take forever to clean up."

Hank shook his head at that. "Well, you don't have forever. Go on. We'll take care of the mess."

Vince pushed the dress and bag into her arms. Aubrey must have mentioned those as well.

"Go do your thing and get all dolled up," he said. "But I have to say our guy Jasper likes you just as well in your jeans and best muck boots."

"Thanks, you guys." Her heart squeezed as she started to head in for a shower. Then she stopped. She returned to her dresser and folded the tiny quilt her mom made for her and tucked it in her drawer.

Kayla clutched the dress and bag and raced by her coworkers, who were also her friends. Time was ticking away, and she needed to do a quick makeover.

She had a party to go to.

Chapter 21

Jasper stared up at the rafters of the main lodge, where thousands of white holiday lights twinkled down on the first Colton Christmas party in twenty years, his heart anything but merry.

With Elvis crooning about a "Blue Christmas," kids chasing each other with jingle bells and all eleven of his siblings and their spouses and partners on hand for a good time, he figured that even he was bound to scare up some holiday spirit eventually. Since it hadn't happened yet, he straightened his Santa hat, pasted on a smile and played the role of host, while waiting for a Christmas miracle.

His mother appeared beside him, looking up at the same sparkly lights.

"You really pulled this off, honey," Isa said. "When you mentioned it, I wasn't so sure you would have enough time to put it together. But you surprised me."

"It did turn out all right, didn't it?" he said.

He took in the massive, decorated Douglas fir in the corner, the red-covered buffet table with its line of chafing dishes and the twenty small tables with red linens, candles and garland, not to mention the huge, raised floor right in the center, where they would dance the night away.

"Bandit's feeling festive." He pointed to his dog, romping in a Santa costume with several children trailing after it.

"As for the party, I had a lot of help, though I wouldn't say that Aubrey was all that surprised."

"The good and bad of a big family," Isa said. "Plenty of help. No secrets."

"It's mostly good." Jasper wrapped his arm around his mother.

He gestured around the room. "Do you think it's as nice as the annual Colton holiday parties you used to host when we were little?"

She spread her arms and spun in a circle. "This is so much better. Look at *all* of us."

"We are an impressive bunch," he agreed. "I'm so glad that Dom and Sami and Philip and Naomi were able to make it this time."

Isa leaned closer to him. "I'm sorry that Kayla didn't."

"How do you…?"

"I got tired of waiting for you to tell me about her, so I asked your brothers and sisters. Several had some good details."

"I'm sure they did," he said with a frown.

"They all care about you."

As if they'd timed it, the whole family drew in close, and the noise practically exploded in the smaller circle.

Caleb and his twin, Morgan, sidled over to Jasper, both appearing full of questions.

Morgan leaned in first. "Any more sightings of Spence on the Gemini since you and Kayla had your run-in with him?"

"Not since then," Jasper said. "But he threatened our whole family, so we need to be diligent in watching for him. Good thing Kayla slowed him down with that injury, but we all know he's coming back."

"Better keep her around if she's a good shot," Morgan said, grinning.

He answered with a shrug. What else could he say? He'd messed up, and now he would never have her.

The crowd expanded as Ezra and Dom joined them. Alexa and Dane weren't far behind.

Dom, with his inside information as an FBI special agent, stepped to the center. "We had a pretty cool update at the Denver office. Some of Spence's colleagues have turned against him since he threatened Mom and Alexa in broad daylight. It appears that no one wants to be associated with someone who endangered the lives of a mother and her US marshal daughter."

Caleb clapped his hands. "I love hearing that the man has no allies."

Dane leaned in as well. "Unofficially, Spence is suspect number one for the Blue Larkspur PD. We don't know where he'll go next, but if he has to use the money from The Rock Solid, he'll be hunting for a place to launder it."

Morgan raised her hand, but she pursed her lips as if she wasn't happy about volunteering. "I might have a lead where I can get some information about that element."

Jasper was laughing along with the stories and one-upmanship integral to a large family, when he glanced at the large glass doors that led into the foyer. All those discordant sounds became white noise as he caught sight of Kayla standing in the doorway, a red dress flowing over her curves, her hair falling in soft waves past her shoulders. He'd never seen her in heels before.

He crossed the room to her as slowly as he could, which, he was ashamed to admit, clocked just short of a run.

"What are you doing here?" he asked when he reached her. He stuffed his hands in the pockets of his suit jacket to keep from touching her.

"I believe I was invited." She smiled but then lowered her gaze. "Is there somewhere else that we can talk?"

"You mean because there's close to thirty pairs of eyes staring at us right now?" He didn't have to look back to know that was true. He'd lived it his whole life.

"Yeah. That's why."

Jasper glanced back and found just what he'd expected, but he caught a few thumbs-up signals as well. He guided her down the hall and into one of the smaller conference rooms and closed the door. Though he was beginning to be optimistic, it was too soon for celebration just yet.

"Why did you decide to come?"

She pressed her lips together. "Would you mind if I went first? And wait until I'm finished, okay?"

He nodded and gestured for her to continue, his

stomach still tight, though hope lay almost in reach. She'd come to the party. That was something.

"I said a lot of things two weeks ago," she began. "I know I can't take any of them back. But please know that I would if I could."

"I know. Me, too."

At her grin over his interruption, he gestured for her to go ahead. "Sorry."

"I will always be a product of my family, just as you are a product of yours. And sometimes I'll fall short and question when I should have complete confidence in you. But I want you to know that I do trust you."

She crossed her arms, her hands gripping her triceps. "I came to you first. Somehow, I instinctively knew I could trust you. I just didn't expect to fall in love with you, too. So if you're still willing to have me, I would love to be your date tonight."

When he didn't answer, she moved her hand in a circular motion for him to get started.

"Would it be okay if I didn't say anything at all?"

At her confused look, he grinned, pulled her to him and told her at least some of what he needed to say with his lips. He hoped she could feel it all—the commitment, the passion, and, yes, the trust. Both were breathless when he pulled back minutes later.

"We don't need all the answers tonight, but this is a good starting point, don't you think?" He kissed her once more. "I love you, too. I do have one important question though."

She smiled at him, their noses nearly touching.

"Where did you get that dress?"

She leaned her head back and laughed. "You can

thank Alexa for that one, and Aubrey for bringing it to me."

"I will. They're my two new favorites."

Jasper reached for her hand, laced their fingers and guided her back through the main lobby.

"You know Aubrey knew about the surprise, right?"

He scoffed at that. "I'm her twin. I know when she's lying."

As they entered the dining room, the booming sound softened to a low rumble, and the circle of conversation opened to include them.

"Everyone," he paused, waiting for quiet, "I'd like to introduce Kayla St. James, my date."

A chorus of "Hi again, Kayla" followed and then hugs in true Colton fashion.

On the other side of the circle, Dom raised his hand. "Sami and I have an announcement to make as well."

He drew his fiancée forward to stand next to him. "I've decided to retire from the FBI and go into the security business with Ezra. I'll be leaving my position by the end of January."

Sami clapped her hands. "And we're moving to Blue Larkspur."

After the applause ended for that, Oliver stepped up, drawing a heavily pregnant Hilary forward with him. "We have an announcement, too," he said. "We eloped!"

Oliver waited for the cheers and applause to die down before adding, "And we'll be building a house not far from the Gemini, so Marian and Robin can have a great place to grow up like we all did."

Isa stepped to the center of the circle and spun around, sending smiles to all of her children, their significant others, grandchildren and all the other little ones she'd welcomed into the family. She stopped for an extra-large smile at the woman on her first date with Jasper.

"Have we gotten all the announcements out of the way so that we can get the music and dancing started? Or has one of you secretly been elected president, and you're ready to go public?"

Theo stepped to the center next to her. "I have an announcement. Or rather, it's a request, for you, Caleb, Morgan, Oliver, Ezra, Dom, Rachel, Gideon, Jasper, Aubrey, Gavin, Alexa and Naomi." He met the gaze of each one as he continued through the list, and then he puffed up his cheeks and blew out again. "I would like to ask for your blessing to propose to my beloved Isa."

A chorus of cheers and applause filled the room.

"He gets points for just remembering all the names," Ezra said.

"And in order," Dom added.

"I think they agree," Theo said to Isa, who already had tears streaming down her face.

"Hold on a second," Jasper called out. He dragged a chair away from one of the tables and set it in the center of the circle.

Theo guided Isa to sit and then bent on one knee in front of her. He removed a box from his pocket and popped it open, revealing a sparkling solitaire diamond.

Another chorus, this one of *oohs* and *aahs*, broke out.

"I guess I might have to get used to hearing everything in chorus when I join this family," Theo said with a laugh. "Oh. I'd better ask the girl first."

He turned back to Isa, who shook her head, smiling.

"Isadora Colton, you light up my life. I breathe easier in this world just knowing you're in it. I can't wait to be a part of your loud, boisterous and incredibly loving family." He paused and looked deep into her eyes. "Be my wife, sweet Isa. Let's make our golden years the best ones ever. Will you marry me?"

"Yes. I thought you'd never ask," she said, earning groans from their audience.

Theo slid the ring on her finger, and as they both stood, she threw herself into his arms. They kissed until hoots and whistles announced her children's discomfort.

"Argh. Too much PDA," Dom said for them all.

Isa laughed. "Careful, or we'll do it again."

"No," her children chorused.

"Another wedding to plan on the Gemini," Aubrey called out to yet another round of cheers.

Slowly, the circle unfolded as Ezra went to plug his phone into the speaker and be the first to pick a song and hit the dance floor. He picked a slow one.

Jasper pointed to Ezra as he guided Kayla out on the floor for their first dance ever.

"He's my new favorite brother, too."

"Sure sounds as if you like your brothers and sisters a lot."

"I like you," he said.

She grinned, her eyes shining in the twinkling lights.

"I like you."

He stared at her lips and then couldn't resist dipping his head for just one kiss. Maybe two. When they pulled back, the whole dance floor was filled with Coltons and all the people they loved. Including the one *he* loved.

Theo and Isa took their place in the center, dancing

and staring into each other's eyes as if they were the only couple in the room. Perhaps, to them, they were.

Kayla smiled over at them. "They're so cute."

"Maybe we'll be like them one day." His heart pounded with that hope as her real presence filled his arms.

"But no rush." She lifted her chin and brushed her lips over his again. "No rush at all."

* * * * *

HARLEQUIN
PLUS

Announcing a **BRAND-NEW** multimedia subscription service for romance fans like you!

Read, Watch and Play.

Experience the easiest way to get the romance content you crave.

Start your **FREE 7 DAY TRIAL** at <u>www.harlequinplus.com/freetrial</u>.